STORYHACK

ACTION & ADVENTURE, ISSUE ONE

Contents

Hello friends,

It's been another whirlwind of adventure and learning for me as I've put this issue together. I'll get the whole process smoother and smoother with each issue.

In the meantime, I hope you enjoy the stories that follow. There are a few returning authors from issue 0 and several new faces. I am so grateful for all of you who have backed on Kickstarter, submitted stories, edited a story, passed along the word via social media, and done anything else to help me get this out the door. I could not have done it without you.

Also, when you're done reading, I'd love it if you would leave an honest review somewhere.

Cheers,

Bryce Beattie

Bryce Beattie, editor

A recently dismissed recruit watches in horror as an alien race betrays and massacres his former classmates. Now he may be the only person capable of stopping the first wave of an interstellar war.

New Rules for Rocket Nauts

BY MICHAEL DeCAROLIS

If he were to peer through the window of The Eagle's Cup, Leo would have known the time by the thickening Ganymedian frost on the outer surface of the biodome. Instead, he knew the time intuitively—he had been counting down to this specific hour for all the purposeful years of his life. This was the hour that the nauts of Rocket Training Squadron 3 received their pins.

Leo, however, was not with his classmates on the synchro-orbital training base that floated just outside Ganymede's thin atmosphere.

"Yuri," Leo growled with one eye on the monitor, "turn it up. I wanna hear every name. And you can top me off, too, if y'please." The bartender—a former naut himself, who even now kept his white hair in a regulation buzzcut—complied knowingly. As his glass was refilled, Leo listened to the names being called. Already

on the E's. It wouldn't be much longer to the spot where his name should be.

Other than Leo and Yuri, there was no one else in the bar. Ganymede Base 3 was nearly a ghost town at this time of day, and on this day more than usual. Since there was no such thing as a day off at any of the Jovian settlements, everyone would be working for another hour basewide. GB3 supported two main divisions: Squadron 3's training platform, held directly overhead by a massive ion reactor that shone like a constant noontime sun, and the Xenobiology and Linguistics Division, which occupied an expansive system of tunnels that extended deep below the icy surface.

For the time being, Leo enjoyed the solitude of the bar. He knew from experience that as soon as the working day was over, The Eagle's Cup would be filled by no small percentage of the hundreds of humans stationed there. Until then, though, the bar was his. Or so he thought.

"Galileo Glass! How did I know I'd find you here?" Leo didn't have to turn around to know whose voice was carried on the balmy artificial air that burst through the door. "How're you holding up?"

"Cassie, I told you on the comm this morning—I'm fine. What're you doing here?"

"I snuck out early. I'm not the only one. You know pinning day is like a holiday around here, and this year is a hallmark occasion if there ever was one." She paused, thought for a moment, then put her hand on his shoulder. "I'm sorry. You should be up there."

"I mean it, I'm fine."

When Leo downed his drink, Cassie asked Yuri, an old friend of her father's, for two more before asking Leo: "What're you drinking, anyway?"

"Dihydrogen monoxide. Neat."

"Great. Hey, we don't have to watch this here. Do you want to come back to my pod and watch it? No one'll be home, obviously."

"Cassie. I promise you, I don't feel bad. I almost think it'd be worse watching it in private. It would feel like I'm ashamed. But the truth is, the minute I knew I was out, I became okay with it. I realized that I didn't really love it, anyway. Being a naut isn't like it used to be. Now it's all rules and regulations. Procedures. It's like driving a damn bus."

"Do you really mean that? You're fine?"

"Yeah. It's not like back in the day, when being a naut was really an adventure. You remember the stories my grandfather used to tell about the Second Unification War? These days it's mostly just political. Half our training was about how to work with cephies, and none of it was about tactics or skill. There's been such a push for the cephies, I'm surprised there are any humans graduating in this class at all."

"Don't be like that," Cassie said, almost defensively. "The cephies are a great addition to the fleet. Besides, I'm only able to stay here because of them."

"Yeah, I know, but—" Leo had no real rational point to make, just a vague notion that people were overlooking something obvious. "After today's graduation, over half of our wing will be cephy pilots. There'll be enough of them to man every mission, if need be. There's something off about that."

"Now you're starting to sound cephalophobic, Leo. They're a remarkable species. The speed at which they adapted to us is amazing. Did you know that in the sealed report from the first contact, they were described as 'timid cuttlefish-like creatures that exhibited *some* curiosity?' In less than a decade the entire population was walking—*walking,* as in upright on two legs—and above the surface, no less."

"I know, I know. You can spare me the PSA. I was rooming with one, you know. For the last 2 months. I kinda liked the fact that they can't talk, but that damn lightshow kept me up every night. He was the biggest damn ceph' you ever saw, too. He could barely even squeeze into the modified uniform. I called him Tiny, not that he had any idea what that meant."

"Oh, Leo! That's what I wanted to tell you. I had a breakthrough last week at work!"

"Did you finally figure out how to decipher those color changes?"

"No, that's just it. The color changes look completely random to us because they *are* completely random. That's not how they're communicating at all."

"Then what?" Leo really was curious at this point, but he was still trying to mind the broadcast of the ceremony on the bar's monitor. As a result, he gave the distinct, albeit false, impression that he was ignoring Cassie's every word.

While he listened to Cassie, Leo eyed row after row of his former classmates, soon-to-be and just-pinned nauts. The humans, in their form-fitting blue jumpsuits that covered everything below the chin, stood united alongside the polychromatic cephalopods in their modified jumpsuits: sleeveless, so that two tentacle-like limbs could hang from each shoulder, and hemmed at the thigh, where thick, boneless appendages mimicked the actions of human legs. The humans had tight collars that bore their rank and insignia in orange. The cephies had no collars, so they wore their rank and insignia on their shoulders. Their bulbous heads, protruding eyes, and constantly flapping sidefins could accommodate a collar easily enough, but the only solid part of a cephy's bioluminescent body—a pair of large chitinous mandibles that hung down from the front of their faces—could not. If not for his unreasonable suspicion of them, Leo would have admitted that he partly agreed with Cassie: the Ganymedian Cephalopods, with their constantly shifting emission of light, were an incredible species.

"They communicate *outside* the visible spectrum!" Cassie exclaimed triumphantly. "They can control their emission of electromagnetic waves that we can't see. And guess who cracked it. Yours truly! It seems obvious, really, but isn't that how it always is? Right under your nose—or in this case, right before your eyes—the whole time. They mostly communicate in IR, I think, but I'm pretty sure they can modulate UV as well. I just haven't seen it yet."

"But how'd you figure it out?"

A slow smile spread across her lips. "Implants. Sub-corneal. I got 'em a few weeks ago." Cassie tapped next to her left eye, "infrared," then her right, "and ultraviolet." Leo hadn't noticed before, but now the electric blue circuits in the whites of her eyes were as clear as the red veins they replaced. "Don't tell Daddy—he doesn't know he paid for 'em."

"Well, you don't have to worry about that. 'Captain Daddy' and I aren't on speaking terms." Leo paused, then: "He's the one who signed my separation papers."

"Oh! Leo, I—I'm sorry. He and I haven't spoken. He hasn't been down here for weeks. I didn't realize—"

"Baby, it's okay. That's not even what's bothering me. Anyway, congrats on the big break. Maybe we should be drinking something a bit harder, after all."

"What is it, then? What *is* bothering you?"

"It's just that—" Leo felt self-conscious about what he wanted to say, but he knew that if he could tell anyone, it was Cassie. "It's just that I feel like I'm the only one who doesn't think we should be rolling out the red carpet for the cephies so quickly. I mean, yeah, let's work with them. That's great. But let's understand them first. Your work in the XLD is important. We should get that squared away before we hand over the keys to the kingdom. We don't even know if they have a culture. Or if they do, if their culture is compatible with ours." Leo was getting worked up. "Look at human history. It wasn't until the twenty-second century that we stopped killing each other in the quest for cultural dominance—and that was only after we had nearly destroyed ourselves. We were a species ninety percent off our home planet by the time we really unified.

But now we're bending over backwards—what, to make up for past mistakes? For a different species that we still know almost nothing about?" He had to stop to catch his breath. "I'm sorry. I know that sounds awful. But that's how I feel. It seems like common sense."

"Leo! Leo, look. My dad's up there. He's part of this. I am, too, in my own way. But Dad's on the ground floor with this, and no matter what happened between the two of you, I still trust him. He's personally overseeing this graduation, and he wouldn't be doing that if he didn't believe in a Human-Cephalopod Coalition. He's up there right now next to the admiral, determined to do better with this species than we did with our own. Look—"

They had both taken their eyes off the monitor, but when they looked at it now, they knew that something was wrong.

RULE #1: TRUST YOUR GUT

Cassie didn't even hear herself say, "I've never seen that before." It was true, though. No human had seen this before.

The kaleidoscopic skin changes of every cephy visible on the monitor were suddenly in sync, modulating as one organism and settling on a single solid hue. They weren't the only species changing color, however. Every human visible on the monitor was turning a shade of pink, then dark red, as though they had instantaneously gotten an intense sunburn. An agonizing cry broke out, then men and women fell to the floor. As the video feed turned a slight bluish-purple, it looked as though the humans aboard the training base were being roasted alive. That's when the feed cut out.

"Dad!" Cassie saw him before the monitor went blank. He had fallen to his knees and begun tearing at his uniform as though he were feverish.

Yuri, who never showed any emotion, stood bug-eyed and gap-mouthed behind the bar. Leo was the opposite. He narrowed his eyes, gritted his teeth, and clenched his fists. Then he grabbed Cassie by the shoulders.

"Cassie, we've got to get up there!"

"Wha—what?" She was in shock. Leo shook her gently.

"We've got to get up to the base. We've got to—check on your dad, of course. But listen: that grad ceremony was being broadcast to every Jovian settlement, and the cephies knew that. We might not be able to understand them, but that was a declaration of war in any language. It was an *act* of war. And I would bet my separation pay that the civilians down here are their next target."

"I don't—" Cassie took a deep breath, swallowed, and wiped her eyes. "Oh my God. Okay. Okay, you're right. But how do we get up there now? Every single surface ferry is already at that base, waiting to take dignitaries back down."

"I don't know, Cass. We've got to find something."

"Well, if you're goin' up there," Yuri interjected, "you're gonna need this." He reached under the bar and pulled out a bundle of rags, then tossed it to Leo, who unwrapped it and smiled. "Mark 32 Ion Blaster, fully charged."

"Thanks, Yuri. I'll bring it back soon."

"Wait, I've got it," Cassie said. "C'mon."

RULE #2: GET OFF YOUR ASS

Cassie grabbed Leo's hand and raced outside. As they sprinted along the edge of the biodome to Officer's Row, nearly halfway to the other side of the compound, Cassie explained. "Dad's got something."

"What do you mean? He's a stickler for the rules, there's no way he has a private craft."

"You only knew—know. You only *know* one side of him. Inside, he was as much of a wildcard and a romantic as you! Do you think he *asked permission* to have his cutlass custom-made from the hull of the ES Roosevelt? Anyway, I remember when I was a girl, right before we were transferred here from GB1. There was a salvage yard right outside the base. He bought this thing on the sly and had it sent ahead of us in pieces. He's spent the last decade rebuilding it."

"Rebuilding what?"

"You'll see!"

"Hey Cassie. Your dad's gonna be alright." Leo always struggled with delivering comforting sentiments that he didn't believe, and he worried that Cassie would see right through him.

They ran the rest of the way in silence.

When they arrived, Cassie punched a code into the storage pod and an entire wall receded into the ground. Inside, with a pristine red and yellow paint job, sat a small, sleek rocket.

"Retro!" Despite the tragedy they were facing, Leo could not hold back his excitement. "This is a Phaethon One! I didn't know there were any of these left. This is amazing! Okay, your dad's a little cooler than I thought." Then he pulled himself together. "This'll run, right?"

"Yeah. I mean, I don't think Dad's had the chance to test it; there was no way to start it up without everyone in Officer's Row knowing that he was breaking the law. But he's a great engineer, so I'm sure it'll be fine. One thing, though—we have to wear spacesuits."

"Oh, I know! This generation sacrificed safety for speed and maneuverability. That's just what we need right now, anyway."

"Here." Cassie handed Leo a suit. "It came with the Phaethon, so I hope you *really* like retro."

Leo smirked, then got changed. The ochre suit reflected an era when asymmetry was all the rage, with its one large, grey shoulder pad over the right shoulder connected by a strap to the left hip that kept the suit fastened. The shoulder pad matched the thick grey boots and gloves, and the whole thing was topped by a bucket-shaped helmet with a clear faceplate. Leo strapped Yuri's blaster to his right hip and climbed inside. Meanwhile, Cassie slipped into a modern, formfitting green suit that had been modified to connect to the Phaethon. She climbed in next to Leo, leaving two empty seats behind them in the tight cockpit.

Leo began the pre-launch checklist reflexively as he taxied outside.

"Wait—" asked Cassie, "how are we going to get out of the biodome? It'll take way too long to taxi out to the spaceport."

"We're gonna launch from right here, straight to the top of the dome. The one-way vent valve should sense us approaching from this side and automatically open."

"Should?"

"Did I ever tell you about how my grandfather earned his Cosmic Star? He was stationed on Mars when Unification War Two broke out—and remember, Mars was just an outpost at the time. They didn't even have a fully operational spaceport on the surface. He knew he had to get off-planet, but there was no rocket with its own vertical launch capabilities —everything back then needed a tower. You know what he did? He commandeered a land-rocket, pointed it at Olympus Mons, and punched it to full-throttle. He used the damn volcano as a ramp to propel himself off the surface. You know the rest of the story."

"And what's your point?"

"My point is: here we go! Three. Two. One. Blastoff!"

RULE #3: FLY BY THE SEAT OF YOUR PANTS

Leo's head hit the back of the seat as the Phaethon One hurtled towards the vent valve above. The quick calculations he performed in his head—which would have been more of a comfort if he had done them before they mattered—confirmed that the valve would have just enough time to open fully between the moment the sensor picked them up and the moment they reached the vent. Of course, this all relied on the sensor picking them up at speed in the first place. If it didn't, Leo would have no time to avert a collision with the biodome's outer shell. Between the biodome and the Phaethon, only one was built to survive such a collision—and it wasn't the Phaethon.

"It's not opening!"

"Wait, Cassie."

"It's not opening!"

"Wait—there!"

There was a heartbeat's worth of stillness inside the cockpit before they both breathed a sigh of relief. The vent valve opened for a second as the Phaethon punched through the aperture into the Ganymedian night, then shut again behind it. The silence continued as the ice, stone, and human structures on the surface fell away. If not for the high stakes, Leo thought, this moment would be serene: below them, the tranquility of Ganymede; above them, the floating training base; and out the window, a full view of majestic Jupiter looming above the horizon, with the shadow of Callisto casting a dark circle on the swirling peach clouds, Io glinting alongside the planet, and the constantly-moving Red Storm that would be menacing instead of beautiful if they were any closer to it.

Leo's moment of serenity didn't last long. From the disk-shaped training base, which was now about five minutes away, poured several dozen Ursa-class rockets. Leo didn't point out to Cassie what this said about any human resistance, or lack thereof, aboard the platform.

"Can you outfly them?"

"Well... no. They're born better pilots than me. Every single one of them. They've evolved operating in three dimensions, while we have to get the hang of it. But the Phaethon *can* outfly an Ursa. This was built for the days when there were still dogfights. We can move and accelerate in ways they can't. Those Ursas are basically armed transports. They're heavy and slow, but they do pack a punch. I think I can get past them without getting hit, but we can't take them all on."

"Where do you think they're going?"

"Where else? Did nobody ever stop to ask why there is no biodiversity on Ganymede? Why the cephies are the only species we've encountered? I think they don't play well with others. I think they're going to raze GB3 to the ground."

"How can they hope to do that? The biodome is too strong—"

"Too strong for a few hits, yeah. Hell, they could all crash right into the thing and it'd be fine. But sustained can-ion fire? They'll breach the dome in a few hours, tops. Long before any reinforcements can get here."

"God. My God, what are we going to do?"

"Well, first things first, we get up there and get your dad. Maybe he'll know what to do."

"Leo, wait. I think you've nailed it."

"What?"

"You said they could all crash into the dome, and it'd be fine, right? Well, we can make them crash!"

"How? Quickly now, we're getting close."

"I'm not sure, but—I'm looking at them communicate right now. There's no UV, but there are waves, patterns of IR coming from each cockpit. And I'm sure they're using IR to see the surface below, too. Can we—can we 'blind' them somehow? Is there anything on the training base that can emit a strong enough wave of IR?"

"Baby, you're a genius! Okay, when we get up there, we're going to have to split up. You go find your dad. Start in the auditorium. I'm going to head for the reactor—" Leo was interrupted as a can-ion blast pulsed towards them from an Ursa on the edge of the formation. With a flick of his wrist on the control stick, Leo induced a tight spin that narrowly avoided the blast. "Well, they see us."

"Can we fight back at all?"

"We don't have anything as strong as can-ion, but we do have this!" Leo tapped the trigger, releasing a burst of titanium rounds from the Phaethon's railgun that tore through the outer hull of the nearest Ursa. "If we were just one-on-one, I could get around behind it and take out its engine. As it is, we'll just have to hope that's enough to hold them off, make 'em realize we're not worth their while." After a moment, Leo confirmed: "It looks like they're going to stick to their mission. We're nothing but an annoyance to them."

The Ursas fired a few more blasts—which were easily dodged by the Phaethon—but maintained their trajectory towards the surface. Leo itched to fly right through the center of their formation and take out anything he could, but he knew it would be fruitless. *If your gut says get to the base, get to the base.* Leo pushed the throttle to full and circled around to the base's landing port.

From inside the cockpit, Leo verified that the base's systems still functioned correctly. That meant that he could leave his helmet in the ship and rely on the atmosphere and artificial gravity of the base, but it also told him that the cephies had not shut off the comms after the attack. He didn't like the implications.

The lack of any communication or distress signal from the control tower strengthened Leo's suspicions, but they were absolutely confirmed when Leo and Cassie disembarked from the Phaethon and moved through the base. Everywhere they looked, burnt human remains told them all they needed to know.

"You know what's waiting for you. Are you sure you want to see that?"

"I have to get Dad. Even if—I just can't leave him here."

"Okay. The auditorium is that way," Leo pointed down a short hallway. "Get your dad, then get back to the ship and take off. I have to go downstairs to the main reactor. If I can blow it, it'll give us just what we need: an old-fashioned kaboom that'll release a burst of energy strong enough and long enough to blind the cephies, even when they're near the surface. Those Ursas can't hover, so they'll be constantly swooping down towards the biosphere. If we can blind them like you said,

most of them should crash into the dome, or even into each other."

"Wait—" Cassie blinked her left eye three times, switching on her IR lens. "There are still a few of them aboard. Be careful."

Leo decided it would be cruel to say nothing, so he responded with "you be careful" before turning the corner and descending the steps.

His footsteps echoed eerily in the deserted hallway. Leo tried to slow down to move more silently even though he now knew that the cephies could see him in total darkness and through walls, no matter how quietly he moved. Still, his survival training nagged at him and kept him cautious below the flickering lights.

The tentacle tightened as it rotated Leo around to face its owner.

He managed to squeeze out a few...

As he approached the reactor core that protruded from the lowest part of the station, Leo had a sneaking suspicion that he wasn't alone. He was right. While moving down the last hallway before reaching the control room, Leo was stopped dead in his tracks when a powerful tentacle whipped around his neck and lifted him off the ground.

The tentacle tightened as it rotated Leo around to face its owner. He managed to squeeze out a few words while the massive cephalopod lowered itself to the floor from the ducts that ran along the ceiling: "Tiny. I had... no idea... you could... walk on the ceiling."

Once on the floor, Leo's former roommate used two more of its tentacles to stop Leo from struggling to free his throat, pulling his hands away and holding them down at his sides.

"Wait... can we... talk this over?" Tiny's response came in the form of an extremely rapid display of pink, blue, and yellow bands spreading across its body. Cassie had said that the color patterns were random, but to Leo this looked like a clear display of aggression. Leo wondered if it would be the last thing he saw, as his vision began to tunnel from lack of oxygen. Unable to look at what he was doing, Leo reached as far as he could with the fingers on his right hand.

RULE #4: SHOOT FROM THE HIP

Blam! The tip of Leo's middle finger reached the trigger of Yuri's blaster to fire off a shot at the floor. The shot was enough to startle Tiny, who loosened his grip.

Blam! Blam! Leo pulled his right arm free, fired a round at the tentacle that was choking him, and another at Tiny's massive head.

Leo stood, freed from his captor, and watched as the cephalopod re-formed his misshapen head and limb.

"I didn't know you could do that, either." Leo fired another shot at Tiny's head, only for the crater left by the blast to steadily morph back into its original shape. "Yep, that changes things."

Without a second thought, Leo turned to run down the hallway towards the reactor door, away from Tiny. He didn't even make it a full step before Tiny had hoisted him up by his ankles. Hanging upside down, Leo felt an intense heat washing over him, and saw that Tiny was now a solid, vibrant purple.

Before Leo could fire another useless shot, though, a long, dark blade pierced Tiny's abdomen from behind. The thick lifeblood of the cephalopod spurted out as the blade jerked quickly to the left and to the right. Leo fell to the ground.

"Right there," came Cassie's voice from behind the slumping cephalopod, "lower half of the torso. That's where all their vital organs are. Brain, heart, everything. You can shoot them a hundred times and just piss them off, but slice that up and they're done."

"Thank God! How'd you find me?" Leo ran over to Cassie and hugged her tightly, then kissed her forehead.

"I found Dad pretty quickly. Once I got him strapped into the ship, I came after you. I was following your IR signature when I saw a UV surge. I got here just in time."

"Wait—so your dad's okay? Oh, Cassie, that's wonderful. I didn't think—" Leo hadn't thought. He stopped himself when he saw Cassie's face.

"I—I just couldn't leave his body like that. I want to give him a proper burial back home. Next to Mom." She held Leo tight for a long second, then focused on the task at hand.

"Here, I want you to have Dad's cutlass. It's a cobalt superalloy, nearly unbreakable" -Cassie smiled as she thought of her father-

"and Dad named her Queen Mab."

Leo told Cassie how sorry he was, thanked her, and strapped Queen Mab to his left hip. "You've got to get back to the ship and get out of here. Head towards GB1. With any luck you'll meet the relief force halfway there."

"You're nuts if you think I'm leaving you here. This isn't a suicide mission."

"There's no way I'll make it back to the ship in time. The end of the road is right in there," Leo said, pointing to the closed door at the end of the hallway. "Once I trigger the reactor, I'm going to have to hold off the cephies to make sure they don't shut it down. My life is inconsequential. I'm a naut washout; I've got nothing else to give the world. There are hundreds of lives down there, and each one is worth more than mine."

Cassie, fuming, said "Fine!" and turned away. As she stormed off, Leo was puzzled. This is not the hero's farewell he expected.

"Aren't you going to at least say goodbye?"

"I didn't get to say goodbye to Dad," she yelled over her shoulder, "what makes you think I'm going to say goodbye to you?"

No time to get hung up now, Leo thought. Turning towards the door to the reactor room, Leo drew Queen Mab in his right hand and Yuri's blaster in his left.

Leo blasted the biometric lock, and the door slid open. When he stepped inside, he was beset by two cephies, one from each side. Dispassionately, he blasted the one to his right in the face—barely harming it, but knocking it backwards. Then, Leo turned to the cephy on his left and hacked off three of its upper tentacles before slicing it through the abdomen as Cassie had taught him. As the first cephy grabbed him from behind and pulled him towards its snapping mandibles, Leo realized how angry he was at Cassie for not even giving him a goodbye kiss.

"I'm going down with the damn ship," Leo said aloud as he twisted around to face the cephy, "and *she* gets mad at *me!*" Leo took out his aggression by blasting the jaws off the cephy, then disemboweling it. "Unbelievable."

Leo ran across the narrow platform that stretched suspended through the center of the reactor room. His footsteps clanged on the metal grates of the catwalk, stopping only when he reached the console in the center. In front of him hung the massive ion reactor.

RULE #5: IF YOU'RE GONNA PLAY, PLAY TO WIN

Leo leaned heavily on the Reactor Core Temperature control lever in the center of the console. Within seconds, the reactor began humming. *Thanks for the emergency procedure lessons,* Leo thought. *Every naut is also an engineer, they said.* Leo flipped a sequence of switches that shut down the computerized safety regulators. The reactor began vibrating, then shaking violently. *Every naut is also a safety officer, they said.* Finally, Leo stepped to the side and lifted a panel in the grated walkway at his feet. Below the walkway ran a final safety measure, a bundle of wires that connected the core thermometer to a cooling reservoir that would automatically flood the reactor if it ever reached a critical temperature. Queen Mab severed this connection. All Leo had to do now was wait.

At that moment, the door at the far end of the walkway slid open. Half a dozen cephies rushed towards him, tentacles flailing in his direction and colors flashing across their slick skin. He fired a few blasts their way to slow them down. Then, three more cephies burst through the open door through which he had entered. *Sixty seconds until this can't be reversed. Then a bit longer until it blows. I can hold them off.*

Leo got into a fighting stance, but the cephies moved no closer. Instead, they all turned the same color that Tiny had displayed when he went ultraviolet. Leo fired a few blasts at the large group, but even when they were hit, they were unfazed. Soon, Leo felt a wave of heat hitting him from both sides. He fell to his knees as his strength was replaced by pain. But Leo didn't scream—he laughed.

"Whaddya think I came here for?" he shouted, mustering all the false bravado he could. "I'm blowing the reactor! You don't think I knew it was going to get hot?" Soon, though, all Leo could do was shut his eyes and focus on taking one breath at a time. Leo knew what fate awaited him. His spacesuit would allow him to survive a bit longer than the nauts he saw roasted alive at the graduation ceremony, but that was merely delaying the inevitable.

Well, I guess I'll be joining my classmates, after all. But I've got to stay alive as long as I can, Leo commanded himself. *Dying would be nice, but as long as I'm alive, they aren't coming over here to shut this off. Stay alive.*

As time slowed down for Leo, and death drew nearer, he thought of Cassie one last time. The strange guilt he felt for dying told him that he had truly loved her.

Suddenly, a quick blast of cold struck him and shocked him awake. He felt himself being pulled off the walkway. With his eyes now wide open, he saw that a hole had been torn through the base's hull, which was causing the reactor room to depressurize. His reflexes taking over, Leo drove Queen Mab through the floor of the walkway and held on with both hands. The reactor in front of him was beginning to glow red-hot. Looking over his shoulder, Leo watched as the cephies assailing him were sucked into space one-by-one through the tear in the hull. Then, a bright red and yellow rocket burst through the opening, slid wildly in the emptiness of the reactor chamber, and finally came to an unsteady hover beside the walkway.

"Need a lift?" Cassie shouted to Leo as the cockpit opened.

"Get out of here! The reactor's about to blow!"

"Come on! I'm between you and the breach. Let go and I'll grab you."

"There's no time!"

"Please!"

Leo looked at Cassie in the Phaethon, with the horrid figure that he could only assume was her father strapped in behind her. He realized she wasn't just saving him for his sake. Leo placed his left hand down on the walkway, and with his right hand, pulled Queen Mab free. He floated up into the air and was drawn towards the fissure. A second later, Cassie grabbed his free hand and pulled him down into the seat next to her. She slammed the cockpit shut, handed Leo his helmet, and said, "The controls are yours."

Leo turned the Phaethon towards its self-made exit and pushed the throttle forward. As they rocketed away from the training base, the reactor blew. The force of the explosion completely destroyed the bottom of the base, while the platform above was pushed farther away from Ganymede, out into space. Leo watched shrapnel from the base whiz past them as the Phaethon tumbled end over end away from the blast. Cassie, on the other hand, could see a magnificent wave—invisible to Leo's unaided eyes—rush towards Ganymede's surface instantly. They were both able to see ship after ship crash into the shell of the biodome below.

"Now what?" Cassie asked.

"'Now what?' Are you kidding? We just saved the human race! Maybe a drink. And a parade." Leo smiled at his own exaggeration, but knew that this was just the beginning. "Okay, before the parade: there are bound to be a few Ursas that made it through that, but we should be able to take them out ourselves. Then we get to the surface and see to your dad." He reached over and took Cassie's hand.

Somehow, when Cassie squeezed his hand in return, Leo felt like he really could save the whole human race.

"But after that—well, a war has just started. The fleet will be mobilizing. But they're going to need to learn to play by a whole new set of rules if they want to win. And we're the only ones who can teach them."

"New Rules for Rocket Nauts" is copyright © Michael DeCarolis.

Michael lives in Navarre, Florida, with his wonderful wife, Julalak, and their cat, Othello. Michael loves traveling, spending time with his family, and reading everything from classic literature to comic books-especially Thor.

Michael only writes part time. He works full time as a high school English teacher. Before teaching in Florida, Michael taught middle school English in Maryland; before that, he taught English as a foreign language in Thailand. He earned his Bachelor's Degree in English from the United States Naval Academy, and his Master's Degree in Teaching from the Johns Hopkins University.

To contact Michael or follow his writing, visit:

decarolismichael.wordpress.com

A desperate chase through the woods leads to an occupied cabin. Has Fred Moose doomed everyone to be slaughtered by the Wendigo outside?

The Price of Hunger

BY KEVYN WINKLESS

Fred Moose stumbled when the crust of snow gave way beneath him. He clutched at jack pine on the way down, felt the needles whip his face. Felt his ankle wrench as the snowshoe twisted under him.

Snow seared his cheek. Sweat trickled cold in the small of his back. He lay there panting, wide eyed, frozen with panic for a moment before thrusting against the crumbling snow, scrambling to his feet.

He swayed, exhausted, a knife in his side with every shallow breath. He swallowed, mouth dry, willed himself to move.

His ankle burned, but he ground his teeth together, and pushed on. If he could just make it to the road–

Somewhere behind him, he heard it crashing through the bush, swallowed the animal whine in the back of his throat. The ounce of gold in his pocket felt like a ton.

How far was the creature now? Too close, but was there still a chance?

The snowshoes flapped against his boots as he limped on. His breath seemed loud enough to echo in the dark. The air was still and frigid. It burned with every breath, and he knew he'd pay later, but –

Another crack as somewhere the thing that had once been Ernie Blacksmith toppled a tree. Fred's fingers and toes were losing feeling, but he had to push on.

He had to escape.

Suddenly, the spaces between the black spruce seemed thick with birch and poplar saplings, and then –

He stumbled to a stop, caromed heavily against a slick, leaning trunk. His breath came in rasps.

He stood a moment, looking blankly over the open space, feeling the fringe of hair under his hood crackle with freezing sweat.

His chest felt empty.

There was no Moon, but the frozen lake seemed to glow with a pearly light under the stars. Above, the sky had that dark glow only visible on the coldest nights. The stars barely twinkled. The snow rippled like frozen waves, whipped into weird shapes in places where drifts had collapsed on themselves.

There was no road.

Stumbling through the bush, he'd gotten turned. He was heading the wrong way. The road and the possibility of meeting a truck or Bombardier heading into Ilford had been his only chance to get away – slim as it was so far out and at this time of night.

There was another crash behind him, and a cry that made his skin crawl: the mushy voice didn't understand the words it was dredging up from Ernie's long-dead mind, he knew. He prayed.

But now he had to move: he broke the paralysis of despair with a mindless sprint across the open ice.

Half-way across, gasping, teeth grinding with every impact on his twisted ankle, he felt a sudden prickle on his spine: then the wordless howl echoed across the darkness as the thing broke out of the bush in pursuit. His mouth filled with the dry, metallic taste of fear, and adrenaline washed away some of the exhaustion as he surged forward.

Perhaps it was chance, or perhaps he'd glimpsed it in the shadows of the trees and his body had guided him, but as he scrambled up the drifts along the opposite shore he was suddenly in the golden wash of light streaming from the tiny window of a trapper's lodge, hidden in among the trees.

His heart leapt as he slammed against the door, fumbled with the latch. His hands shook as he threw the door open and fell into the warmth. Behind him, he heard the thing's hungry moans, heard the noise as it scrabbled at the crusted snow where he'd been.

He jerked to his feet, spun unseeing to the door and slammed it tight against the darkness, knowing the door wouldn't hold.

There was silence, except for his pounding heart and rasping breath. Then behind him: the crackle as someone shifted on the pine strewn floor, the metallic *snick-snack* as a bullet was chambered. Then Mary Cook spoke:

"Fred Moose! What the *hell* are you doing?"

He twisted his head to look at her just as the creature reached the lodge. The door bucked against his grip on the handle. He gritted his teeth, braced his shoulder against the frame and prayed he could hold it long enough.

"Mary! The table! Fast!"

She stared for a moment, then slung her rifle and scrambled to shove the heavy table across the floor as he strained and dug his heels down to the packed dirt of the floor, shouted as his twisted ankle objected and his leg threatened to give.

There was a pause in the thing's assault – Fred leapt away, and together they jammed the table tight under the handle, wedging the door shut. The two of them slumped, panting. The storm lantern swung in a slow circle overhead, making shadows twist in the corners of vision.

Mary stared at him wide-eyed, then spoke in a voice heavy with dread.

"What did you bring here, Fred?"

He shook his head. It was too much to explain. His fist wrapped around the weight in his pocket. It was as cold as ice.

He held out his hand: "Give me your rifle."

Wordlessly, she unslung the battered Ross and passed it to him before turning to where her grandmother hunched under a pile of blankets and furs by the stove.

He'd hardly checked the bolt and chamber when the creature's assault started again. The little window cut into the logs was unshuttered: when the thing threw itself against the oiled canvas stretched over it against the weather, it simply shredded.

The lodge filled suddenly with the fetid reek of putrid flesh. For a moment he flinched from the claw-like hand as the thing's arm flailed wildly through the gap – then he sprang forward, hammering at the ragged moose-hide that wrapped the arm, each blow tugging another tuft of insulation from the rents. The thing howled and tore at the window, nails gouging up splinters as it struggled to thrust its head through the gap. Behind him, Mary screamed at the sight of the drawn, grey face, the wild eyes that held no trace of the man.

The hooked fingers snatched again, tangling in Fred's sleeve and dragging him close with inhuman strength. His breath whooshed with the impact as he slammed against the wall. The stench of its breath as it snapped at him made his eyes water and he choked down gags as he struggled. The thing's eyes rolled back, foam flecked the corners of its mouth, a hungry gurgle rose in the back of its throat as it pulled him inexorably closer, oblivious to Mary's blows as she fought to help Fred free himself.

At last Fred got his feet up against the wall and thrust against it with all the strength adrenaline could give his abused body. He jerked back when the thing's grip slipped, slammed his head against the edge of the bed. Through the stars clouding his vision he thumbed the safety.

"Mary! Down!"

She dropped to her belly in the pine branches carpeting the floor a split second before he fired.

The report was deafening in the one-room lodge, but then the silence stretched. The thing was gone. When the pounding of his heart slowed and his breath was less ragged, Fred realized Mary was still huddled on the floor, weeping in the wash of emotions of the aftermath.

He struggled up, reached down to help her, and was startled by the fierceness with which she clung to him. He set her on the bed beside her grandmother, and waited nervously for her to calm. His ears strained for the first signs of the thing's return.

After a time, she pushed him away, scrubbed at her face with her sleeve, and looked up at him. Her throat worked for a moment as she swallowed the fear. "Was that...was that *thing* Ernie Blacksmith?"

Fred shook his head, staring out the window as he remembered the desperate rush through the bush. "No. It was, but that's not him. Not now."

Mary's eyes crinkled with incomprehension. "What happened to him?" she asked quietly.

He shook his head again. "We were working his trap line. We found...something."

He swallowed, remembering the scene: the shredded prospectors' camp, cabin door hanging loose. The devastation inside. The blood, frozen in streaks on the wall and in the snow drifting on the floor. The deep cold that had filled him when he saw them: so much worse even than the twisted, blistered bodies that had haunted him since the Great War. The feel of paper-dry flesh as he'd pried open fingers clutching some treasure. And then the little, misshapen ingot that was every prospector's dream, glowing in the grey, desiccated claw of the last man to hold it.

Fred shuddered at the memory of the dead man's face, lips drawn back, eyes wide, staring at nothing. Not even the foxes had dared to cross the threshold of the cabin.

He wished he hadn't.

"Ernie found something. I told him to leave it, but he couldn't." he lied. He swallowed again. "And then he...changed."

Mary stared at him, wide eyed. She shook her head slowly. But her hands clutched again, and he knew she believed him.

"Wendigo."

They jumped at the cracked, old voice – Granny Queskekapow had been so silent and still they'd both forgotten she was there. Now they stared at her weathered face among the blankets that wrapped her.

"It is Wendigo, child. Not Ernie. No more Ernie. Only hunger. Only envy." She pinned Fred with her dark eyes. "Fred Moose. You know."

Mary shook her head. "Those are just stories!"

He blinked back the memory of the bodies they'd found: the mangled flesh, the spattered blood. The smears of it on fingers and faces. No ordinary disagreement over shares among men hoping for the next strike. He looked from the shredded window, to the table wedged against the door, and back to the old woman huddled on the bed. Granny's eyes glowed in the lantern light. He knew.

"It'll be back," he said firmly. "We have to get to town."

Mary looked slowly between them questioningly, but nodded slowly. "I have Dad's Bombardier by the road." Her eyes widened. "What about Dad? He's out there walking his line!"

Fred shook his head. "If he was close enough to be in danger he would have heard and come all the way to the lodge. This time of year he'd walk his North line first, right? In that case he's closer to town than we are." She

swallowed but didn't argue. "He'd want you both safe, so that's what we do."

His eyes narrowed as he remembered the thing that had been one of his best friends in the years since he'd returned from the trenches, and Mary's cousin. "And then I round up a few of the men and we come back to make sure you *stay* safe."

He scoured the cabin while Mary and her grandmother hunched into parkas and gathered together blankets and furs into a bundle. When they were finished, he handed Mary the rifle and jammed the hatchet he'd found into his belt. He flipped his heavy hunting knife and offered the handle to Granny Queskekapow. "In case."

She cackled. "If it comes to that I've seen enough winters, Fred Moose!" Still, she took the knife and it disappeared into her wrapping.

Carefully, he listened at the door, the hair prickling on his neck. Silence. He motioned to Mary and the two of them strained at the table, moving it back just far enough for them to file out the door.

"Mary, you lead." He winced to hear his voice come as a hoarse whisper, and cleared his throat. "Then you, ma'am." He glanced one last time around the tiny trapper's lodge, but there seemed to be nothing more for them here.

He turned back to the women. "Let's go."

The creak of the snow under their feet sounded like thunder in the deadly still. Fred's eyes flicked back and forth, his ears straining to hear above the noise. Granny stumbled once, but Fred caught her easily before she fell. Her eyes caught him, glittering in the dark. For a long moment he stood with his hands clutching her shoulders, staring into those eyes: there was something in them - a deeper fear than he'd expected, but trust too.

And a sadness he hadn't seen in her since he'd come back from the War and told her that John wouldn't.

Ahead, he heard Mary stop. Suddenly, the look in Granny Queskekapow's eyes vanished and she chuckled silently. "She'll be jealous, Fred Moose," she whispered hoarsely.

He flushed and let her go. She patted his side as she turned back to the trail, gnarled hand pausing on the deep outer pocket of his coat. He swallowed hard, and flushed deeper thinking of what was there. His hand clenched, hungry to feel the reassuring weight.

Then he cursed himself for being distracted and hurried to catch up with Mary, who had continued on when she'd seen Granny start moving again.

They were only a handful of yards from the Bombardier when the thing burst from the bush behind them with a howl that made their skin crawl: it was sharp with rage and hunger, heavy with despair as though Ernie was still inside somewhere and afraid of what he would do when he reached them.

It scrambled through the thigh-deep snow to the trail more quickly than he could believe.

"Go!" he screamed, turning to face it, imagining Mary struggling to pull Granny Queskekapow into the vehicle. He jerked the hatchet from his belt and braced to slow the thing at least long enough for the women to escape.

It lurched out of the snow and onto the packed trail, scrambled to its feet and forward -and it was on him.

The thing hit like a freight train, exploding the breath from his chest. All that saved him was how *much* stronger it was: the blow threw him back beyond its clutching fingers and into the deeper snow. He struggled to stand, but it was on him again too fast. He got his snowshoed feet up against its chest, but even with both legs straining the creature twisted its fingers into the canvas of his jacket and pulled inexorably closer, and the reek of it covered him like a smothering blanket.

Somewhere behind, he heard the Bombardier's engine cough into life. The thing didn't even look: its eyes rolled back to show the whites, its jaws dripped foam as they worked. His hair prickled when he realized it was mouthing a constant stream of words:

coldsohungryneeditgiveittomesohungryw antitsocoldsobrightsobeautifulgiveittomegiveit tome

He jerked up his arm, hesitated as the thing inched closer, then brought the hatchet down into the neck below Ernie Blacksmith's dead face.

The thing's eyes snapped back to pin him, black with rage, and it snarled. He yanked the hatchet free, gagged on the stench that bubbled from the wound along with the thick blood. It oozed: dark and sticky, left black splotches on Ernie's ragged moose-hide parka, smeared over the beadwork.

Fred hacked again, and again. The thing howled and jerked, head flailing in its *need* to catch him in its teeth. The axe came down again, and the arm hung loose, broken. Fred gave a desperate heave with his legs, and felt his sleeve tear in the thing's grip. He brought his knees back and kicked. He howled in agony as he felt his abused ankle give at last, but the creature's claw tore free with a handful of canvas and insulation and it staggered back into the snow.

He twisted, desperate to get to his feet before it could be back on him, breath coming in rasps as he struggled to untangle his snowshoes through the searing pain of his ankle as it twisted in the straps. The frozen crust broke under him as he twisted to lever upright, swallowing his arm to the shoulder. He foundered in the powder underneath. His breath came in desperate clouds as he flailed, fighting back to the packed snow of the path.

Then the thing was up, shaking itself like a wounded bear but ignoring the oozing wound in its neck and useless left arm. Fred tried to scramble back on his elbows and fumbled in the snow for the dropped axe. The thing's eyes focused on him again as his fingers closed on the haft. It hunched forward, coiled to spring and –

CRACK!

The report hit the creature like lightning, and it crumpled back into the snow. Suddenly Mary was there, sobbing as she struggled to cut the straps off his boots. At last she had the snowshoes off, him on his feet and was dragging him toward the Bombardier. Granny Queskekapow stood in the rear door fighting with the bolt of the rifle.

He hobbled as best he could, but something made him crane his head back - just in time to see the thing struggling to its feet. Its head was ruined, hair matted on the right side with dark blood. Yet still it moved. And for a moment Fred felt sure those dark eyes met his.

The thing staggered toward them. Mary thrust him clumsily into the back of the Bombardier and scrambled into the front. The engine screamed as she gunned the gas, forgetting the clutch. She cursed. He struggled up as Granny Queskekapow pressed the rifle into his hands.

Still the thing came on.

Mary finally got into gear, and the tracks threw up snow as they lurched forward. She leaned on the wheel, shouting at the machine to turn more tightly. But the skis caught in the pack on the narrow lane and the whole thing shuddered sideways as the tracks shoved them forward.

Fred was nearly thrown from the door as he fought with the bolt of the rifle. The creature was almost on them as he shoved a round into the chamber and brought the weapon up.

CRACK!

It staggered with the point-blank force, but this time it didn't fall. As it twisted back toward them he could see the ragged hole in its left shoulder where the bullet had gone through its heart. Something dark oozed down its back, but the creature seemed oblivious.

Still it came on.

He yanked back the bolt again, and cursed when the third round jammed fast. The Bombardier jerked and shuddered as Mary urged it through the brush at the side of the lane in a series of blasts from the tracks. He prayed the skis and their struts would survive the abuse.

The thing's face twisted in an obscene grin as it clutched for him – missed when the Bombardier lurched forward a yard, then caught him in its claw. He jammed himself against the door frame as another lurch jerked the creature forward and threatened to tear him out into the night. Behind him, he heard the clatter as Granny Queskekapow fumbled in the locker.

He braced himself with his back and his good leg and swung the butt of the rifle at the thing's face. Tooth and bone crunched under his blow, twisting the thing's snarl into a leer. The stench of its putrid blood swirled around him and he felt bile rising to mix with the metal of his fear.

The Bombardier was free. He felt the jerk as Mary forced it into second gear too soon. She was shouting back at him over her shoulder, frantic, but he couldn't hear her over the roaring in his ears. He pounded at the thing again and again, but even one-handed it pulled itself closer and got one foot up onto the running-board. Its lips moved, and he could hear Ernie Blacksmith's twisted voice in his mind:

coldsohungryneeditgiveittomesohungryw antitsocoldsobrightsobeautifulgiveittomegiveit tome

Suddenly there was light behind him,

yellow as butter and throwing the shadow of his blows crazily over the thing's face.

Fred felt the heat on his face as Granny thrust the kerosene lamp at the thing's face.

It flinched back, eyes wide – the black suddenly rimed with white. She thrust past him again, spattering flaming droplets across his sleeve as she tried to get as close to the creature as she could.

Mary screamed something at him, and the Bombardier surged forward. Fred clung to the frame of the door, dropped the rifle, and snagged Granny Queskekapow's arm to hold her firm. The thing lurched off its feet, struggled to keep hold of him with its unruined arm and get itself upright. He lifted both his feet and kicked.

With a howl, the thing's fingers tore loose and it stumbled.

He snatched the lamp from Granny's gnarled fingers and launched it at the creature's chest. It burst with a "whoof" of sudden conflagration.

He stared at the pillar of fire that had been Ernie Blacksmith as the Bombardier picked up speed, craning out the door to see the burning shape stumble against a pine as they tore toward the road.

Mary took the turn so sharply the machine nearly keeled over, but then they were on the roughly packed snow of the road and accelerating toward town – and safety.

Fred pulled the door shut against the cold and slumped onto the bench. Granny Queskekapow was fumbling in the locker again, pulling out what she needed to start the stove, and through the window at the back of the cabin he saw a line of smoke trailing up into the sky.

He reached forward to put his hands gently on Mary's shoulders. She flinched and hunched down tighter over the wheel.

"Pull over," he said. "We're safe."

She nodded uncertainly, but let the Bombardier coast to a stop where the road turned at the north point of the lake. In the silence when she turned off the engine, the hiss of the kerosene stove was deafening. Fred thought about the fire behind them.

He threw open the door and stepped out into the cold. Mary followed him as he limped through the bush to stand at the edge of the lake, staring south to where that thin trail had already disappeared into the darkness. His fist clenched around the gold in the pocket of his coat.

Mary clutched his arm, pulling herself close. "Do you think it's really over?"

He nodded slowly, then pulled it out of his pocket, opened his hand to watch the little, misshapen lozenge glitter under the stars.

He thought about what he had seen in the prospectors' camp: the devastation and mangled bodies, faces twisted into expressions that had no place on any man.

He thought about how that look had come over Ernie's face when he'd pried the gold from that dead, dry hand. How the *hunger* had come over him.

Staring at the gold, it suddenly seemed heavier than the world.

"That must be worth more than you make in a year!" Mary breathed. "Give it to me."

He glanced up at her, startled, saw the fever glitter in her eyes. A chill washed over him.

His fist squeezed the gold tight, and in a single spasm he hurled the thing far out over the lake.

"Fred! Why!" Mary shouted, jerking forward to snatch at it, but it was gone.

For a moment, he was almost overcome by the urge to scramble out over the ice and dig through the windswept snow for treasure. But then the moment passed, and he felt the tension drain out of him.

He led her back to the Bombardier over her protests. In the window, he saw Granny Queskekapow's eyes glittering as she watched them. She nodded.

He pressed Mary into the back, ducked forward to the driver's seat. The road stretched straight on as far as he could see.

"*Now* it's over," he said.

"*The Price of Hunger*" is copyright © *Kevyn Winkless.*

Kevyn has been writing SFF for decades, boasting his first green "no thanks" from Asimov's in 1989, and that wasn't even the beginning. Since then, he has published poetry in a number of amateur anthologies, flash fiction and studies online, and occasional fragments of longer projects. In recent years, Kevyn has returned to focus on SFF by putting his training in anthropology to work, sifting through digital archives of pulp era greats to learn what made them tick. He shares what he's learned and its results in various places online, including on Google+, on his blog Actually..., and in occasional rants on Twitter where he appears as @WhenUrukFell. Kevyn's current project is the upcoming pulp-style magazine: EXTANT!, which he is working on in his ample spare time living and working with his family in Japan, where for 20 years he has often lived the future he likes to read about. Learn more about Kevyn at his blog: http://intellectdevourer.blogspot.ca/

TOTALLY RANDOM FACTS

1. The people who backed StoryHack issue 1 on Kickstarter have been scientifically* proven to be 15% better looking than the general population.

2. This one time Bryce (the editor) had tickets to go to Neil Diamond, but forgot to go to the show.

3. There is no Dana, only Zuul.

4. Coming up with space fillers late at night when you're half asleep is probably a bad idea.

* Making stuff up is a science, right?

Lydia Madison is the daughter of a dragon hunter, and the second of three wives in a plural marriage in a tiny village in the Utah Territory. When her husband is abducted by a dragon, only Lydia can rescue him... even if it means trading her own life for his.

Retrieving Abe

BY JAY BARNSON

Two days after her husband's abduction, Lydia Madison took it upon herself to rescue him. She slung the knapsack across her back, took her father's rifle in her hand, and closed the door of her tiny house for perhaps the last time.

Her path through the tiny Utah village of Shiblon took her past the home of her neighbor Phoebe, Abraham Madison's first wife. Phoebe hung laundry in the morning sun as her three tiny children played in the yard. Her swollen, red eyes belied the normalcy of her chores. She and Lydia had never gotten along well, although they now suffered similarly in grief, if not equally. Lydia hadn't been able to shed tears yet.

Phoebe glanced at the rifle, and asked, "Are you going hunting, Lydia?"

Lydia shook her head. "Not for food. I'm going to retrieve our husband."

Phoebe responded in a dull monotone. "You'll just get yourself killed, or hurt like the Miller boy. I heard the council has put together a reward. Someone may come."

"Nobody is coming. Saint George has offered twice as much for more than a month, and nobody's come. Unless Brother Porter's back from Colorado, I don't think there's a dragon hunter anywhere in the Utah Territory right now. I'm going to fetch Abe."

"Then I will mourn you both."

Lydia took it as some measure of kindness, rather than an insult. Lydia knew the danger better than anyone. She had scant chance of success, or even survival. "Will you let Grace know?"

"Grace went back to her family in Manti. She took her baby and left for the train earlier this morning. I doubt she'll return unless Abraham does."

Lydia almost smiled. So Grace, Abraham's third wife, showed some practicality after all. Phoebe's family lived in Shiblon, and would provide for her the best that their meager means allowed. The rest of the community would, of course, assist. Lydia had no other family to aid or mourn her. Just Phoebe. "If he still lives, I'll do what I can to bring him back."

"Do you think he is still alive?"

"I do. But I don't know for how long. Dragons rarely kill their captives immediately. But in the end, they always kill them."

The able-bodied men of Shiblon had mounted a rescue expedition two days earlier, hours after the dragon had snatched Abe from his fields. The expedition ended in disaster. The dragon attacked them, setting fire to the mountainside and forcing the men to flee. Sixteen-year-old Isaac Miller had run the wrong way. The doctor expected him to live, but he'd endure weeks of pain and a lifetime of scarring from his burns.

The march of over two dozen men and boys both ways left an obvious trail for Lydia to follow up the mountain. By early afternoon, it came to an abrupt end. Beyond a depression lay the dead, charred remains of the forest. The dragon had contained the burned area well, as dragons do. They possessed an understanding of wind and flame far beyond man's comprehension. The inferno had consumed hundreds of acres of mountainside, but left the surrounding area untouched, protected by wind and natural fire breaks. A section of forest was now a field of ash and dead, blackened tree husks, filled with the odor of stale smoke and ash.

Lydia unslung her rifle as she passed through the haunted, scorched land of gray. The air glowed as the afternoon sunlight illuminated the thick, unsettled dust. Soot and ash caked her boots and the hem of her homemade dress, and coated the inside of her mouth and nose. While it was less than a mile across the wasteland, the steep incline and foul air made it feel like five.

The ridge on the far side overlooked a steep, rocky gully, crossed by a well-constructed bridge to her left. Beyond lay a shallow valley with a small lake in its center, dotted by trees and overgrown green fields. A small herd of deer drank from the southern side of the lake. On the east bank stood a cottage.

Who would live in a dragon's hunting ground? Were they victims of the dragon's appetite? Rubbing her thumb nervously over the ridges of the untested rifle's hammer, she crossed the ridge and made her way to the bridge.

She'd fired every one of her father's guns except this one. A young gun maker in Ogden named John Browning designed the single-shot lever-action weapon, customizing it for dragon-hunting. The gun's stock contained a mechanism of springs and gears to reduce the perceived recoil for its heavy, powerful ammunition.

It arrived the day after her father left for his final hunt. She didn't know how much Brother Browning knew about dragons, but folks claimed that he and his father had known plenty about guns. Browning included six bullets of her father's design. A brass jacket over the round penetrated the dragon's scales, then peeled away. A reservoir in the lead core contained a poisonous compound the dragon hunters called "dragonsbane." The poison hindered a dragon's ability to create flame. Her father had incorporated the poison into all of his hunting rounds over the years.

Lydia's father had taught her to shoot as soon as she'd grown enough to handle the recoil of his muzzle-loaders. She proved to be an excellent shot, and a decent hunter. While her father hunted dragons, she hunted food. Her mother protested that such activities were improper for a young lady, but she eagerly prepared the rabbits and squirrels Lydia brought home.

Lydia grew up knowing her father's vocation. Young Lydia eavesdropped on conversations, and listened eagerly when her father slipped into stories of his adventures, often over her mother's protests. Lydia learned that dragons were cunning and soulless, and often as intelligent as men. They could fly, and many were large enough to snatch a fully-grown cow from its pasture. Some dragons could speak, and were as skilled at deceit as they were with fire. They took human captives for amusement and as slaves before killing them. Some dragons could even change their form, to appear as animals, or even as humans.

Her father often said that if you looked into a dragon's eyes, you could see the fires of Hell.

Most importantly, Lydia learned how dangerous they were. While she understood the possibility that he might not return, she took her father's success for granted. Shortly after her mother's death, he set out on a job and never came back. After the dragon moved on to another territory, a search party found only his broken rifle and the sheath of his prized hunting knife. Lydia wished they'd kept searching for the knife. Of all her father's tools and weapons, the Damascus-steel Bowie knife was what she thought of when she remembered her father. He wore it everywhere, even to church.

Months after her father's death, Lydia married Abraham Madison. She hadn't fired a gun in her three years of marriage. She'd planned on making babies, not killing dragons, but unlike riflery she hadn't gotten the knack of that one. Her one pregnancy terminated early, and what had issued out of her had resembled a tiny wingless dragon more than a human child. The midwife told her it had probably been dead inside her for weeks.

Lydia secretly believed it must have had a twin, because she still felt something dead inside her ever since.

The bridge was well-made and well-maintained. Dragons had no need of bridges, but her quarry had allowed this one to stand, like the cottage. The bridge spanned a twenty-foot gap that was more than half as deep as it was wide. While not strictly necessary to cross the gully, it was far more convenient.

When Lydia had made it halfway across the bridge, the wide boards snapped beneath her. She frantically reached out as she fell, grabbing hold of a support beam as her rifle tumbled onto the rocks below. The beam and her tenuous grasp held for the moment. She looked up to where she might get a stronger handhold to pull herself up, and looked down at the ground below. A six-foot drop from her dangling feet seemed dangerous but not life-threatening. A jagged boulder directly beneath her presented the greatest danger, and the other rocks threatened to turn her ankles if she landed wrong. But a controlled drop seemed far less dangerous than an accidental one. With a little bit of a swing to land clear of the boulder, she let go of the bridge.

She collapsed rather than let her ankles take the full measure of the drop. One of the jagged stones caught her arm and carved a nasty gash through her sleeve and skin, but otherwise she escaped harm. She took off the knapsack and opened it. Aside from the all-important collection of bullets, it contained some morsels of dried food, fresh water, a clean washcloth, and a bottle of rubbing alcohol. The bottle had taken no damage in the fall.

She tore the sleeve off along the rip. If she rescued Mr. Madison, she'd prevail upon him to buy her cloth to make a new dress. For once, Phoebe and Grace would be unable to object. She opened the bottle of alcohol and dribbled it across her injury, wincing and sucking in air through her teeth at the sting. Then she covered the wound with clean cloth from her pack, and tied it in place with the remnants of her sleeve.

Next to the rifle lay the broken halves of the board that had snapped beneath her. The supports had not been connected at all to the beams on either side of the bridge, and the underside had been carefully scored to weaken it. The bridge was a trap for an unwary dragon hunter, and she had literally fallen for it. Only luck had saved her from falling with full force onto the jagged boulder beneath it.

She could almost hear her father's voice in her ear telling her, "Dragons lie." She vowed not to be victim to such treachery again. She retrieved the rifle and searched for a way to scramble out of the gully.

After a short but challenging climb, she continued down into the small valley. She circled around the lake–little more than a large pond, less than a quarter mile in diameter–and made her way carefully towards the house. She scanned the sky as she went, expecting a swooping dragon at any moment, but spied only birds. For all of her father's stories, she'd only seen a living dragon once, and then at a distance.

As she approached the house, the door opened. A beautiful, tan-skinned woman stepped out onto the porch, dressed in a buckskin dress with elaborate beadwork. She looked directly at Lydia, and Lydia spotted the red glare in her eyes, like a cat's eyes at night looking into a flame. Lydia raised the rifle, and hooked her finger onto the trigger.

"Do you mean to kill me, young woman?" the woman asked in precise, educated English. Her voice betrayed no fear as she stared down the barrel of the rifle.

Lydia closed the distance in several slow, careful paces, her aim unwavering in spite of the weight of the weapon. "I mean to bring my husband back home. Does he still live?"

The woman arched an eyebrow. "Ah, you must be Lydia," she said. "He told me about you. He's in the house, alive and well. I imagine he'll be out momentarily, now that he's heard us. He's my guest, not my prisoner."

"You'd let him return?"

"If he chooses."

Lydia lowered her stance, aiming at the woman's horrible, confident smile through the gun sights. "Are you suggesting he doesn't want to come back?"

The woman didn't answer. Abraham emerged from the doorway, dressed as he'd been the day he'd been abducted. His clothes were clean and pressed, and his coat bore gleaming new cufflinks. His beard and mustache were freshly trimmed. Clearly he'd been well taken care of while the town below mourned him.

"What's going on here?" he asked. "Lydia, what are you doing here? And why are you pointing a gun at Clementine? Put that thing down before you hurt someone!"

Lydia lowered the muzzle slowly, narrowing her eyes at the woman. "Clementine, is it? That doesn't sound like a dragon's name."

The woman narrowed her eyes at Lydia and hesitated before answering. "It's not. But it's easier to pronounce with human tongues. I have difficulty saying it myself when I am in this form."

Abraham turned his astonished gaze at Clementine. "What are you saying? What about your dragon?"

Clementine sighed. "I'm afraid I've been dishonest with you, darling. The dragon is not my pet. It is me. I can change into this form."

"But... you said..."

"I said a lot of things, Abe, dear. I'm sorry. I lie. I wanted to get to know you better before

I told you the truth. I also lied about my age. I'm not twenty-five. I'm almost two hundred years old. Your town was my hunting ground long before you were born. I've been to your much-vaunted Eastern cities when they were still trading villages. Those golden cufflinks I gave you were gifts from a young French nobleman I met about eighty years ago in New York who had escaped the guillotine during the revolution."

Abraham moved his hand self-consciously as if to cover the cufflinks, but stopped himself.

"Mister Madison," Lydia addressed her husband formally, "Have you been in a sinful relationship with this woman?"

Abraham's momentarily bewildered expression told Lydia all she needed to know. Rather than take offense, he answered, "No, I'd never do such a thing. But I can see how this arrangement might give the appearance of impropriety, and for that, I apologize."

Clementine aimed her smug half-smile at Lydia. "Yes, your morals and your religion. Speaking of which, what exactly does your religion say about the state of your soul if you murder me? I'm not threatening you. I've committed no crime against you."

"You stole my husband."

"Borrowed."

"Will you return him now?"

"Let's not let temper get the best of us." Abraham objected. "True, that thing carried me away. But Clementine has been nothing but a gracious hostess these two days. I planned to return soon now that the mountain fires have burned out."

Lydia frowned. While Abraham was a skilled farmer and businessman, she'd always known an over-abundance of brains had not been one of his gifts. But had the woman's beauty beguiled him beyond common sense? "Clementine set that fire to attack your rescuers."

Clementine looked apologetically at Abraham. "They were coming to kill me, Abe. None of them died. But I did lie about the size and duration of the fire. I'm sorry. I lie. It's a terrible habit of mine. But I wanted so desperately for you to stay with me just a little longer."

"So may I take him home?" asked Lydia.

Clementine turned her palms upward, smiling at the man. "Your presence has done wonders to calm me. But if I were to be thrust so soon back into loneliness, I'm not sure what I would do. However, if your dear wife Lydia would be willing to stay with me for just a few days, I'm certain her company would satisfy my cravings for companionship. You can then leave, and even keep those gold cufflinks as a reminder of our delightful visit."

"Nonsense. I'll be leaving with my wife. I've enjoyed my stay here, but now that I know it was all deception, I'm afraid it has poisoned the memory of it."

"I am sorry, Abraham," said Clementine. "But that is not an option."

Lydia raised the rifle again, aiming squarely at Clementine's heart, and asked, "Is that a threat, dragon?" Lydia's index finger brushed the trigger, yet she could still not bring herself to pull it. Whether her hesitation was born of fear for her soul, or fear of Clementine's wrath should she fail, she wasn't sure. She knew from her father's unguarded stories how swift and hardy dragons could be. She wished she could recall any story about whether or not that applied to them in human form as well.

Clementine's eyes flashed red as she turned back to Lydia, arms down, hands half-clenched like claws. "Are you sure of your skills, girl? I promise safety. If you attack me, I will not show mercy to either of you. Is that what you want?"

Abraham stood firm. "Now that I know what you truly are, fiend, I will not leave my wife in danger."

"Please, Abraham. I'll be fine," Lydia said, hoping that she could be forgiven for this lie. "Phoebe and Grace and your children need you. Go now, and you should be able to get to them before dark. Keep to the side of the bridge across the gully, because some of the boards may be weak."

"I can't leave you with this thing, Lydia." Abraham stated simple truth, she realized. His sense of responsibility meant that he would rather die than leave her captive with the dragon.

"Abraham," Lydia spoke flatly, feigning more confidence than she felt. "I promised to honor you, but in this matter, you must trust me. If you do not leave right now, we will both die."

Lydia's eyes riveted on Clementine, who simpered at them. Abraham hesitated, shifting his eyes between the two women. Finally, he answered in a half-whisper, "I'll get help, Lydia. Don't fear."

"I won't." Another lie.

Abraham turned and retreated, retracing Lydia's path along the lake.

Lydia lowered the heavy rifle before it began to shake from her fatigue and fear. Dragons rarely kill their captives immediately, she reminded herself. She had until Clementine got bored with her. She reminded herself that she only need keep the dragon distracted for a few hours to allow Abraham time to return home. After that, she could worry about keeping herself alive.

Clementine cast a final glance at Abraham, pressing her lips together as if tasting something sour. Then she turned her full attention on Lydia. "You must be tired from your journey," she said. "Would you like to come in and sit a spell, perhaps have some tea?"

"I don't drink tea," Lydia said, gently lowering the rifle's hammer. "I suppose I could sit a while." Fighting her instinctive urge to flee, she followed Clementine into the house.

While small, the cottage proved to be immaculately clean. The eclectic decorations were tastefully arranged, varying from works of art to unusual crafts to weaponry. The house's furnishings were simple yet well-made. Lydia could not hide her surprise. "Do you live here?"

"Where did you think I lived? A cave?"

"I didn't really think about it."

"I've had to resort to caves from time to time, I confess. But I've taken on human form so often that I've grown accustomed to human comforts. And companionship," she noted as she seated herself on a wooden chair with a silk cushion. She pointed to its duplicate on the other side of the room.

Lydia shrugged off the knapsack and sat, propping her rifle carefully against the wall under a painting of a mansion.

"That was Helena House in Georgia," Clementine said with a back-handed wave towards the painting. "Lovely place before the war. I lived there almost a year."

"If you lived in all these places, why did you come back here?" Lydia asked. She felt nervous without the gun in her hands, but knew that in close quarters, it made little difference. With or without it, she was at the dragon's mercy for now.

Clementine didn't answer right away. "I came back because the world became too big. Your kind became too big. My kind, we must have freedom to take wing. And that's what this desert land means to you, isn't it? Liberty, freedom?"

Lydia nodded. "People out east weren't fond of our religion."

"Or your system of marriage, I understand. Tell me about Abraham. I admit, in spending time with him, I've had trouble understanding how such a boring man might manage to convince not just one woman, but three, to marry him."

Lydia felt her cheeks grow hot. "He's a good man and a good provider. He took me in by way of calling, as I was unwed and had recently lost my parents, and had no great skills. He had plenty to share."

"And so now you share him. Tell me, is that enough for you?"

Lydia had asked herself the same question many times in the last three years, and already knew the answer, although it still hurt. "Faith manages. But I think it would have been better if I'd been able to have children of my own." It felt somehow easier to confess this to an enemy. Lydia didn't regret it, even knowing that Clementine would use this information to twist the knife in the coming hours or days. The key to extending survival was to keep the dragon entertained, after all.

Clementine nodded, her expression almost sympathetic. "He told me about that. I'm sorry to have guided the discussion to such a sensitive topic. Perhaps you'd feel better if you had something to eat. It's nearly suppertime. Is stew okay?"

"Are you feeding me?"

"Of course. You are my guest, after all. It's nothing fancy, though. There's stew left in the pot that we can heat up, if that is acceptable."

"More than acceptable. Thank you." A meal would provide another hour or two of distraction, and Lydia realized how hungry she'd become hiking up the mountain.

"It will take a while to heat. There's bread in the oven, baked fresh this morning. For dessert, how about some fresh berries? There are some that grow in the woods just behind this house."

"Oh, I don't need dessert, ma'am."

"Call me Clementine. And I insist. It will only take a few minutes. Would you be so kind as to start the stove? It already has wood and kindling. You can use the matchsticks on the wall."

With that, Clementine grabbed a basket and left out the back door. Lydia stood and walked to the stove in the kitchen. This turn of events confused her, but she had to admit that Clementine played the part of the hostess well. Lydia found the tin container holding the matchsticks on the wall. As she reached for it, she noticed the knife hanging beside it, and her hand froze.

It was not a kitchen knife. It was an oversized, quality Bowie knife like her father's. He'd used his to behead dragons for proof of payment. She peered at it closely. The riveted buckskin sheath was new. She'd almost forgotten the markings and imperfections on the hilt, the dent in the pommel. She pulled the blade halfway out of the sheath, and immediately recognized the unique swirls along the Damascus steel blade.

Her vision swam.

The hanging ornaments on the walls weren't simply eclectic decorations. They were trophies from Clementine's victims, including Lydia's father. What French nobleman would give a woman a gift of cufflinks, after all?

Of course, Clementine lied. By her own admission, she lied constantly. Why should being honest about previous deceptions validate any new promises? Lydia had known what Clementine was from the beginning. A dragon. Dragons always kill their captives. Not instantly, but eventually.

And now she claimed to be gathering berries.

She lies.

Lydia cursed herself with words she'd rarely heard her father use after he'd joined the faith. She snatched the rifle and the knapsack containing the extra bullets, and raced out the door towards the mountain path. In the brilliant light of the late-afternoon sun, she caught the silhouette of giant wings disappearing behind the ridgeline. Her panic forced her exhausted body forward as she willed herself up the trail, despairing that no matter how fast she ran, she'd be too late.

This time, the bridge provided a quick path across the gully as she kept to one side, walking along the beam. When she topped the ridge, she squinted into the late sun across the ashen graveyard where blackened trees stood like tombstones. The defoliated field provided an excellent view of the dragon in its true form down the slope from her. Its leathery, scale-covered back was turned to Lydia. The beast's folded wings and body shielded most of whatever it ate from Lydia's view, but the late sun glinted off a golden cufflink half-buried in blood-soaked ash.

Beneath her horror and guilt, a fury rose within her, seeming to lift the gun barrel with it. With old habit she brought the stock up to her cheek and simultaneously thumbed back the hammer. Without hesitation or compassion, she took aim at the spine where the serpentine neck joined the shoulders, and gently squeezed the trigger.

The explosion was her own voice, a deafening scream of rage and defiance. The creature whipped its snakelike head up and around, fangs dripping crimson. The round missed the spine, but blossomed at the base of its thick neck. The hole seemed a pinprick against the creature's bulk, but Lydia knew the sledgehammer force against her shoulder—partly cushioned by Browning's springs and gears in the stock—had been concentrated into a nearly half-inch lead point that expanded inside the wound. It would drop a buffalo if it hit a critical area, but a dragon—easily a match for a buffalo in size—was a different beast entirely.

The dragon that called itself Clementine shrieked. It beat its mighty wings, whipping up a billowing cloud of gray ash as its great mass lifted impossibly into the air.

Lydia shook off the knapsack, and dug inside. Her hasty grasp secured two bullets. She jammed one round between her teeth as she watched the dragon soar above the dead trees and circle towards her. She glanced down briefly to work the gun's lever to eject the spent casing, slid another round into the chamber, and slammed the block closed.

She glanced up just as Clementine dove towards her, wings outstretched. While every instinct told her to run the other way, she heeded vaguely-remembered advice from her father, and ran at an angle towards the dragon.

Dragon fire, contrary to the legends, is neither extremely hot, nor does it possess great range. Lydia's father referred to it as "dragon spit." While more than enough to kill a man with a direct hit, dragons more often relied upon their ability to precisely generate and predict the secondary fires. A target's sudden move at an angle towards them confused their aim, forcing an early, less precise shot. Dragons also didn't turn very well in flight, forcing another pass–which allowed a skilled hunter another shot. The ash field provided one more advantage for Lydia: there was nothing else near her left to burn.

Even so, the heat from Clementine's blast struck Lydia's back so hard she thought for a moment that she'd been hit. Behind her, a glob of burning ooze settled into the ash.

Clementine had already turned for a second pass. Lydia spun and fired a snapshot, but couldn't tell if the round hit before throwing herself to the side.

Small flaming globs rained down around her in a scattered pattern, but none hit her. An ash cloud from the buffeting wings sprayed around her, coating her mouth as it entered around the teeth clenching the bullet. Lydia coughed, nearly losing the bullet.

The dragonsbane must have begun working, she realized, causing the dragonfire to lose cohesion. Lydia ejected the spent brass from the rifle, pulled the bullet from between her teeth, and locked it in place inside the rifle's chamber. She tried to spot her knapsack, but the ash cloud blocked her vision. She didn't even see Clementine until a moment before the dragon landed in front of her.

Lydia stumbled backwards from the creature and raised the rifle as the snakelike head inhaled for a nearly point-blank shot. A short, insubstantial spray of flame mingled with the muzzle flash from the rifle. The shot went straight through the top of its mouth and into its brain. Clementine the dragon collapsed instantly.

Lydia, singed by the heat but untouched by the direct flame, fell to her knees and sobbed.

It was nearly noon the following day when Lydia returned to town. The sentries watching for the dragon's return nearly took her for a monster due to her ghoulish appearance. Her dress was torn and blackened from soot and flame. Ash, dirt, and blood covered what the dress no longer did. Her shriveled, brittle hair wildly framed a dirty, almost unrecognizable face marked by tear-streak paths. Her father's hunting knife dangled on a makeshift belt around her waist, and his rifle was still slung on her back. Behind her, she dragged a rudely crafted travois. It held two bloody bundles wrapped in bedclothes from Clementine's house: one, the remains of her husband; the other, the head of the dragon. Her knapsack, filled with small treasures liberated from Clementine's house, jostled alongside the grislier cargo.

She stopped at the Bishop's home first, to drop off the dragon's head, collect her reward, pay her tithes, and to ask for help burying her husband.

The day after the funeral, Lydia slung her father's rifle over her shoulder alongside her knapsack, with her father's knife hanging from her waist on one of Abraham's belts. She paid one last visit to Phoebe.

Phoebe glanced at the rifle. "Are you hunting again, Lydia?" she asked.

"In a manner of speaking." She handed a wad of greenbacks to Phoebe. "This is the reward money I collected for the dragon. Please see that Grace gets half."

"What about you?"

Lydia adjusted the rifle on her shoulder, its weight now strangely comforting. "I'm heading down to Saint George. I understand they have an unclaimed reward and a need for a dragon hunter."

"Retrieving Abe" is copyright © Jay Barnson.

Jay Barnson is a writer, software engineer, and an award-winning video game developer. He has written for The Escapist and Cirsova magazines, and has been published in several anthologies. He is the first place winner in the 2016 DragonComet writing award. Most importantly, this is Jay's second time appearing in the hallowed pages of StoryHack. His first novel, "The Blood Creek Witch," will be released in early 2018 from Immortal Works Press.

A wealthy inventor has been discretely sponsoring do-gooders in steam-powered suits for years. When another of his heroes faces death, can he just stand by and watch a good man die?

Protector of Newington

BY JOHN M OLSEN

The brass and steel suit wasn't meant to take bullets. I cringed as I watched from the far side of the intersection as Donald waded into the fight, metal-encased arms tossing Arnold Tucker's thugs around like dolls as they fired deafening shot after shot at him. They didn't seem to care they were as likely to shoot each other as the armored suit. Not an intelligent lot, those men.

A shot clipped a pressure line, and an oily squelch of steam burst up into the air. The smells of burned gunpowder and oil wafted across the street.

One man said, "Got 'im. He'll be out of power soon now." At least Donald had enough control left to knock the man's teeth out before the suit tipped and fell.

The remaining men gathered as Donald tried to get up and collapsed back to the ground in the heavy suit, scraping on the cobbles. Tentatively at first, one of them poked his downed opponent with a toe. Then Tucker cracked his knuckles and said, "Stretch him out flat. I'm goin' ta see what makes him tick."

The situation left me with no choice. I waited until the thugs touched the suit, then pulled out my chain with three ultrasonic whistles. A sharp puff on the first whistle triggered the Tesla battery. A dog howled two streets over. With luck, Donald wouldn't have any idea I'd intervened. He was the hero, after all.

The electrical blast dropped the men senseless as if hit between the eyes with a bat.

The second whistle opened the valve to an emergency pressure tank. Donald creaked to his feet and looked around at the men as they twitched on the ground, then held his clenched gauntlets up in victory.

Donald's amplified voice came out through a megaphone cone on the front of his helmet. "Citizens, please send for the bobbies. These miscreants shall no longer accost you."

Shopkeepers and pedestrians filed out of their hiding places in nearby stores. They knew how to detain men who didn't fight back. By the time bobbies arrived, Tucker's unarmed thugs lined the side of the street with their hands and feet tied.

The crowd grew, so I approached to pick up Donald now that I couldn't be associated with his heroics. Not everyone wanted Moroccans in London, let alone a cripple like me. But when I played the part of a Hansom steam cab driver, they never looked twice at a one-legged man in a fez. I was invisible to them.

By the time I pulled up within easy listening distance, Donald spoke to a newsman, still upright. "And that's how I singlehandedly took down these hoodlums who demanded protection money from local businesses. They won't bother these good people anymore. In this modern day and age, we must all use technology to our advantage to promote civility, since the criminal element won't hesitate to use machines to do their nefarious work."

He always had a good speech handy when he worked. I'd seen this newsman speak to him before. The paper that ran on the south shore of the Thames described him as the mysterious Protector of Newington.

The bobby captain strolled up wearing a fresh-pressed uniform, baton in hand. "Thank you again, sir, for your help. We'll get these men off to the county jail over on Horsemonger Lane. I imagine it will be a short stop before we walk them over to the Queen's Bench Prison for a long stay." It seemed the policeman wanted to be in the newspaper article as well. I suppressed a smile.

"I'm glad to assist our fine police force, since it's impossible for you to be everywhere despite your best efforts. We are lucky these men were simple footpads, rather than machinists and metalworkers bent to evil."

I waved to Donald and got his attention, motioning him to come with me.

"Good people, I must leave you now." He clanked over to my cab and climbed in, barely fitting through the door. "If you ever need me, I'll—" His power failed completely, and he slumped into the passenger compartment as I closed the door.

The next morning, Donald arrived for breakfast. "See how well it went? It's right here in the paper, Fahim. They're calling me the Protector again." Donald beamed as he sipped his steaming tea, flavored with bergamot oil and far too much sugar for my taste.

I nodded. "As they should. You do your job well, but you took too many risks. The suit will take days to repair. You can't go out until the suit is whole again. Last time, you sunk it in the Thames. I warned you about water. Now bullets. You risk not only the metal suit, but your own life. Those men could have hurt or killed you."

"But it worked. We beat them. Right here it says all six men went to jail. It gives their names." Donald read through the list.

I turned. "Wasn't Arnold Tucker among them? You didn't read his name. He was the one who wanted to tear you apart."

Donald's eyebrows rose and his eyes grew wide, "If he escaped, then we have to go back out for him. Can the suit be ready tonight?"

I held back a sharp retort. After a steadying breath, I said, "We took a month to get him and his men all in one spot. The suit is a mess. I told you it would take days to fix. We need more time, more information, and a plan."

"We know where he lives. I can follow him and see where he goes. He never saw my face since I had the full suit on."

I raised an eyebrow.

"Fine, fine," he said. "I won't apprehend him yet. I'll only watch and follow, I promise. From a distance. Do you want me to wear a fake beard, too?"

Worry clung to me like a sweaty blanket. It would be easier if he actually ever tried to stay safe. "I will repair the suit as quickly as I can, inshallah." If God wills it. It would take long hours, but I had everything on hand in the warehouse. I picked up a wrench and made good use of my time while Donald played at being a spy.

Donald returned from his day's expedition as I patched up yet another hole in the mechanized armor with a loud spark from the welding rod. A haze of smoke lingered in the air from my work. The pressure lines would hold for now, but several struts had bent, and might succumb to metal fatigue if I bent them back into shape yet again.

"I tracked him to an orphanage between the Church Street dirigible ferry and St. Mary's Chapel. Funny, that. I've never noticed an orphanage at the docks before, but the place was lousy with children when I peeked through the window. He made the trip to the building this morning, and back home in the evening. Steam trucks made deliveries and picked things up all day. He took a satchel of some sort home."

I glanced up from the large workbench, with my magnifiers still in place. "I understand deliveries. Children must eat. But shipments? What would he ship from an orphanage?" I removed the lenses and sat back rubbing my chin. I looked at my hand and realized I had just rubbed bearing grease all over myself.

"Does it matter? We know how to get him. I can put the suit on, collar his scurvy carcass as he arrives at the orphanage, and drop him off at the jail with a nice note."

I shook my head. "Scurvy happens to sailors with bad diets. It makes a poor insult."

I pointed toward the distant docks with my welder. "And what he does always matters. It's the reason we went after him in the first place. The police wanted him, but they were too busy with bigger criminals like the sky pirates north of London and that fellow who murdered several families. Maybe Tucker is one of those bigger criminals, but we don't know enough about him yet. Your new information is critical, but is not sufficient."

Donald strolled toward the door. "If I follow him again, he might get suspicious. If you need more information, I know where we can get it. Have the suit ready at first light. If we find the additional clues you need, we can apprehend him as he arrives. It's been a long, hard day and I need to get some rest to prepare for tomorrow."

His plan was sound. I would work through the night if I had to.

The armor still held pressure as the pre-dawn sky lightened, but would fail if mistreated. Donald wore it anyway.

Why had I built the armor? There had to be a better way to bring justice to the world and make a better life for people. Better than my life had been in the Madina as a child. Now I had enough money to make my own path, but the mechanical suit had been my only real plan. The suit was both a wonder and a burden.

My heroes invariably asked me why I never used the armor myself. I cringed at the thought of creating an imperfect machine leg, fitted to my imperfect flesh. They always said the machine would be as beautiful if it was built for me, but I knew they agreed with me deep down. It was more important for them to wear it than for me to do so.

Some of them had tired of fighting crime after a season. Others sustained injuries and retired from the work. One unfortunate chap assumed it could break a hundred-foot fall. I was good, but I couldn't work magic. Donald lasted like the best of them, staying with me for months as the man in the suit.

I once considered adding wings to the suit, but then I thought of the poor heroes. It was bad enough that one of my friends had already died wearing it. Wings would be too dangerous. I couldn't live with myself if I subjected them to the added danger. We would have to stay firmly planted on the ground.

I steered the steam cab as Donald called out directions from inside. The sky turned from dark purple to deep shades of orange and blue as the dew-dampened streets reflected the occasional glow of gas lamps. Only bakers and delivery trucks plied the streets at such an early hour.

Donald called a stop on a street lined with warehouses. The cab let out a belch of black coal smoke and settled into place.

The face of the building across the street was more that of a shipping or manufacturing facility. Tall windows lined the front to let in light for what appeared to be office space and a shop floor. All the buildings on the street had docks in the back, accessed through a wide alley. It was nothing like an orphanage.

I asked, "You're sure this is where he went?"

He couldn't nod in the suit, but he tilted forward and back. "I peeked in through the window to the left of the door. There were more than a dozen children in there. If we go out back, we can search their large rubbish bin for evidence. I still don't see why we need to do any more than collar him, but we'll go your way. I shall keep watch while you search."

Donald wasn't the brightest hero I'd ever had, but he was observant and he put his whole heart into the work. If Donald claimed to have seen children here, there must be children. The front of the building had no dormitory windows, so the housing would be toward the back.

I said, "Yes. Let's go out back to look things over."

Donald tilted again in agreement. "You would be amazed at what you can learn about a business by what they throw out. I'm sure you can find some evidence to make you happy."

The city streets came to life in slow fits and starts as I steered into the alley and along the back of the buildings to find truck docks and rubbish bins left for pickup. I climbed down, and with the aid of my crutch made my way over to the bin behind our target warehouse.

Donald sometimes came across as a brash risk taker, but he was also a perfect match for the suit. His delicate touch on the controls was beyond reproach. He hoisted me up and lowered me into the bin with utmost care.

He said, "I'll be at the corner watching. I'll come back if I see anything."

The rotting food was of no interest. The remains of shipping crates and metal scraps covered the floor. A sheet of tin covered a large section of the bin, so I tilted it up and reeled back in horror. The body of a child about eight years of age lay in a box, discarded with the trash.

I clenched my jaw. I had no need to search any further. We would take them down and assure that Tucker and anyone else here was charged with murder. The metal scraps and papers, though incriminating, were frosting on the cake. Charges of child slavery had shut down factories in the past. The mayor of London had gone to great lengths to remove the most egregious forms of indentured servitude, but these murderers were proof that the mayor needed more help. Heroes had to step up to cleanse the city of these vile monsters.

If need be, I could donate money so the children would have a chance at a normal life, rather than being worked to death.

I peered over the edge of the rubbish bin's tall walls. My crutch leaned against the outside of the bin, out of reach.

Donald wasn't at the corner, and my heart skipped a beat.

Movement caught my eye, and I spotted him in the shadows as he approached.

Donald breathed hard from the strain of controlling the still-damaged suit. He said, "Tucker's here. He and some others met out front to talk, then they went inside. This is our chance."

"There's something you should see, Donald." I held the tin sheet back as he peered over the edge of the bin.

"Is that—" His voice choked off into silence.

"They are working children to death here."

The gauntlets clenched until pistons strained at the exertion, threatening to bend rods and burst pipes.

"You can't charge in and beat them to a pulp, Donald. We must be careful, quiet, and precise. The machine isn't ready for anything more."

Donald said, "I never told you the real reason I joined you. It wasn't for the thrills. You were my best chance at delivering justice. My wife and daughter won't have died at the hands of pirates for nothing."

I knew of his dedication, but we'd never spoken of his motivation before.

He turned and clanked back toward the corner, increasing in speed as he moved.

"But these are not those same men! They may kill you!"

He turned the corner. I was powerless to stop his righteous wrath, and I had no idea to what extremes he might go. To top it off, I was still in the bin.

A glance up at the back of the building showed a second floor with little square windows. A small face occupied one window. It must be the dormitories.

A crash echoed through the alley, strong enough to be felt through the ground. Metal screeched on metal. What was Donald up to? It sounded like he was tearing something apart. A vehicle? The suit? I had no way to tell.

I levered myself up with my arms to hang over the edge of the bin, then dropped down on the other side. I stumbled and fell in a heap, but found my crutch where I had left it. I could do nothing more to help Donald. Well, almost nothing. I pulled out my second whistle and gave it a solid but silent blast. At least he would have power to spare for a few minutes, whatever he was doing.

The ground shook again, followed by a long, slow rumble of stonework collapsing. Gunfire erupted in bursts from within the building. If he took out any supports on the front of the building, it might not handle the structural loss. These rickety constructions often stood only through sheer accident. The whole building shuddered.

I peered back up at the dormitory windows. The windows were now all lined with small faces. How many children did he have in there? If the building came down, it would trap or kill them all, and Donald was busy tearing things apart, oblivious to their need.

I would have to take care of the children myself. There was no other way.

The locked back door was too sturdy for me to break down. I peered through a large window next to the door. The early morning light was bright enough to see a shipping room closed off from the factory floor. I could still hide once I climbed inside. I broke the window with my crutch and cleared as much of the jagged glass from the frame as I could before draping my jacket over the edge. Bits of glass crunched underfoot.

As I had with the edge of the bin, I levered myself across and fell through the broken window. Another impact hit the building, and my crutch clattered to the ground outside. Was there time to go back out to retrieve it? I had no idea, but things didn't look good. I had to press onward without it. The children were in danger.

From deeper within the building, Donald's amplified voice rang out. "Tucker, your doom is upon you! Surrender, or I will destroy you!"

Donald was as dramatic as ever, but this time there was a dangerous edge to his amplified voice. Donald sounded as if he had nothing to lose and would go to any length to succeed. But what would he consider a success? Arrest? Destruction of the building? Tucker's death?

Holding to the wall, I hopped over to the door and opened it, careful to peek around before exposing myself to the dangers of Donald's rampage and the responding gunfire. Shapes moved in the dark to the far side. To my left was a stair going up with a rail on the outside, visible to the whole floor should they look my way.

A large shadow moved with rapid clanking steps. Donald. He ran across the factory floor and leaped over some floor-mounted machines. It was a beauty to behold how he controlled the suit like a dancer at the ballet despite its weakened state. As he landed, he pivoted and kicked out a support. A catwalk crashed to the ground. Several men screamed, and much of the gunfire ceased.

I crept up the stairway and stopped at a large landing at the top where I found another door. Based on what I had seen outside, the dormitory should be on the far side of the door. It was locked.

The building shifted, and I leaned against the wall to keep my balance. Wood creaked and groaned around me. On the far side of the heavy oak door children cried out with each new movement or noise. Some called for help. Others whimpered as their furnishings shifted and scraped on the floor with the shifts of the structure.

The door between us mocked my inability to open it. I didn't even have my crutch to use as a lever. I rammed my shoulder into the door and fell, useless. The wood groaned once more. The door frame twisted, and it was clear that the door wouldn't open even if it had no lock. The bent frame held it in place.

Children cried once more at the noise and movement. I needed tools, or at least someone to help me.

That was it! They had everything necessary to free themselves. "Children! I'm here let you out, but I need your help." I risked being overheard from below, but I only saw one option. This was likely the only stairway, the only way out.

A voice from the far side said, "Who are you? Can you open the door?"

"I'm a friend, not from the factory. The door is stuck. We can get it open if we work together."

A second voice asked, "Who is it, Emily?"

Emily, the first voice, said, "I don't know. He says he can help us get out." She bent down to speak through the growing crack under the door. "What do we do, sir?"

"Get the oldest children, the strongest, and bring a bed over to the door. Can you wedge part of the bed frame into that crack under the door?"

"I'm the oldest, but James, he's the strongest. James! Get the others and bring a bed here. Janet, gather the little ones."

I smiled. I had a small hero working for me on the other side of the door. Her assurance and commanding voice told me all I needed to know. They would do whatever they could under her direction. It might be enough.

A loud bellow reached me from the floor below. "Unhand me, you fiends!" The building continued to settle and groan. It might collapse on its own with no further help, but what could I do besides work to get the door open? My safety mattered little if I left the children behind. It would haunt me to the end of my days if I didn't give my best for the children and for Donald.

With a start I realized I could do more. I pulled out my first whistle and gave it a blast to trigger the recharged Tesla battery, assuming the suit still functioned. The loud electrical pop and screams from below were oddly satisfying.

"We got a bed. Now what?"

I wiggled my fingers under the door. "Can you fit a headboard, a leg or something under here? If so, you can pull on the bed and pry the door open. Do you know what a lever is?"

"I see what you mean. James, help me tip it up."

The tip of a bed's headboard jutted out underneath the door. The bed was narrow and made of thin pipe and slats, but it might work.

"Fantastic! Now pull on the top." I threw my shoulder into the door again as the headboard shifted. The door creaked, but didn't come loose. Metal groaned, and something clanked and crashed on the far side of the door.

"The bed broke. Will they punish us?"

"Not if I get you out. We can do this." I pulled the broken headboard through to my side and got my arms in place underneath it to pry from my side while on my hands and knee.

I continued, "If you can get another pipe under, lift at the same time I do."

The rampage and gunfire resumed downstairs. Donald must have broken free. Another great crash from below tilted the floor, and children screamed.

"Is everyone okay in there?"

Emily said, "Yes. It shook us around a bit is all. Janet, line them up over to the window side. It might be safer to wait there. We're all leaving when the man opens the door."

Such confidence. I hoped with all my heart it wasn't misplaced. The building was coming apart, and time was short.

I said, "You can call me Fahim. Now if you are ready, lift!" I groaned against the headboard as children on the far side pried with a pipe broken free from the bed. "Keep going."

The frame groaned, then splintered as the heavy oak door tore free from its hinges. It leaned outward and collapsed on top of me pinning me to the floor of the landing. A sharp pain flared in my ankle where it had pounded into the floor.

"Now go, children! Down the stairs, and out the back door to the docks. Hold tight to the rail as you go." I counted as the smaller children herded past through the door and down the stairway which tilted at a new angle. "There's a steam cab parked across the alley. Climb into it and hide the small children as best you can."

More children filed past, shepherded I supposed by Janet who lined them up and came out behind them. They wouldn't all fit in the cab. Finally, a girl of about fourteen and a large boy came out of the dormitory. It had to be Emily. She said, "James, help me. He's trapped."

I said, "No, you go. I'll manage." I reached for the edge of the fallen door. The thought of them risking their lives to stay and help was too much.

"Nonsense." She dropped to the floor with James and they levered the door off and leaned it against the wall.

James gawked. "It took your leg right off!"

"No, my leg was like that before, but I've hurt my ankle. I can't walk. You must hurry and get out. Stop wasting time on me."

The two of them each grabbed an arm and hoisted me up despite my protests. Hard factory labor had built James into a wiry bundle of muscle, far stronger than myself. Emily wasn't far behind, even with her lighter frame.

Another rumble echoed through the building, and the floor shifted to a steeper angle. The dormitory dropped to the floor below with a huge crash as its supports gave way. The stair and our landing still clung to the wall of the shipping room, but we swayed and teetered as we stumbled to the top of the stairway.

They hauled me down the delicate stairs, my foot barely touching on the way down.

We reached the main floor, and I peered through the dust toward the front of the building. Light came in via the gaping hole Donald had entered where the facade had fallen away. Inside, Donald stood with his back to a pillar. He faced four men with guns and two with clubs. Donald stood tall and fearless.

He braced himself against a machine mounted to the floor next to the pillar. "Today, justice will prevail. It's time you dogs got what you deserved."

Tucker leveled his pistol and said, "Kill him now."

The frame groaned, then splintered as the heavy oak door tore free from its hinges. It leaned outward and collapsed on top of me pinning me to the floor of the landing. A sharp pain flared in my ankle where it had pounded into the floor.

Steam released as Donald gave out a great cry. He put all of his effort into one last action. The surface of the pillar crumbled behind him as his bunched legs pushed against it, irreparably deforming the suit in a burst of power.

"Run, children! He means to bring the whole building down."

James said, "Not without you, sir. You saved us, now we'll save you."

Donald stood up from the rubble of the pillar and gave a salute in my direction as clouds of dust billowed up. The men all fired at him from point blank range as I lost sight in the clouds of debris and dust. Emily and James supported me as I hobbled out of the building. Stars filled my vision from the pain in my ankle at each step.

The children stopped as I cried out in pain, but I said, "We aren't safe yet. Go over by the steam cab with the other children."

The entire front collapsed, bringing the roof down as we reached the middle of the alley. The rear wall held for a moment, then tipped and fell inward leaving nothing but a pile of twisted metal, wood and rubble. I'm embarrassed to say that the last thought to cross my mind as I collapsed into unconsciousness was of shoddy structural engineering.

I awoke to the sound of a child's voice. "No, you can't take him. He saved us." I opened my eyes and there was Emily, fists on hips. She glared at the bobby as she and the other children formed a protective circle around me.

"Now, miss, we need to take him with us for a bit. He came from that building, and we looked up the men that owned it. A bad lot, they are."

I propped myself up on my elbows. "It's all right, Emily. I'll talk to him."

"If you'll come with us, now, we'll sort this out." He got a closer view of my face, clothing, and missing leg. He shook his head as if he'd been burdened with the short end of the stick at the crime scene.

"If I might explain first, this will go much more smoothly." I sat up and held the hands offered by Emily and James.

The bobby rolled his eyes, but got out a notepad and pencil. "Right then. Before I arrest you, I'll take a statement. For the sake of the children, you see."

I spoke carefully to avoid entangling myself in the investigation. I didn't want the notoriety that would come from the newspapers or police attaching me to the armor.

"Thank you. I came here in my cab two hours ago. I brought a man in an iron suit. The paper calls him the Protector of Newington. You know of him? Ah, good."

The bobby put his notepad away with no notes taken. "So you will blame all of this on him, then? I think it's time we haul you in. Now shoo, children. The grown-ups have work to do."

I held up my hand. "If he ran into grave trouble, I was to blow this whistle." I pulled out the third whistle. The one I hoped never to use. The one I always knew I would use in the end. "It will help find him."

I put it to my lips and blew. The periodic chirping of an air horn sounded in reply from deep within the rubble. It would last for an hour, maybe long enough to find what was left of him and Tucker's men.

I bowed my head. "He was a true hero, as the paper said. He looked into that rubbish bin over there and flew into a rage. My last sight of him was as he fought several armed men inside the collapsing building. All I did was help the children find their way out."

It was all true, and it was the truth which would best suit the death of a hero, companion, and coworker in the fight for goodness and light.

After another hour and the discovery of several corpses, the children were restless, scared and hungry. "Officer, might I take the children for some food and shelter? If you need anything else from me, you can get a message to me at this pneumatic tube address." I handed him a card.

The address itself was a dead drop which could be rerouted to reach me, but not allow them to find my warehouses or factory. I had no reason to expose myself to their scrutiny.

He read the card and gave a gruff nod of assent. "Right, Fahim. Is that your first or last name? Never mind. Get them over to Saint Mary's. They will be able to find food and space for them at orphanages. We'll be in touch. Such a terrible thing, losing a good man like that. We'll see to it he's buried proper as an honored citizen with the suit as a memorial."

The children's grips on my hands tightened, and they glanced down at me questioningly. I gave them a reassuring wink and squeezed their hands as they helped me to stand on my sore ankle. James handed my crutch to me. I have no idea how he found it in the mess.

My face reflected the sad situation as I spoke to the bobby. "Yes, a terrible loss of a good man. It is well to honor him."

My days of recruiting heroes to run a powered mechanical suit were at an end. Hurt and loss weighed on me. I didn't have the heart to put another good man through all that again. Two had died already and others had been hurt saving a city that didn't always want to be saved.

I was surrounded by children. My next step formed in my mind so clearly it would be a travesty to do anything else. It was time to stand up for these downtrodden and abused orphans. I would form and run an orphanage myself to take care of them and teach them everything I knew of science and humanity.

I would never be the hero Donald was, but Emily, James and the other children were heroes in their own right. They showed great promise and could surpass Donald with time. My heart would always carry the burden of the good and ill I had wrought through the armored suit, but perhaps with the children I could find peace instead of merely finding justice.

"Protector of Newington" is copyright © John M Olsen

John M Olsen reads and writes fantasy, science-fiction, steampunk, and horror as the mood strikes, and his short fiction is part of several anthologies. He devoured his father's library in his teen years and has since inherited that formidable collection and merged it with his own growing library in order to pass a love of learning on to the next generation.

He loves to create things, whether writing novels or short stories or working in his secret lair equipped with dangerous power tools. In either case, he applies engineering principles and processes to the task at hand, often in unpredictable ways.

He lives near the Oquirrh Mountains in Utah with his lovely wife and a variable number of mostly grown children and a constantly changing subset of extended family.

When the latest issue of StoryHack finally got delivered to Starbase Theta Lugosi IX, the crew started to dance.

 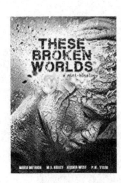  

Ben is a PI with PTSD who also just happens to be a werewolf. He is handed a repo job that seems too easy to be true. Of course things go awry and an accident flings him into a grim future. Will he be able to make it back to his wife and friends, or will he be doomed to die among total strangers?

Brave Day Sunk in Hideous Night

BY JULIE FROST

The dream started like they always did, with me behind the wheel of my Jeep, under a light pole in a parking lot. The engine was off, "Don't Fear the Reaper" blasted over the speakers, and a 9mm semi-auto Ruger rested in my hand. Whether or not it was a nightmare depended on what happened next. Nowadays, they were at the half-and-half point.

People streamed out of the reception center, and cars jockeyed their way out of the lot. Finally, a lone figure–tiny, female, and African-American–exited the building, hesitated a moment, then made her way to her little blue Hyundai, the last vehicle there. As I watched it drive away, the gun weighed heavy, but my life weighed heavier. I'd write a note, but no one would care enough to read it–my parents had died and my entire unit had been slaughtered at the hands of insurgents in Afghanistan. I'd been home for five months, after seven months of hell at the hands of those same insurgents, and I had nothing left.

"I'm sorry," I said, although I had no idea who I was talking to.

The gunshot yanked me bodily out of sleep, gasping into my wife's riot of curly black hair while her strong arms enfolded me. "Nightmare, then," I croaked, and shivered against her, struggling to put my claws and fangs and fur back where they belonged. The full moon wasn't for another week, but apparently my inner wolf didn't care. I hadn't hurt Janni–I would never hurt Janni–but I'd shredded my pillow.

Janni pulled the blanket over my shoulders and stroked my scarred back. "Easy, Ben. It wasn't real."

"At least I know that if you die in a dream, you don't really die. God, I hate that one." I inhaled her scent, grounding myself in Mate and Home and Not Alone.

Her fingers rubbed circles between my shoulder blades. "Which one was it?" There were several, a greatest-hits reel of failures and horrors.

I swallowed hard and squeezed my eyes shut. "The one where you didn't tap on my window that night at the veteran's dinner. You didn't stop me from eating my gun."

"Well." She kissed my forehead. "Your subconscious is a mean bastard, sugar, because here I am and here you are."

"It's been four years. You'd think it would know that by now." I felt limp and exhausted. "Anniversary Syndrome sucks."

"You won't get an argument from me on that score. But you're better this year than you were last year. Next year will be better still. You'll see."

"Couldn't do it without you, honey. Just. Couldn't." Sometimes how much I depended on her scared me. I wondered if it scared her too. I hated being a burden, but Janni didn't seem to mind holding me up when I couldn't do it on my own. I thanked God for her, fervently, every day.

The alarm buzzed and dragged me out of the rabbit hole I was in danger of falling into again, and I managed a shaky smile. "What good timing."

She sent me off to work at the PI firm with a handkerchief imbued with her scent. Pam–my partner and mother-in-law–had gotten there first, and she eyed me shrewdly from beside the perking coffeemaker. "Rough night, baby boy?" The cadence of her Texas accent was soothing, in its own way, because she, too, was part of Home and Pack. I felt immediately better.

I made a beeline for caffeinated goodness.

"What gave me away?" Mmm, hazelnut creamer.

"You forgot to shave, and you look like a grouchy blond raccoon. Your dark circles have dark circles." She enfolded me in a hug, which was a little overwhelming since she had three inches and fifty pounds on me. "I know this time of year is bad. How you holding up?"

"I've been worse," I said, my voice muffled against her more-than-ample bosom. "Pam, seriously, I'm all right. It was just the one nightmare. Give me something to do to take my mind off it, and I'll slurp down some coffee and try for normal."

"Mmph. If you say so." She let me go and held me at arm's length, shaking her head. "There's a case file on your desk you can work your digital magic on." She'd called me her "pet hacker" even before the werewolf thing.

"Yes, ma'am." Stirring my coffee, I sat behind my desk and woke my computer up. Untangling paper trails was its own kind of relaxing, and I was soon buried contentedly in data–although my hand strayed to Janni's handkerchief on occasion, where I'd put it beside my mouse pad.

I was so engrossed that when the door opened, I didn't quite register it until someone cleared his throat, making me twitch violently and sprout claws, scooting my chair back until it smacked the wall. His eyebrows crawled up his forehead while I took a second to catch my breath and made a mental note to tell Pam that we should increase the volume on the electronic bell. "May I–" I stopped. Breathing was supposed to be an autonomic function. "Sorry. May I help you?"

"Your website says you do all kinds of jobs, including repossession and bounty hunting?"

"Oh, sure, have a seat." I moved my chair back and grabbed Janni's handkerchief for a second. "I'm Ben Lockwood. What've you got for us?"

"Josh Henderson." Henderson had short-cropped dark hair and a neatly-trimmed beard, and wore elegantly-tailored pants and a jacket that looked like it cost more than I paid myself in a month. He passed me a folder. "Here are copies of the lien on the vehicle and the arrest warrant for the fugitive, Gilberto Montoya. We're pretty sure he's still driving it."

That would make him stupid, I didn't say, and then blinked when I opened the folder and saw what the "vehicle" was. "This is a–" My eyes came up. Henderson's expression was bland, and my brow creased in confusion. "It's a 1971 Winnebago. I'm pretty sure it's worth less than we'd charge you for the repo."

"The book on them is about five grand. This one in particular has some special equipment. There's a nice bonus if you can bring it in, and another if you can get our fugitive at the same time." He produced a bundle of bills. "Say, five hundred up front? Bring it to the address in the paperwork, and don't touch anything, whatever you do."

"Sure." I printed out our standard repo and bounty-hunting contracts. "I just need you to initial here, and here, and then sign here, if you would."

He read them over. "I can trust your discretion?"

"If you couldn't, we wouldn't be in business."

"Thank you, Mr. Lockwood. It's a pleasure doing business with you." He rose, and we shook hands. "Call me when you have the Winnie and my prisoner."

After he left, I tapped on Pam's office door and went in. "We gotta new job. Repoing a motor home and apprehension of a fugitive, in one tidy package."

"Well, I don't feel like driving one of them things in LA traffic, so I'll let you have it. How dangerous is the fugitive?"

I shuffled through the papers. "Mostly petty crap and not showing up in court. Nothing super-violent, and even if he was, well." I popped my claws and admired them. "I'm a big bad wolf. I'm pretty sure I could take him."

"You ain't so big and bad as that. Be careful, hear me?"

"I'm always careful, Pam." This was a barefaced lie, and she gave me a Look. "I'll take the Ruger along with the Micro Desert Eagle?" The Ruger carried eighteen rounds, in blatant violation of California state law, but I'd decided that when the legislators dealt with the same shit I did on a daily basis, they could tell me how many bullets I could have in my mag. Pam pretended she didn't know.

"That makes me feel better. You never know how these deals are gonna go."

"Yes'm. I still need to track the thing down anyway. It's a little motor home and a big city."

"Let me know when you head out to corral the guy."

"Will do." Back at my computer, I fired up another thing the legislature didn't know I had, an app that let me hack into traffic cams and hunt for specific license plates. Since LA was a veritable warren of cameras, this little program had served me well over the years. While it was doing its thing, I scrolled through campground databases, which also kept track of license plates.

"Oh. There you are." I frowned at the screen. "That was suspiciously easy." The motor home resided at the Castaic Lake State Recreation Area, which I had a passing familiarity with because we sometimes ran there on full moon nights. It had a reservoir, a bunch of hiking trails, and plenty of wildlife to interest the wolves.

Pam came out of her office. "You find him?"

I stood up, pulling my Jeep keys and the Ruger out of my desk drawer. Checking to make sure it had one in the chamber, I holstered it for a cross draw under my jacket, since the Micro Desert Eagle was already concealed in my right jeans pocket. "He's checked in at Castaic Lake. Either he doesn't know he's being hunted, or he thinks he won't be found there. So I guess I'll show him the error of his ways, and scoop him up." After a moment's thought, I stuffed Janni's handkerchief into my inside jacket pocket.

"You stop at a burger joint on your way, baby boy. Because I know you didn't have breakfast." When I was stressed, I couldn't eat, and she worried. I didn't pack a lot of extra pounds around as it was, and couldn't really afford to lose any.

"Yes'm." I pecked her on the cheek. "With any luck, I'll be done before dinner and we can all go out, okay?"

"I'll hold you to that."

It always slowed the brain hamster if I had something to do, so I was actually pretty happy when I headed out the door. As promised, I hit a drive-thru and munched on a burger and fries while I set out to the lake.

This time of year, the Recreation Area wasn't crowded, and I easily found my target. They had a parking area for the tent campers, and I pulled in and assessed the Winnebago. It was about as nondescript and beat-up as I'd expected something from that era to be, with faded paint that used to be green and white, and a dent in the right front fender.

I had a sniff around, staying below the windows and keeping as silent as I could. Noises and scents told me that Montoya was alone inside, and that he was just a regular human and nothing I really needed to worry about. A weird burnt smell I couldn't place surrounded the thing too, making the hairs on my arms stand on end.

Satisfied that I could take him if I needed to, I rapped on the door with the knuckles of my left hand. Montoya, after going quiet, let out a stifled curse and a hesitant, "May I help you?" He had the suggestion of an odd accent—and didn't open the door.

"Mr. Montoya, I need to speak with you, please." I always started out polite. No sense getting nasty unless I had to.

"I'm very busy. Can you come back tomorrow?"

"I'm afraid it can't wait."

A beat. "Just a minute."

Yeah, no. Even locked, the flimsy door of a motorhome this old was no match for werewolf strength, and it practically came off the hinges when I ripped it open. Montoya was in the back, crouched over a machine that emitted a painfully high-pitched whine. Instruments and dials spat out data. I stared for half a second, then grabbed him by his shirt collar and jerked him back from the thing, which was about all I could do in the cramped confines of the Winnie.

He yelped and swung, but it was clumsy and telegraphed, and I kicked him in the knee, making him stagger. He aimed an elbow strike at my jaw, but I blocked it aside and caught his wrist. Spinning him around and twisting the arm behind his back, I slammed my booted heel into his knee again, and this time he went down to his stomach, with me on top of him. "I really wish you hadn't done that." I wasn't even breathing hard, although he was. The machine's whine switched to a powering-down sound and went silent, much to my relief.

"Who–" He let out a pained grunt as I pulled a set of plastic handcuffs from my back pocket and secured his wrists. "Who're you?"

"I'm the bounty hunter hired to bring you and your Winnebago in. Really, Mr. Montoya, you need to pay your bills and show up to court." I lifted him effortlessly to his feet, although he was much taller and heavier than me. This wasn't new; everyone was.

"Is that what they told you?"

I steered him to the passenger seat and let him sit down. "The paperwork was in order. I know it's not a pleasant thing, but this is why I get paid the big bucks."

"You have no idea, man. None."

"Nor am I interested," I said, fastening his seat belt. I didn't buckle myself in, because I never did, my relationship with restraints being what it was. The keys, handily enough, were in the ignition already. In my recon, I had noticed that the Winnie wasn't hooked into an electric outlet or a sewer pipe, so it was nice and easy to start the thing and pull out of the space. It handled like a drunken whale on Ecstasy, and I didn't blame Pam for not wanting to drive it.

Montoya went broody and silent until we hit LA proper, and then he started sweating. "So nothing I can say will change your mind about this?"

"Can't really think of anything, man. I'm sorry, I know it sucks, but try not breaking the law." Traffic, as always, was a cast-iron bitch, and navigating turns with this thing was no fun.

"Henderson's an asshole," he muttered. "I can't believe he got one of the natives involved, this is not cool."

The phrasing was a bit odd, and I looked at him out of the corner of my eye while evading a taxi who clearly had no idea that this behemoth couldn't actually stop on a dime. Waiting my turn at a red light, I tilted my head. "What do you mean, 'natives'?"

"He and I aren't from here. The gizmo in the back is a–"

The light turned green, I started to go...

And something slammed into our midsection from the side. We spun around, hit something else, and tipped way too far over before the Winnie decided it didn't want to be on its side today and landed back on all fours. It spilled me out of the seat anyway, and I made a grab for the steering wheel, hanging on with all my considerable strength.

And that high-pitched whine that I'd interrupted was suddenly loud and insistent, and I clapped my hands over my ears and clenched my fangs, because it was actively painful. The world went dark and spinny and upside-down for several seconds, and when it stopped my stomach opted out of the burger and fries. A handy plastic receptacle beside the seat received my offering.

Montoya, too, was being quietly sick in his own receptacle. We finished at about the same time. A box of tissues sat on the floor between the seats, and I availed myself of one and stared out the windshield.

A blasted cityscape greeted me. The buildings slumped, the pavement was jagged and uneven, and weeds and trees grew from cracks in the sidewalk. Not a single person or intact car was in sight, besides us. Los Angeles stank of people, normally, but I couldn't smell any humans through my open side window. I might have thrown up again if my stomach wasn't already empty.

I let out an inelegant, involuntary, and unprofessional cussword, and turned a steely glare on Montoya. "Talk fast, Sparky. What the hell just happened?"

He had gone positively green. "You broke. You broke my time machine."

Every synapse in my brain screeched to a halt. Even the wheel hamster stopped. "Your what, now?"

"My time machine." He jerked his head toward the wrecked city. "You think this happens in two seconds? No. This is the future. About a hundred years from your time, if I'm calculating right, but I might be off either way by a decade."

"Well." I waved my arm, a little wildly. "*Un*break it! I have a life I need to get back to. My wife is going to *freak*." I was freaking pretty hard myself.

"I'd love to, but I have this little issue with my hands being cuffed behind me." His lips tightened. "And, if it's all the same to you, I'd just as soon not be turned over to the Time Wardens when I manage to get you home."

"Time Wardens," I said, deadpan.

"Henderson. Of course he didn't tell you who you were really chasing, because you wouldn't have believed him anyway, so he ginned up some good-looking paperwork and plopped it on your desk. Spun a story about me being a fugitive." He barked out an entirely humorless laugh. "Well, I am, but not the kind of fugitive your people chase."

I sputtered. "Time travel. Is possible."

"If ill-advised." He jerked his chin at the ruins again. "But like hell do I want to stay here. I like your time a lot better. The Wardens, though, they get really anally retentive about corrupting the time stream, so they don't like it when someone goes back to stay."

"And I walked right into that." A

headache started pounding behind my eyes. "Awesome."

"I might be able to fix it and send us back. But you gotta promise that you won't hand me over to Henderson. He played you, man."

Yes, he had. I didn't like being played. I gritted my teeth and unfastened his belt, then pointed at him. "You rabbit, and you will regret it."

"I won't. I don't like it here any better than you do, promise."

"Okay." I let the fangs come out, and his eyes widened. "Because I *can* track you, and I *will* find you. Got me?"

He nodded rapidly. "Yes. Very much so."

The multitool in my back pocket sheared through his plastic cuffs. "Now. Fix it."

H e tried. I gave him credit for that. Apparently the mechanism in the back dining area was just a small section; the part in the bathroom where the car had hit us was the Vital Component, and he sat back on his heels and shook his head. "I'm sorry, Ben, but I need parts."

"And where the hell are you going to get them *here*?"

"Oh, you'd be surprised."

"Then surprise me."

"You won't accuse me of rabbiting?" The display of fangs and claws, as I hoped, had intimidated him. I would never use them, because I wasn't That Guy. But, at this point, he didn't need to know that.

"Not if you come ba–"

I stopped, because I'd been testing the air for quite some time, checking for threats. God knew who or what had colonized the remains of Los Angeles. And someone–a wolfy someone–was sniffing around the Winnie. I raised my hand, and Montoya cringed and went quiet as I stalked toward the door and yanked it open.

My hand flashed out and grabbed a guy by the scruff of his neck, pulling him inside while I loomed over him in the same motion.

Which was when I realized that he was about twice my size. He had black hair and green eyes, and wore a pair of cargo jeans along with a torn T-shirt that strained to hold his muscles at bay. He didn't take kindly to being hauled in or loomed over, and he snarled and knocked my arm away. "What the hell are you doing here?" he asked.

I recoiled, having no desire to mix it up with a wolf that big. He'd take me apart and spit out my bones in close quarters like this. "We had an accident."

His nostrils flared. "Wait... Ben? What? Aren't you back with–" He stopped in confusion.

"Who are you?" I demanded.

"Did you hit your head? I'm Ray. Part of your pack? Or, you know. What's left of your pack."

Now I was the one who was confused. "My pack has all of six people in it, and you're not one of them."

His nose worked furiously. "No, I can smell that. Now. But." He squeezed his eyes shut. "This is way above my pay grade. I'm just on recon duty. You'd better come with me."

"What about me?" Montoya asked. Squeaked, really.

Raw hatred twisted Ray's features. "You too. *Human.*"

R ay led us through the broken ruins. I could sense people and other things watching us, and it made me itch, glad I had the Ruger and the Eagle. "What happened?" I said.

"What always happens?" Ray answered bitterly. "War. Werewolves got outed, and people decided we were dangerous and broke out the wolfsbane and silver, and it was *on*. LA was Ground Zero. Most of us live here now. Every once in a while, the military comes through and makes sure we don't have enough to mount an offensive."

"But. We're not dangerous. My wife has never hurt a human in her li–"

He interrupted me with a look filled with pity, opened his mouth to say something, then closed it firmly. "You'll see. We might not have *been* dangerous, but we sure as hell are now."

The office building they'd made their home in wasn't far away, and Ray whistled a signal between his teeth. A few seconds later, we were surrounded by a group of four male and three female wolves, in various states of repair. The alpha was the biggest werewolf I'd ever seen; he was built like a granite cliff with about the same amount of body fat, a mountain of muscle wrapped in dark brown skin, wearing a short-sleeved camo shirt, trousers to match, and combat boots.

For all his alpha assurance, however, he

stopped short when he saw me. His chin came up, and he sniffed warily. "I found him in a Winnebago with this human," Ray said. "He didn't know me."

"No," the alpha said slowly, "I don't imagine he did. How are you, Ben?"

"Confused. I think it's safe to say I'm confused."

He made a motion with his head dismissing the others, who took charge of Montoya. He gave me a desperate look before they disappeared into the bowels of the building, but what the hell could I do? I just hoped they wouldn't hurt him; I felt kind of responsible for him, and I couldn't get home without his expertise.

I wouldn't have accused an alpha like that of being sensitive, but he steered me gently toward a sofa and sat me down. "You don't know me, either, do you?" he said.

I shook my head. "No, sir. You're clearly the alpha, but I've never seen you before."

"Jamaal Poulson. What are you doing here?"

"I seem to have had a time-traveling accident." He opened his mouth, and I raised a hand. "I don't even know. It's Montoya's machine, not mine. I was doing a repo-and-bounty-hunt job for someone who obviously didn't tell me everything I needed to know, and it went south. We got hit by a car in an intersection and wound up here." I tilted my head. "What I really want to know is, how do you know me?"

He sighed and scrubbed a massive hand over his face. "There's no easy way to tell you this, Ben."

A chill skittered up my spine and sat at the base of my skull. "Tell me what?" My voice was remarkably steady, but I had the feeling that my bad day was about to get much, much worse.

He took a breath. "When we found you, you were wolfed. Refused to go back to human." A pause. "Cuddled up next to the body of a woman, little tiny African-American thing. She'd bled out."

His last word faded into a roaring in my ears, and black fireworks exploded across my vision. I couldn't breathe, and I felt hot and cold and numb, all at the same time. Recoiling back into the sofa cushion and pulling my knees into my chest, I whispered, "Janni."

"You attacked anyone who tried to come near her." He wasn't touching me, which was smart. "But you were wounded yourself, and weak from hunger, so we eventually got you away and buried her for you. It's been a year, and you're still not talking, much. Enough to tell us your first name, and that's all. Sometimes you wake up from a nightmare, calling for her. Mostly, you still stay wolfed."

"I'm not surprised." My voice was a hoarse croak, muffled into my arms. "What about the rest of my pack? Megan and Alex, Pam and Chambliss." A thousand possibilities tumbled through my scattered mind, each more horrific than the last.

"You were alone. No one's come looking for you. I'm sorry, Ben."

I nodded, at a loss for words. My hand hunted of its own accord for my inside jacket pocket, coming out with Janni's handkerchief. I buried my nose in it, reminding myself that she was waiting for me and would be incredibly put out if I didn't make home it in time for dinner.

My breathing eased, and my head came up. "I need to talk to the human I was with. He's my ticket back. I can't. Can't stay here, Jamaal. Just. Can't."

His mouth twisted. "I don't blame you. Come with me."

I followed him up three flights of stairs, and he led me down a hallway to a door guarded by a blonde Valkyrie, who shot me a sympathetic look and stepped aside. Montoya was pacing back and forth when we walked in, and he slumped with relief when he saw me. "This is a terrible place, Lockwood. One of them threatened to eat me."

"We don't like humans much around here," Jamaal said, baring a fang. "Considering the fact that we're trapped in this hellhole because humans are *stupid*, I'm not sure you can blame us."

"Fine! I'll be more than happy to get out of your fur." He threw up his hands. "Just get me the parts I need to fix my machine." He frowned and looked at his watch. "And it needs to be soon. The longer we wait, the more the time streams get mixed and separated, the harder it is to get back to the right place."

I strode across the room and grabbed him by the shirt collar, yanking his ear down next to my mouth, which was full of fangs. "Tell me this isn't set in stone."

He froze. "I don't know, man! But I'll be

more than happy to go back to your own time and stay there to find out. Like I said, I don't like it here either."

I shook him a little. "Do you have a list of what you need?"

He tapped his forehead. "Right here."

Jamaal spoke up. "We'll send Ray with you in case of accidents. We've got someone on overwatch on your motorhome too. Scavengers might strip it, otherwise."

"That would be bad," I said. "Let's go, Montoya."

"Ray's not going to eat me, is he?"

Jamaal rolled his eyes. "No, dumbass."

"But I might if you don't get me the hell back home," I told him, and he gulped.

Jamaal handed us off to Ray, and we went scrounging through auto parts and electronic stores. Pickings were thin, and we had to hit more than one of each to get what he needed. The whole time, I had an itch on the back of my neck, and Ray cast several unfriendly glances around.

"Someone's watching us," I said.

"Someone's always watching," he growled back. "But this one's new."

"Well, let's see what he thinks of my little friend." And the Ruger was in my hand before Ray quite knew I was armed.

"What the hell, where did you get *that*? Wolves aren't allowed–"

"Fuck them, wolves aren't allowed," I snarled. "They murdered my wife because, I'm assuming, wolves aren't allowed. A disarmed populace is a docile one, and I'll be damned if I'll ever be docile again." I had Opinions about guns, and I wasn't particularly shy about sharing them with the class. "What happened to 'the right of the people to keep and bear arms shall not be infringed'?"

"It went out the window when they decided we weren't *people*."

"Is it this way all over America?"

"Pretty much. There are enclaves of wolves here and there, and they do their best to keep us contained. It doesn't always work, but we pick our battles."

My lips tightened. "And I bet it would be real handy to have a combat veteran with his wits about him on the team."

"Jamaal was in the Marines."

"I could tell. I was an Army Ranger, myself." I shook my head. "Tell you what, I'll have a talk with my. . . other self, see if I can yank him out of that spiral of self-pity he's trapped in."

"We've tried. He's half out of his head most of the time, poor bastard."

I barked out a humorless laugh. "Well, I know what that's like. And what it might take to buck him up."

"Uh." Montoya's mouth pulled down. "That might not be the best idea."

I huffed and crossed my arms, not holstering my gun. "Why not." I didn't inflect it like a question.

"Don't you read? Meeting yourself is bad. It can damage the time stream irreparably. And strand you here." He shivered. "Strand *us* here."

My jaw clenched. "If my other self is as bad as they say, I can't just leave him like that. I'll be messing up a future, not my own past."

"Every second you spend here messes up the past and diverges this timeline from yours." He waved an arm. "It'll inform your choices going forward, assuming you get back. Just being here means that this future is iffy."

My head hurt. "But–" I rubbed my forehead. "You know what, I don't care. Just get your parts and fix the machine. We'll worry about it later.

"Don't say I didn't warn you," Montoya said, and went back to poking around shelves.

"I hope whatever your plan is works, Ben," Ray said. "He doesn't sleep much, or eat, or even move, and a couple of the pack are making noises about supporting someone who can't contribute, you know? It's a hardscrabble life out here."

"He might think he's better off dead. We'll see if we can disabuse him of the notion and make him useful again."

"Jamaal won't let anyone hurt him. That's what separates us from them, he says. Because if we take care of the ones who can't take care of themselves, it proves we're not the monsters that the humans think we are, if only to ourselves."

"He's right. He's a good alpha, I can tell." I thought of Megan, my own alpha, and twitched. I hoped I'd see her again. Soon.

"Hah!" Montoya waved a... thing over his head that he'd fished out of a drawer in the radio control hobby shop we'd been roaming around in. "This is the last component I need. I think."

I let him and Ray head to the motorhome to get started on repairs, while I wandered back to the office building to have a chat with my future self. "Do you think that's a good idea?" Jamaal asked dubiously.

"I think it's the best shot you've got of shaking him out of this, is what I think." I shrugged. I had a pretty good idea the state I'd be in after losing Janni, and leaving without trying to do something about it was inconceivable. "And if it doesn't work, I doubt it'll make things worse, anyway."

"Point." He led me upstairs again, to a corner office with wall-to-wall windows. "He likes it better here than in the dark, for some reason."

"Yeah, there's some history there." Like the insurgents dragging me to a lightless part of the cave and leaving me trapped for days on end, in an attempt to break me into giving them information. I didn't have the damn information they wanted, but try convincing them. They'd let me out after I started hallucinating. I rubbed the handcuff scars ringing my wrists in a tic I'd never quite gotten rid of.

The other me was crouched in a corner wrapped in a blanket. He smelled more wolf than human, although he was human-shaped. I shivered at the idea of becoming that. A woman I hadn't seen yet sat in a chair across the room from him, reading out loud from *The Hobbit*, of all things. I supposed the classics were best, and I'd always had a fondness for that one. She twitched violently when she saw me. "Jamaal?"

"I'll explain later, Sarah. For now, he thinks he can help."

"Well, nothing else has."

My eyes were locked on my other self, and I walked over to him, making sure he saw me coming so it didn't give the appearance of sneaking up on him. I squatted in front of him, and he stared hard, then shook his head wordlessly.

"Hey," I said softly.

"You're not real." His voice was a rusty whisper, like it was unused to speaking.

"I'm as real as you are." I held my left hand out to him, the one with the large and ostentatious wedding band on it, and he zeroed in on that with the intensity of a snake staring down a mongoose. He reached his own left hand out, and I saw with a pang that the ring was gone.

"They took it. They took everything. And then they took her, too."

"I know. Jamaal told me. The idea of my world without her in it haunts my nightmares. But, look." I kept my gaze steady. "It's been a year. If you let them make you into this. If you let them break you this hard. Then they win."

"I was never. Never the strong one. You know that."

My breath caught. I did know that. I knew that better than anyone. I leaned on Janni and the rest of the pack way more than was good for me—or them, for that matter. Four years since my own trauma, and maybe I wasn't a puddle of goo crouched in a corner anymore, but I wasn't as put-together as I should've been either. I still went without a seat belt more often than not because restraints freaked me out. I'd rather have been shot with a gun than be poked with a syringe. I needed to work on both those issues.

"She knew that too. And *you* know that it would break her heart to see you this wrecked, this long after it happened. She worked long and hard so that we could stand up on our hind legs again."

"Well." He barked out a harsh sound that only a psychopath would mistake for a laugh. "Losing her knocked them right out from under me, didn't it."

At least it was a somewhat long and complete sentence. "And that's fine. But it can't be a permanent state. Your pack is worried about you, and they need you. You have skills that would help them out."

He blinked. "My... pack." It seemed like a revelation to him.

"They saved your life and kept you alive when they didn't have to. I know Jamaal's not Megan, but he's a good alpha. Pack takes care of its own, you know that." I put a little steel in my voice. Just a little. He was at a delicate tipping point, and I didn't want to spill him over to the wrong side. "It's time to start giving back. Can you do that, for me? For them?" I reached into my jacket pocket and came out with Janni's handkerchief, pressing it into his hand. "For her?"

His eyes widened, and he brought the scrap of cloth to his face, inhaling. Scent was more important than sight to a werewolf, and Janni's scent was the most evocative of all. He curled forward, and a sob tore its way from his throat. And another, and another.

I heard a sharp gasp from behind me, and Sarah came over and knelt beside him, wrapping her arms around his shoulders, kissing his wild and curly hair, which hadn't been cut in a long time. Tall redheads weren't usually my type, but it seemed to me that she had more than just a passing pack interest in him. I wondered how many days she'd sat with him, reading, just letting him know that he wasn't alone, and a pang went through me.

"He hasn't cried. Ever, since we found him," she said.

No, he wouldn't have. I didn't, very often, because I was frankly afraid of unleashing that much emotion, so I kept it on a tight rein. I certainly didn't like losing my shit in front of strangers, even if they had adopted me. But the grief and loss poured out of him, and he leaned into her hard and cried like a child who'd been abandoned in a dark and scary place and had just been rescued. It was release and relief, all at once, and I stepped back and let him do it. Sarah just held him, petting his back. She had some tears herself, even.

He eventually cried himself out and fell into an exhausted slumber, pillowing his head on Sarah's legs. "Thank you for taking care of him. Me," I said, somewhat awkward.

"He was so lost for so long," she whispered, wiping her eyes. "Maybe now he'll come back."

"Won't happen all at once. He'll have setbacks. But I think he might be on the road, at least."

She stroked his hair, and he sighed and leaned into it a little, even in his sleep. "He hasn't wanted anyone to touch him. At all. It's a breakthrough."

"Yeah, I'm not real touchy with anyone but—" But my pack. And if Other Me thought of these people as a bunch of strangers instead of pack, then that was just another obstacle. "What a mess. I can be an idiot, sometimes. Sorry?"

She gave me a tremulous smile. "It's all right. If you—"

Ray picked that moment to burst into the room with no ceremony whatsoever. "You'd better come," he said to me, panting.

Jamaal came off the wall he'd been leaning against, watching the whole thing. "What's going on?" he asked.

"There's a guy at the motorhome making noises about time violations. He's waving some kind of gun around."

I bared a fang. "Henderson. Good. I've been wanting to talk to that bastard." But before I left, I pulled my wedding ring off and put it on Other Me's finger. It was loose; he'd lost a lot of weight.

Sarah stared. "What—"

"I can get another one made when I get home." If I got home, I studiously did not say and tried very hard not to think. Talking to myself like this might have irreparably messed up the timeline, but I couldn't have left him like that. Just. Couldn't. "He needs it more than I do. Make sure he doesn't lose it, okay?"

A tear trickled down her cheek. "Thank you."

"Thank *you*, Sarah." I stood up. "Now. Let's see about these Time Warden shenanigans."

Henderson was in the midst of haranguing Montoya when Jamaal and I came around the end of the Winnie. I didn't even stop; I just stalked right up to Henderson, grabbed him by the shirtfront, and slammed him against the engine compartment with one hand while grabbing the wrist of his gun hand in the other and squeezing, making him drop it with a pained yelp.

"You gotta problem with him fixing my ride home, jackass?" I snarled in his face, fangs foremost.

Henderson gabbled at me, but I was on a roll. "I do not like being thought of as *stupid*. I especially do not like when the client withholds *important information* from me. I like it even less when the client thinks he can *play me* so I'll do his dirty work for him." I pushed in closer. "I really, *really*, do not like it when the client attempts to clean up his *mess* by *stranding me* in a future in which my wife is *dead*."

"I'm not allowed to tell people who don't know about it about time travel!" he said, struggling fruitlessly. "You wouldn't have believed me anyway."

"You would be *amazed* what a *werewolf* with a *mad scientist* for a best friend would believe."

Jamaal put a hand on my shoulder. "Ben. Eating him will not solve your problem."

"Oh, won't it?" I pushed in closer to Henderson's face. My fangs dripped on his shirt.

"Ben." Jamaal was relentless. "Are you That Guy? Are you the guy who'd rip a man's throat out because he upset you? Because if you are, I've misjudged you. Bad enough having one of you off the rails around here. Two would be too much."

I took a breath, closed my eyes–

And let Henderson go, stepping back. It scared people who knew me when I started emphasizing words. I could only imagine the effect it had on near-total strangers. "No. Janni didn't marry That Guy." Breathing. I could do that. Not deeply, or well, but I could do it. "That being said, I want this slimy bastard to explain to me just why I can't go back to my own time."

Henderson leaned away from me. "Montoya's in violation of at least six different statutes I can think of off the top of my head. You weren't supposed to play with the damn machine, that's why I told you not to touch anything."

"Henderson," I said slowly. "I am being very patient with you right now." Then I waved my arm wildly at the smashed side of the Winnie and stepped right back into his personal space. "What in the everlivin' *fuck* makes you think I touched anything on *purpose*? Some idiot ran a red light and t-boned us in the middle of an intersection! Maybe if you hadn't wanted me to drive your fucking *time machine* all over Hell and Los Angeles, this wouldn't have happened!" Building up a head of steam again was a go.

"I can see you're upset. . ."

"Oh, you think?" I made an effort and put the fangs away. "I have had. A very stressful day. Which culminated in trying to talk my crazy future self into some semblance of sense. And now you come here, brandishing your statutes, telling me I can't go *home*?"

"Wait, you talked–" Henderson rounded on Montoya. "You let him talk to his future self? What the hell were you thinking?"

"Yes, Henderson." Montoya didn't quite roll his eyes. "I'm going to stop an armed werewolf, who kicked my ass without even breaking a sweat, from doing whatever he wants. You try it, see how it works out for you."

"I can't even tell you how many violations you've got, Montoya. I don't have enough fingers. Best for everyone if you just stay here with your broken machine and make the best of it."

"That. Is not. An *option*," I said, and there were my fangs again. "How did you get here, anyway?"

"I stepped through the rift that opened when you had your acci–"

He stopped short, horror dawning on his face, while Montoya positively grinned with evil glee. He pointed at the Time Warden. "So you don't have a way back either. How many statutes does that put you in violation of, Henderson?"

Henderson sputtered for a moment. "Look," I said. "You're already stuck with a paradox. I met my future self, and it was pretty terrible for my state of mind, which–let's be honest–isn't great on the best of days. If you don't let me go home, that will not be good for anyone. Not me, not this pack, and definitely not you."

"But if you go back to your own time, then this will change. The paradox–"

"Fuck your paradox, damn right it will, if I have anything to say about it. I mean, obviously I make it home again, because if I hadn't then they wouldn't have found me *holding my wife's dead body*." I got up in his face again. "We are fixing the machine. With or without you. I am going home. With or without you. What you do after that is up to you. I wouldn't be too heartbroken to just leave you here, honestly. Officious assholes get right up my nose. That is not a place you want to be. Is it." I didn't inflect it like a question. I'd been doing that a lot lately.

"I don't suppose it is." He looked sulky, but it was good enough for me.

"And if you try to sabotage this process, then I will *bite* you, and then *leave* you here. Got me?" I wouldn't, or, at least, I wouldn't bite him, but he didn't need to know that. I pointed at a piece of rubble. "You can sit over there, and shut your trap."

Montoya stared at me as Henderson did exactly what I told him. "Wow, I wish he'd sent you after me a long time ago."

"I'm not real happy with you either," I growled. "How close are we to fixing your gizmo?"

"Pretty close. I've got some screws to tighten and a couple of tests to run before I know it's ready."

"Then what are you waiting for." I didn't

inflect that like a question either, and he nodded rapidly and retreated inside to work his magic.

"Well. If that's what you're like when you're all there, I hope our Ben recovers," Jamaal said. "He could be a real asset to this pack."

"I hope he does too. Last time something knocked me for that much of a loop, I took a long while to come back from it. I'm still not all the way back, but I've got a pack and a family to keep me grounded." I tipped my head at him. "He's in good hands. And, you know. . ." My mouth twisted. "I don't know what the whole time thing will do to you guys, if it'll just. . . calve off another piece of the multiverse or what, but you've got my best wishes."

He offered his hand, and I shook it. "Wolves live a long while," he pointed out. "And humans? Well. They don't. If all else fails, we've got time on our side. This didn't happen in a day, and it won't be fixed in one either."

"I suppose." The motorhome emitted a high-pitched whine. "That's my cue, I think. Take care, Jamaal."

"You too."

I poked my head inside the Winnie, with Henderson right beside me. "Is it fixed?" I asked.

"Pretty sure," Montoya said. "I've got it set to send us back to about five seconds after we left, although it might be off by a few seconds. Or. . . minutes. Maybe an hour? It's a hell of a jury-rig, and who knows what happened to your timeline while we were gone."

I frowned. "But if you're off by that much, you might appear in the same space as a person who just happens to be standing there. That would be bad, wouldn't it?"

"There's a failsafe." Montoya eyed the machine, which blinked back at him with multicolored lights. "That being said, I'm not sure it would work with the thing half-caved-in like that, so–" He fiddled with a few dials and knobs. "There, now it's set so we'll land in a vacant lot. Or thereabouts. Probably."

It was as good as we could hope for, I supposed. I had no faith that the thing would actually get us anywhere after we ended up wherever we ended up; the wreck had left it undriveable. I sat in the driver's seat and clutched the armrests. "You really should buckle up," Henderson said, strapping himself into the passenger seat.

"Are you kidding me?" Restraints at the best of times were not my friends, and today had been far from the best of times. "I'll be fine. Let's go home, Montoya."

"Say a prayer," Montoya said, flipping switches and twisting dials.

"It's not *his* ho–" Henderson started, and then the world went spinny and loopy and upside-down, and my stomach tried to turn itself inside-out again.

It took longer. Much longer. I wondered if I'd messed the timeline up beyond repair. Henderson's knuckles were white. So was his face. The Winnie shook like a toy in the hand of an angry giant, and the machinery made an awful stuttery buzzing noise. I swallowed hard. "Montoya?"

"Working on it," he said between his teeth.

And then we stopped.

At least this time I knew what the receptacle was for, and my stomach was practically empty anyway. I eyed the cityscape outside the window, which looked and–more importantly–smelled blessedly normal. "So that's fun," I said, grabbing a tissue and wiping my mouth. "You guys do that often?"

"Not very often," Montoya said, shooting a nasty look at Henderson. "Just when I'm being chased."

"Well, it's not my outlook anymore. You two can iron out your differences without me as a referee, because I'm liable to just bang your heads together and call it done." I glared at the Time Warden. "Henderson, I finished your job. Pay me."

Henderson sputtered. "But."

"I found your vehicle and your fugitive. *Pay*. Me. Or we will have. A problem." I was pretty sure my normally-blue eyes had gone amber, because my vision had sharpened. "A bigger problem. Do you really want to have a bigger problem than the one you already have? With a werewolf?"

"I suppose I don't." He gulped a little and reached under his shirt, while I made a warning noise and bared a long, sharp fang. But he came out with a handful of bills, which he handed over to me with alacrity, so I put my teeth back and nodded–after counting it, of course, and making sure they'd actually spend here.

"I'd like to say it was nice doing business with you," I said, "but I frankly hope I never see either of you ever again." I stood up and pointed at both of them. "And if I hear about any more of this idiocy–*and I will,* if it happens in my city–you will not like the results. Got me?"

Montoya nodded, and Henderson squinched his face and looked at the floor. I didn't care, so long as they stayed away from me and mine.

I exited the Winnie, hailed a cab, and went *home.*

Janni's voice came from the kitchen. "Ben? I didn't know you were coming back for lunch." She didn't have time to say any more than that, because I took several long strides that direction, scooped her up like a new bride, and crushed her to me. She laughed breathlessly as I buried my nose in her hair and just inhaled. "What's all this, then, sugar?"

I carried her into the living room and sat us on the sofa with her in my lap. "I've seen the future, and it's awful."

"What are you talking about?"

So I started with the client and told her everything, ending with, "And I gave him my wedding ring, because how could I not? I'll get another one today, but I couldn't just leave him like that. Just. Couldn't."

"Of course you couldn't." She stroked my chest. "Don't worry about it. I would never be mad at you for a thing like that."

Her scent, along with the petting, allowed the tension to bleed out of me. I had no idea how stressed I was until I wasn't, anymore, and I felt like a particularly overcooked noodle. "Love you, babe."

She kissed my cheek. "I love you too. And I made blueberry pie." Probably because of the nightmare. Had that just been this morning? I was exhausted.

But I was also home, with my wife, and werewolves weren't (yet) second-class non-citizens. As I followed her into the kitchen and watched her build me an enormous roast beef sandwich, I realized I had time to turn this relationship less lopsided. Janni actively enjoyed propping me up when I needed it, but I wanted to be a whole person who wouldn't smash into shattered wreckage at her loss– whether that loss happened in a far-off shady future or she got hit by a bus tomorrow. It didn't mean I loved her less, but I needed to stop using her as a crutch.

I counted my blessings... and vowed to be the blessing to Janni that she deserved, for as long as we had left.

Who else seconds the motion
that SHORT STORIES
are supposed to be fun?

**Authors are flocking to this no-hokum formula
because our ads appeal to their intelligence**

Do you dream of writing exciting short stories and selling them to magazines like StoryHack Action & Adventure?

Does your current fiction feel lifeless and boring? Are your main characters so weak that it takes them a whole novel just to solve a problem?

Does your plot fizzle out without even simmering in raw emotion first?

Do you not know what belongs in the first 1500 words of your story?

If you answered "yes" to any of these or any other questions, then the Lester Dent Pulp Paper Master Plot is for YOU!

Once you read and implement these tips and techniques, your fiction with sell like ice cubes in the summertime, ALMOST guaranteed!!!

Don't wait for your writing rivals to discover this long-remembered SECRET formula and sell ALL of their stories while you sell NONE!

THIS IS NOT LESTER DENT BUT IT COULD BE YOU!

THE *FREE* WRITING ADVICE THAT STARTS A CAREER!

The Lester Dent Pulp Paper Master Fiction Plot
is available anywhere fine public domain articles are posted.
Seriously, it's all over the place online. http://bfy.tw/Dzxc

What is a seasoned outlaw to do when she's too worn out to heist?

Taking Control

by Jon Del Arroz

THIS STORY WAS SPONSORED BY PAUL DUFFAU OF PAULDUFFAU.COM

Jolie carried a burlap sack through the streets of Denver, her wide-brimmed hat shadowing her eyes. The bandana she had earlier used as a mask lay circled around her neck. She ducked to avoid eye contact with a man who rocked lazily on the back of his horse, meandering down the dirt street. It was tough being inconspicuous dressed more like a man than a proper lady, but she needed the freedom of movement that pants and a shirt gave compared to a dress.

She continued on her way until she reached an abandoned warehouse, with a faded sign advertising the Colorado Mining Company, boarded windows at eye level and a door that dragged on the ground. The warehouse had been empty since the Pike's Peak gold rush died, save for Jolie using it as her hideout. She circled around the building, pausing at intervals to ensure she spotted anyone attempting to follow.

With no one in sight, Jolie rounded the last corner and pushed open the main door. Hinges creaked and a corner scratched on the dirt, catching after a few inches. Jolie delivered a frustrated kick to the door.

It swung open into a dimly lit area, but her knee overextended with a sickening pop that echoed throughout the warehouse. "Dammit," she muttered, limping the rest of the way inside.

Jolie dropped the sack on the ground, her leg swelling. She reached and slammed the door shut behind her, then sunk to the floor to stretch.

This was a bad sign. Last week, she'd been too slow on a bank job. The police had arrived within moments, and she'd even had to look Police Chief David Cook in the eyes as she'd made her lucky escape. The week before that, she'd forgotten where she'd stashed the goods from a job. Now her knee hurt like hell. Though she'd had a good run, Jolie was getting too old to be an effective outlaw.

"What'd you bring home for supper, mama?" a voice asked from across the warehouse. Connor came out of the shadows where several stacked crates hid their living area.

He wore a fine black cowboy hat and an Indian's buffalo pelt vest over a thin white shirt along with slacks that made him look like a New York City banker. A mismatch to say the least. He claimed he valued their comfort. In truth, he valued whatever he could lift off of the unsuspecting fools he swindled.

"I hate it when you call me that. One, I ain't your mama, makes it creepy. Two, you ain't much younger than me," Jolie said, rubbing a tense muscle in her lower back. "Took some trinkets from the tradin' post downtown. Heavy stuff, made of real silver. Don't remember our takes being so heavy before. I'll need to have Fred fence this."

"Okay, okay. Jolie Nye, notorious criminal mastermind it is," Conner quipped.

The warehouse rattled. Rotting wood bones swayed as rhythmic noise pounded outside. A horn blew. The noise and shaking combined together into an ear-piercing chorus. *Choo-choo*, the train chugged as it passed by, tracks rattling beneath it. After several long moments, the building ceased shaking. Dust and debris filled the air from the rafters.

Connor examined the wall. "One of these days that train's gonna knock this building down, taking us with it," he said, momentarily distracted. He glanced back to Jolie. "You coulda brought me along to carry your payload." He motioned for permission to open the bag.

"You know bringing you along only doubles the chances of getting caught," Jolie said, removing her hat to flick off the dust. Her dirty blonde hair was a sweaty and tangled mess, but she didn't need to impress Connor. "Go ahead, see what I got."

Connor reached inside the burlap bag,

pulling out a silver statue of a cat. The cat had its paw upward, waving hello. It looked like something produced in the Far East, but Jolie didn't have the schooling to place it for certain. If anyone could invent a story behind the statue, Connor could. He whistled. "This'll fetch a pretty penny melted down."

"It'd be a shame. I think it's cute. Was hoping you'd concoct some scheme. Auction it off as some Russian princess's homage to her pet," Jolie said.

"I very much doubt I could convince people this originated in Russia. Now China…"

Pain flared through Jolie's knee. She clenched her teeth as she tightly gripped the pant fabric, bunching it at her thigh.

"Jolie! Are you okay? Need some whiskey for the pain?" Connor watched her with genuine concern. Very little could stop him from brainstorming a good hoodwink.

Jolie bit the inside of her lip and tried to ignore the pain. After several long, unmoving minutes, the pain subsided into something still awful, but livable. "No… no whiskey yet. I need to stop going on runs. My body can't take it anymore."

"Then stop. Retire."

She couldn't help but laugh, though the movement jolted her leg and increased the pain. Jolie righted herself into a seated position, keeping her leg extended. "If I had enough to retire, do you think I'd be doing this?"

Connor returned the statue to the bag. "Maybe you like it. You know, there's other ways of making money," he said. With a flick of a wrist, Connor produced an ace of spades from beneath his sleeve and flicked it at her. "Like the power of magic."

"I can't pull off your tricks. Old, remember? Can't move that quick anymore. Besides, if gambling goes sour, there's just as much running involved."

Another card slid out from Connor's hand, this time bursting ablaze in midair. His fingers followed the card down. It burned into smoke and ash before it hit the ground. "There's more to magic than parlor tricks. I can give you a spell to try."

This nonsense again. Connor had tried to get her to use supposed magic before. Of course, Connor was a con-man. His name likely wasn't even real, and Jolie was certain he intended some bad joke to do with his occupation. Though his heart was often in the

right place, nothing he said could be trusted. They'd been sharing the hideout for months. He'd given her a portion of his take from his rigged gambling games, which had been a nice supplement with her slowing productivity. If only she'd had the foresight years ago to form a real outlaw gang, she'd be able to live off of the spoils by now. Stupid of her, going at it alone for so long.

Jolie sighed. Should she humor him this once? "Even if it worked, I don't even know where I'd use it."

"There's something I've been meaning to try but haven't had the guts to do," Connor said. He crouched down in front of her once more, eyes alive and animated. Whenever he started a new con-job, he had such a brightness and excitement to him. It was odd after all these years in a naturally jaded business, but his enthusiasm was infectious. "I'm small time, always have been. Running Three-card Monte on the street corner or playing poker in a saloon, that's always come easy to me."

"Hit me with it."

"Politics. Think of it as legitimate criminal activity. Best part is, if you go old and grey, they reward you for it."

"I'm not going to win any elections any time soon, Connor." Her leg throbbed again. "On second thought, fetch me some whiskey. Between my leg and listening to your nonsense…"

Connor slid over to a nearby crate and picked up the flask he'd left atop it. He blew dust deposited from the earlier rattling and tossed it to her underhand.

Jolie caught the flask, removed the cap and took a swig. The liquid burned down her throat, but even in that moment it seemed to dull the pain. "Better."

"It's not about elections. It's about controlling the people who win them. Denver is booming. There's construction projects to siphon cash from. Heck, imagine if you ran the cops. How much would people like Bill the Badger pay for a free pass?"

Bill had been run out of town by the police. He'd been too lax and had been seen by half a dozen witnesses. It was either leave or face jail time. Jolie took it as a warning for her fate if she continued on her current path. "How would I gain control? It's not like I could walk up to the Mayor with a gun and threaten him. As soon as I left his office he'd send the police for me and I'd never get paid."

"Like I said, magic. You cast a spell on him."

Jolie stifled another laugh so as not to move, then blinked at Connor's deadpan expression. "Wait, you're serious?"

Connor produced a small bottle from a pocket in his buffalo skin vest. "This is a magic salve I procured from a very reputable Cheyenne medicine man friend. Every summer his tribe gathers with many others for a ritual. They pray to this Great Spirit and he gives them bountiful hunts and heals their sick. This was created during last year's ritual."

"Connor, you're not going to get me to buy that from you. I've seen how you work. Nice detail on the medicine man on this one, by the way. It almost feels real."

"No, no! Come now, Jolie. I wouldn't try something so simple on you. This is free of charge – because it works. I only want a share of the take when you succeed."

Jolie stared at him skeptically. "This is crazy, but my leg hurts badly enough that I may give it a shot. Try me."

"Okay. Here's the plan."

"I can't believe I agreed to do this," Jolie muttered to herself. She waited outside the town hall, which contained the Mayor and Police Chief's respective offices, and a meeting chamber.

Light shone from inside, city officials working diligently to help Denver boom into becoming the capitol of the Colorado Territory. Shadows fell on the steps where Jolie waited for an opportunity to make her move. A few government workers left for the evening, but the Mayor wasn't among them. Jolie slipped inside, dressed in proper lady-like attire, a long crimson dress with petticoats and all. How normal folk went about their daily routines with so much loose material draped over them, she had no idea.

No secretary sat at the front desk, so Jolie opened the door toward the back offices. The hallways were vacant, except for the portraits of former mayors looking down disapprovingly from their frames. Jolie walked through, boots clicking on wood floors even with her soft steps.

The back office at the end had "Mayor Baxter B. Stiles" printed in gilded letters of crushed glass on the door. The door itself was ajar, with light trickling out from the room. Jolie peeked inside.

Mayor Stiles sat behind his desk, engulfed in paperwork. White hair curled down past his ears in a long sideburn that draped over his neck, his cheeks puffy and eyes asymmetric. He turned a page.

Jolie pushed the door further open and stepped inside. It clicked shut behind her.

"Reginald? I thought you went out for a drink with—" The mayor looked up and cut himself off. "You're not Reginald."

Jolie let out a breath, remembering what Connor had told her to say. Her old jobs had been so simple, never having to act a part. Pointing a gun at someone could be oddly relaxing, a certain tension dissipating with the control of a life resting on a trigger finger. Words only caused her stress, never knowing how the intended target might react. But run-and-gun wasn't an option any longer, not with her injured knee. She did her best to curtsey despite the pain, forcing a smile. "Mr. Mayor, I'm Amelia Rose, my husband, uh, Connor..." Dammit. That was the wrong name. She put on her sweetest smile and hoped her pause didn't set off any alarm bells. "... is a hardworking miner, and I wanted to talk about the Union Pacific Railroad Company. They lay their tracks and junctions without thinkin' of the poor people of Denver. I'm afraid that the train running through town in all hours of the night is keepin' my poor husband awake at night, might even knock the house down. I thought we could talk," Jolie said.

Mayor Stiles looked her over. She did have somewhat of an athletic figure from the physical demands of her trade, though she rarely flaunted it. Even in her current attire she considered herself to appear far more proper than suggestive. Whatever his thinking, her appearance managed to soothe the mayor from his tensed shock at the sight of an unexpected visitor. He gave her a political smile. "Mrs. Rose, why don't you come to the town hall meeting next Tuesday?" He stood from his seat and walked around his desk to usher her out, all according to her plan. "That's the proper place to talk about these matters, not that I mind someone of your loveliness paying a visit to my office."

Jolie rubbed the magical salve onto her palm. Connor had helped her to hide the sticky substance, trapping it with a bandage under her blouse sleeve. She reached out as if to shake the mayor's hand, but hesitated with what she saw.

Mayor Styles wore gloves. He offered his hand, but Jolie recoiled hers quickly. She wouldn't be able to apply it. The salve worked only with the touch of skin. Jolie had to think on her feet. Seducing him was out of the question. She wouldn't stoop to that, no matter what the potential gains.

"Is something the matter, Mrs. Rose?" Mayor Stiles asked, glancing down at his hand, left hanging in front of her without the proper shake.

What could she do? Panic filled her, her plan all for naught if she couldn't find a way to touch his exposed skin. One option remained to complete the job tonight. "Yes, yes it is."

Jolie slapped Mayor Stiles across the face.

He recoiled, gingerly touching his red cheek with his gloved hand. The strike reddened his skin in the shape of her fingers and left a white streak of salve across his face that greased his sideburns. "What in the devil, woman?" he asked. "And what's on your hands?"

Jolie stepped forward. The salve should work instantaneously if it was legitimate. Connor had nothing to gain by lying to her, but a magical salve? Preposterous didn't even begin to describe the idea. Why had she agreed to this? His real magic had been manipulating her. Right now he probably would be back at the warehouse, scavenging through her recent gains. She wouldn't be surprised to see him gone when she returned. That double-crosser. But she had other problems to deal with first.

"Mayor Stiles," Jolie said, remembering the script Connor gave her, "with the railroad expansion, a commission needs to be formed for public rail safety. This commission can be paid by taxes from the railroads. You will put me in charge of this commission, and sign a check payable to the order of Amelia Rose in the amount of one thousand dollars to immediately begin this process."

"You think I'll sign over a check to you after this? You'll not be getting a commission, Mrs. Rose. In fact, I will be finding your husband and talking to him about the proper behavior of a woman." His lower lip twitched. "Now get out of my office!"

Jolie stood unmoving for a moment, still holding out hope the salve might take effect.

From the angry glare in the mayor's eyes, it appeared her suspicions had been correct. The substance had no magical properties at all. She was going to kill Connor if she found him again. She still managed to keep composed, holding her face stoic as she could despite her anger. "I don't think you understand, Mr. Mayor. This is not a request, it's a demand." If only she'd brought her gun. He stood at about her height, but the years of a desk job had given him a flabby gut and scrawny arms. If all went sour, Jolie was sure she could overpower him.

"Oh yes?" The mayor laughed incredulously. "Dave!" he hollered.

That word resonated through Jolie, aware of its implications on an instinctual level. Dave could only be one person— Police Chief David J. Cook. Jolie pivoted to run.

Her knee gave way, shooting even more pain through her than the time she'd been struck in the shoulder by a bullet. Jolie collapsed to the floor with a thud, unable to do anything but cradle her knee.

Mayor Stiles loomed over her, frowning. "What in tarnation is the matter with you, woman?"

Denver's oafish police chief bounded into the office. He looked down at the floor where Jolie crumbled in pain. "Baxter, what's going on here?"

"This woman just threatened me, tried to blackmail me," Mayor Stiles said.

"She doesn't seem to be a threat, Baxter. I think she might need a doctor." The police chief crouched down beside her, touching her shoulder softly. "Ma'am, are you all right?"

Jolie bit her bottom lip hard, trying to divert the pain. She looked Cook right in the eyes, something she'd only done before when wearing a mask, outside the Colorado National Bank two weeks ago.

Police Chief Cook froze. "Do I know you?"

"My husband..." Jolie tried to get out, but her body ached so badly it stopped her, forcing her to take a swift breath. She couldn't help but reach out to try to grab something as another wave of pain shot through her knee, clasping Cook's hand and tightly holding onto it.

The police chief went pale like he was about to faint and momentarily lost his footing, though he steadied himself before he fell. When he regained his composure, his eyes had changed. His pupils had entirely expanded into black orbs. He made no move, his hand going limp in hers.

"Dave, what are you doing?"

Cook remained unresponsive.

Jolie's eyes widened. He'd touched her hand with the salve. Did it work this time?

"Point your gun at Mayor Stiles. Don't let him leave."

Cook mechanically removed his gun from his holster, leveling it at the mayor. The magic held him under Jolie's control, just like Connor said it would. The grifter had told her the truth after all.

"Dave? What's going on? Why would you listen to her?!" Terror filled the mayor's eyes.

"Mayor, whiskey," Jolie said, pointing to a bottle resting on a shelf behind his desk. "Then we talk."

Two hours later, Jolie hobbled back into her hideout. She still couldn't walk on her leg, hopping on her good foot until she plopped down on the floor of the warehouse. Cook had carried her half the way at her order, but she didn't want him to know the location of her hideout if he remembered this ordeal. Once more, she leaned her head back against the wall, closing her eyes. "God damn," she said.

"That's not a very Christian thing to say, mama," Connor said with a smirk, sliding out of their living space. He held a deck of playing cards, bending the cards to shoot from one hand to another and back again in rapid succession.

"You're one to talk. Thieving, spell casting. Who knows what else?" Jolie smirked at him despite the pain.

"I only told you about spell casting," Connor said. "I only do parlor tricks, myself. And if people give me money because they think I'm going to do something valuable for them, that's not my fault. I never lie. Not exactly. How'd it go, by the way?"

"It went well," Jolie said. She produced a check from her pocket, from the City of Denver, written to Amelia Rose. "Two-thousand dollars."

"I thought we said one?" Connor missed catching the next shuffling of cards. Several scattered about the floor.

"The Mayor was feeling quite cooperative."

"It worked then? I'm intrigued."

"You said it would."

"Well, I hadn't exactly tested it..." Connor said, scratching the back of his head as he bent down to pick up the fallen cards.

"It didn't work on the mayor though. I touched him, slapped him. But nothing happened. I was shocked when it worked on the police chief." Jolie reached by her, scrunched a blanket together and propped her knee atop it.

"Maybe it doesn't work on the strong-willed. A politician deals with a lot of manipulation on a daily basis."

"And a police chief doesn't?"

Connor shrugged. "He's a grunt at the end of the day. Gets a call, arrives on the scene, and barks orders to his deputies. Not much will involved there, just muscle moving up the ranks over time. A steady payday too. Must be nice."

"We'll live the nice life too for a bit, but we'll need something else in a couple months. You sure you can get cash for this without getting us tossed in jail?" Jolie handed him the mayor's check.

Connor inspected it. "Ah, Amelia Rose. My lovely wife, or should I say that of my forged identity. She done well," he said in reverie, clutching the check to his breast in mock appreciation. "It's no problem. I know a teller who'll manipulate deposits so we should be long gone before it gets back to the mayor. Speaking of which, I have an interesting way we can make the good times last awhile longer."

"How's that?"

"I heard of a guy who can make very realistic illusions..."

"Taking Control" is copyright © Jon Del Arroz.

Jon Del Arroz is known as the leading Hispanic voice in Science Fiction, blogging about sci-fi, geek culture and free speech to more than 10,000 readers per week. His debut novel, Star Realms: Rescue Run was nominated for the Dragon Award for Best Military Science Fiction and his most recent book, For Steam And Country is hailed as the hottest new steampunk series of 2017.

His blind date was kidnapped by Martians. He had no idea why. But he wasn't about to let them keep her.

Some Things Missing from Her Profile

BY DAVID SKINNER

The Martian really didn't want Hamlin Becker to forget its name. As it threw its four-fingered fist into Becker's face, it warbled, "Stigs is me, got it, lug? Stigs. Stigs made meat of you." Stigs clearly didn't care about evading the law. So what? Let the witnesses say it was all Stigs! Stigs it was.

Of course, the law would only *arrest* Stigs. Stigs was risking a very different end, should Becker fail to be killed and someday track Stigs down. Becker was not the arresting sort.

When the other Martian, who prudently had not disclosed his name, told Stigs to forget the damned Terran already – "Stigs, ya moron, we ain't got permission for bodies!" – Becker noted the growing cloudiness in Stigs's two left eyes. Stigs was distracted, looking at its companion, getting annoyed, like maybe its companion wanted to be meat, too. Becker recognized the cloudiness. Several of his coworkers were Martians. They often got that same look. Martians were impatient, and impatience, like most of their emotions, showed in their eyes. With just that coloration.

While Stigs worked up a great fume for its companion, Becker got the chance to collect, pull, and propel his own fist. Which broke something in Stigs's face. Stigs howled. Becker saw the other Martian leaving the restaurant by the back way, dragging Anya easily, hand on her mouth. She was writhing. Her stockinged left foot slipped along the floor, her shoe lost in the ambush. Becker scowled. In other words, in his very moment of actually joining the fight he was losing, Becker let himself get distracted.

Stigs, attention refocused, all four slitted eyes roiling red, pounded Becker with abandon. Becker tried to roll with the barrage, but there was little room among the tables. He might indeed have ended as meat, had Stigs not finally been shot. The already broken parts of its face, and not a little yellow blood, exploded onto Becker. Stigs, being dead, let go of Becker

and crashed down to join a fifty-dollar steak on the table. Stigs, steak, and some rather tasty garlic potatoes, clattered to the floor.

Becker stumbled backward, finding and filling a chair somewhat by mistake. Anya and the other Martian were gone. Becker looked around.

The other patrons had unhelpfully given the Martians more than enough room to be violent. Probably didn't matter; none of the Terrans looked like they'd be much help in a fight. None had a gun, either.

Becker made a decision.

While he was not himself an outlaw, he was the son and grandson of those who had not welcomed the law on Mars. The law, at least, as the Solar Union pretended to practice it. And, being Terran, he generally disregarded the other law (such as it was) of the Martian World-All. Only Nature and God had any authority over Becker, and even those two didn't always get his proper respect.

Becker felt no obligation to wait for cops, paramedics, and commissars, who would only trap him at the restaurant. Whatever help they might be to Anya, he wasn't going to wait on them. Anya was *his* responsibility; it was he who let her be taken. He checked that he had lost nothing from his pockets and, leaving his coat (his best one!) with the coat-check girl, took to the back door as if escaping.

Anya's shoe caught his eye. It was almost a slipper, its heel low. He had liked the simple grace of Anya's feet. *Her graceful little shoes.* This solitary shoe was just *forlorn*. He spent a second retrieving it. He tucked it at his back, in his pants, at his belt.

Then he ran and wiped his face with his tie. His face hurt. Though nothing was broken, everything was tender. And Stigs's blood was hardening. Becker didn't need the crust on his face. There was no helping the stains on his shirt. Absently, with his fingers, he restored the part in his hair, the two low waves like the wake of a ski. Once outside, he threw away the filthy tie.

He quickly looked up and down the alley. He expected nothing and saw it. No Martian kidnapper, no kidnapped Anya, no car fleeing into traffic. No one with a cooling pistol, either. He ran to the street. Only the usual pedestrians, undisturbed; a burgeoning dusk; everywhere the budding electric lights, diminishing shadows in every direction; and noise preventing any proper advance of night. Mars surely lacked a New York but this town aspired nonetheless. And this street was too self-absorbed in its busyness to give Becker a clue.

With his phone he queried for the location of Anya. He wasn't hopeful. The Martians had not seemed especially bright, but even the lowest lowlife knew enough to ditch a phone. Sure enough, the satellites told him that Anya Day, of 347 Geneva Cove, was in the alley. Becker had a sickening flash that perhaps Anya *was* in the alley; that he hadn't just located her abandoned phone; that she herself had been tossed aside, suddenly unnecessary or accidentally dead. He turned back and quickly searched. He didn't find the phone. But at least he also found no body.

He hurried to his car. At his car, before anything else, he went for the Gneiss.

It was his practice never to carry on a first date, especially a blind one. Women either blanched at the Gneiss and prudishly retreated from him; or were inordinately attracted to the badboy he wasn't. Neither sort of woman was ultimately unmalleable, but Becker didn't care for the diversion of either reaction. First dates, for Becker, were soundings at most, and larks by and large. Explaining the Gneiss was for courtship.

The hidden slot was not confused by the residue of Stigs. It recognized Becker's touch and accepted his pass-phrase. The Gneiss was revealed and he withdrew it. From the insecure center cubby, which also held a few music cubes and a book of psalms, he got the thigh strap. With the Gneiss strapped on, he settled into the seat.

So. He did have the name of Stigs.

But honestly, what to do with it? Every urge had him pursuing poor Anya, but he couldn't imagine where she was. The Martians he knew were computer techs, not thugs; he

doubted they knew of any "Stigs." He wished he had spent a second retrieving Stigs's papers, even if they were likely false. Sure, Becker could still go barreling into the Martian district, but to what end? He had never even been there before. Besides, Stigs and his pal were clearly hired. Who's to say their boss wasn't Terran?

Well. He also had the home of Anya. Surely he would find something there. Stigs and Not-Stigs had wanted *her*, after all. She, not Becker, was the point. They'd only really minded Becker after he, in defense of Anya, had grabbed at Stigs.

He had been to Anya's home only once, when he had picked her up at eight o'clock. He hadn't expected to return to her place so early afterwards – unless, of course, their date had gone badly.

Wryly acknowledging the badness of their date, Becker left the lot and sped to Geneva Cove.

I t had actually been a cove, once. One of the great Canals was nearby. The settlers had dug a channel from the Canal to a large crater, creating the cove; not diverting the Canal by any means, only tapping into it. There had been many such attempts to capitalize on the Canals. This one, like all the others, had caused the Martians to attack. The Martians had lost that battle – and the larger war – but, as in all cases where Terrans had tampered with the Canals, the waters eventually withdrew. Defiantly the settlers had closed the channel and filled the crater with shipments of ice from Saturn's rings. The water was regularly topped off by the rain. Geneva Cove was really a lake, now, but it already had its name.

The homes around the Cove were modest ranches and bungalows, separated by driveways, sand gardens, overturned tricycles, and ranks and smatterings of palms, stubby cacti, and citrus trees. Driving slowly, his head still aching, Becker peered into pools of streetlight, at the numbers painted on the curbs. Anya's house was unlit, of course, its windows dark; no one was fussing or lounging behind brightened curtains. As he parked, the porchlight awoke. He would have preferred darkness as he broke in. As it was, the door was unlocked. Anya may have left it so; Geneva Cove was that sort of place. Becker assumed, however, that someone else had already broken in. It was that sort of evening.

He drew the Gneiss discreetly, manifesting it as a small pistol. He slipped inside, quietly moving the door open and shut. He paused in the little foyer, letting his eyes adjust, listening for another intruder. He heard nothing but the fridge in the kitchen. He stepped through the house, surveying from doorways. The windows conveyed a little faraway light – from the porch, the street, and Phobos above. There were only a few rooms, and no basement. There was no one else inside. He returned to the great room. He waited a few heartbeats before finally turning on a lamp. When no one jumped him or shot him, he holstered the Gneiss.

Now in the light he saw the girl on the floor, between the couch and the coffee table. He pushed the table aside and knelt near her head. Before he could check her pulse, he recognized her. It was Anya. But that made no sense. The Martian hadn't been ten minutes ahead of him. And why would it have brought her back *here*? His heart sunk, Becker stared at the girl. She seemed already pale. Then he realized that her cheeks and lips were simply not made up. Her hair was loose; not curled and ribboned. She was in a plain blouse and jeans; not a flattering blue dress. Her only jewelry was a spartan necklace, a cord with an azure crystal teardrop. He touched her face below the bloody gash. She was getting cold. This was not a girl who had been warm and struggling a mere half hour before. Whatever had happened to *this* Anya, the other still needed rescuing. This one, God rest her, could only be avenged.

The dinner conversation had, by the by, touched on family and siblings, and Anya had said she had neither, and was alone on Mars. Becker hadn't sensed she was lying. The conversation and company had been delightful. He also hadn't been looking for lies. So either Anya lied about having a twin or didn't know she had a twin. Or the twin was not a sibling. Whatever the case, the dead girl did not suggest a location for the live one. Though he felt callous leaving her on the floor, Becker did anyway, rather than alter anything. He had already contributed too much to a crime scene. He did say a small prayer.

When Becker had picked Anya up, she had not invited him in. He was seeing the great room for the first time. It was orderly. Simple. The fabrics in the cushions and pillows were solid colors, all pastels. Even the doilies on the endtables, and the antimassacars on the chairs, were barely patterned. The TV was in wall-art mode, displaying a painting of some deeply arboreal valley on Venus. On the mantle were trinkets: a teacup, a sculpture of two children and a dog, a copper urn. To the side of the fireplace was a Martian totem, sculpted from sandstone, of a high-caste female draped by three low-caste neuters. (Becker grinned. Did Anya realize how much this totem would scandalize most Martians?) Such a totem, assuming it was genuine Martian, was not cheap. Geneva Cove told you Anya was middle class; the totem told you she had wherewithal to indulge herself.

Or perhaps the totem had been a gift. Also on the mantle was a photo of Anya with a man, both of them dressed very finely, at some very fine to-do. There were other such framed photos on the walls, even in the kitchen. Always of Anya and this man. There were no photos of others, who might be friends or parents – or a twin sister. Some photos were posed; some candid. In some the man and Anya were kissing. Happily. He, then, was loved.

So why the blind date with Becker?

Becker sighed. Anya might be playing him against this other man. She clearly hadn't trashed his presence in her life – you saw his face wherever you walked in her home. But apparently Anya was stepping out.

Unless all these photos were of the twin.

Or of both girls. Either. Swapping time with one man.

Weirdness really annoyed Becker. Anya had seemed nice. But the implications of these photos were grinding. Sure, he'd wait for Anya's explanation. One should be fair, even to a potential tramp. He still knew there would be no second date.

Especially if he didn't rescue her, of course.

Anya's home presented a persona but no real data. Like most people, Anya kept her life in the Cloud; and though Becker found two devices, one on the kitchen table, another at her bedside, both were password protected. He didn't know enough about Anya even to guess at any passwords. Sure, he worked with computers, but he just wrote intranet apps for human resources; he wasn't a clever hacker.

Becker was left with Anya's omnipresent lover. He found a photo that presented the man in clear portrait. He scanned it with his phone and did an image search. He found the man: Rodion Gorelov. Bachelor. Resident of Mariner Estates. Not quite top register, but hovering around the notably known. While Becker had initially supposed that this man might be a help, now he had to wonder. Wealth, to Becker, usually meant Unionist. A Unionist would be just the rotten sort to hire Martian thugs.

Becker was stepping deeper into something, no doubt.

He started for the door and remembered the girl. He decided to alter things slightly. He gently closed her eyes. He didn't let himself dwell. Thinking of Anya in her curls and blue dress, he hastened to Mariner Estates.

Gorelov's home, like all the others in the Estates, was set back from the road. A little property; a little isolation. His landscaping was a blend of Terran and Martian. Martian plants were difficult to domesticate. When wild they *congested* and overran, and only the nastiness of the desert kept them in check. Martians had cultivated them for food, of course, but never for decoration. Still, they knew how to tame them, in a way Terrans had never quite managed; and Terrans paid well for a Martian hedgerow.

Becker drove unhindered to the small circle at the front door. Either Gorelov had no security at all, or he had fashionably disdained a physical fence and relied on one aetheric. Either way, Becker was not stopped or slowed. Nothing blocked his way, nor was a disabling pulse piped into his car.

Perhaps Gorelov expected midnight visits.

Two lamps in pedestals at the base of the short stairs, and two hanging lamps on either side of the double door, denied Becker any shadows. He was not furtive in any event. He hoped Gorelov clearly saw the Gneiss. That, and Becker's unhesitant gait.

The doors opened – as if the house opened – as if a revelation were being granted. No servant met Becker. No man with an earpiece and an SMG. No Martian with a ready fist. Instead it was Gorelov, alone.

Gorelov looked like his photos. His head was shaved, colored gray by a few days' fuzz. His mustache was splayed as two black daggers.

His ears were oddly small, almost tucked into his head. Indeed his eyes were oddly small, and his nose, and his mouth, as if each had been superficially applied to his brutal skull. For all that, he did not *seem* small. As a whole his gaze seemed rather – honed.

Becker stopped on the landing, a few feet in front of Gorelov. They eyed each other.

Gorelov said, "You look roughed up, friend."

"Argument with a Martian."

"They do argue, don't they? Did you lose the argument?"

Becker squinted. "You could say."

"Forgot you had a gun?"

"Wasn't on me at the time."

"But it is now."

"Yeah. Look. Mr. Gorelov. I don't know what sort of business you normally do at midnight, but that's not what this is about. It's Anya. She's been –"

"Anya?" He suddenly seemed less *composed*. Tightly he asked, "Are you one of Anya's boyfriends?"

One of? Haughtily Becker replied, "No. We just met."

"What are you then?"

Becker snorted. "Her date. We were on a date tonight."

"Tonight?"

"Yeah. Look, she's been -"

"Liar!"

Liar? Becker bristled. He saw Gorelov shift his feet. It was enough to alert Becker. Gorelov launched himself, fist first, at Becker, aiming for Becker's side. Becker stepped aside, planting a foot to balance himself, and swung his arm to deflect Gorelov's. Gorelov, more or less aloft, had to stumble to keep from falling. Meanwhile Becker arced his fist into Gorelov's shoulder. Gorelov was pushed away but stayed upright. They had nearly switched places and were again separated and eyeing each other.

It had been a clumsy attack. Gorelov clearly had been overcome by an unthinking passion. As clearly, he seemed unfinished with it. He was close enough to jab and he did. Becker shifted to shield himself. The jab connected but dissipated into Becker's movement. Luckily Gorelov did not bring the deluge like Stigs. Becker had a moment to grab the Gneiss. Being so close to Gorelov, he manifested it as a short knife. Gorelov saw the knife. Becker had hoped Gorelov would back off. Gorelov didn't. Maybe he thought Becker wouldn't use it; maybe he didn't care. Becker sighed as Gorelov moved in again. You use a weapon to dissuade or kill. Gorelov had not been dissuaded by the sight. Becker was hesitant to kill. So he dissuaded with a plunge into Gorelov's thigh.

Gorelov went down with a cry.

Becker danced aside, holstered the Gneiss, and kicked Gorelov in the kidney. Gorelov balled up and stayed down. Becker did not punish him. He ended the fight by pinning Gorelov to the ground.

Becker shouted, "What the hell, Gorelov?"

A woman's voice answered Becker. "Oh, Rodion loses his cool when it comes to me. He's insanely jealous."

Becker turned his head to find her. She was at the foot of the stairs, half shielded by the pedestal. Her small pistol was aimed at them. No curls; no blue dress. But it was Anya.

Gorelov gasped, "Anya! You're –" He choked. "Um. Honey. Hey. No need to shoot me. Shoot him, yeah. But don't. *Me*. You know I didn't mean to. Damn it. Wait."

Anya frowned. "Didn't mean to what?"

Becker was staring at Anya. It was she. And it wasn't. One of her was kidnapped. One of her was killed. One of her was confronting two men on a porch. And he realized what Gorelov hadn't meant to do. To Anya he explained, "Kill you. You're dead."

Anya glared at Becker.

Becker said, "So there's three of you?"

Her eyes went wide.

Gorelov gasped, "What?"

She stepped forward, thought better of getting too close, and stopped. Her lip was trembling. She waved the pistol at Becker. "Who's dead?"

"You heard me. You are. In your home." Becker looked at Gorelov, who was wincing on the ground. "He called me a liar. He had already pegged me as one of your boyfriends. Yet I tell him you and I were on a date and he furiously calls me a liar. Why? Only because I said *tonight*. He knew you could *not* be on a date tonight, since you had been dead since, oh, a little after eight, no doubt. So what was I doing here? What was I up to? What did I know? Gorelov was a little *fragile*, I think. Ready to pop. Murder can do that to a man."

Gorelov groaned. "I didn't *murder* –"

Becker snapped, "Legal distinctions! I'm sure you've been fretting about them for hours. Got fed up with Anya stepping out, eh? Surprised her at home? Then a little shouting match? A punch? A forehead cracked on a coffee table?"

Gorelov breathed heavily.

Anya, shaking, now pointed the pistol at Gorelov. "What did you do?"

Gorelov was confused. In pain. And very confused. "Made a mistake. I was angry, Pookie. But you're okay! That's great! You can forgive me."

"Anya," said Becker softly. "He doesn't know, does he?"

She shook her head.

"And you understand what he's done to your – sister."

Grimly she nodded.

"Your other sister –"

"Has been kidnapped. I know. I was there."

Becker raised an eyebrow. "Did you see where they went?"

"My... sister has a... locator. Yes. I followed them. But where she is... I can't do anything. I came to see if Rodion might..."

Gorelov growled, "What are you two talking about? What the hell! Let me up before I bleed out."

He struggled under Becker, who smacked him and said, "You'll live. I avoided anything major."

She gazed at Becker. "Why are you here?"

"Looking for a way to find Anya. My Anya."

She smiled crookedly. "We're all your Anya." She tilted her head, as if appraising him. "So you'll help me? This one," she spat at Gorelov, "has been too busy ending my life, it seems."

"Oh yes, I'll help you."

She pocketed her pistol. "Then let's go."

"What about Gorelov?"

She asked, "You a cold-blooded murderer?"

"No."

"Neither am I. Rodion'll get his hanging, one way or another. You can't outrun Justice." Her eyes pleaded. "My sister is in trouble."

Becker thudded Gorelov into the stone tiles and stood up. "Let's go."

"I knew she was dead."

Anya was mournfully watching the passing streetlights. Becker was driving and silently listening.

"I mean, I didn't *know*. But she wasn't answering. And she wasn't moving." She gasped as she fought an impulse to weep. "I figured the Martians had got to her already. She was either safe or... not. And my other sister was still alive." She said angrily, "So, first things first, right? The live sister who's definitely in danger! Rodion'll help. *Ha!* I never figured that he was the one who... Bastard." She glanced at Becker. "Sorry I pointed my gun at you. I wasn't sure what I'd find at Rodion's. When I saw you I wondered... I wondered all sorts of things. Plots and conspiracies. Even after you two started fighting... I didn't know. For sure."

Becker remarked, "Was only prudent."

"Yeah. I guess." She studied him a moment. "Honestly, you're trying to find my sister? You're trying to save her?"

He shrugged. "Yeah."

She smiled slightly, marveling at him. "My sister can really pick them."

"Some algorithm matched our profiles. It was a blind date."

"Fate isn't blind." She inhaled. And exhaled. Not weeping.

When she said nothing further, Becker said carefully, "Look. Anya."

"Yes?"

"You're triplets."

"Yes."

"Living the same life."

"Yes."

"Secretly."

"Yes."

Becker snorted. "Why?"

She sighed. "Now's not the time to explain something so... ah..." She turned back to the streetlights.

He frowned. "Maybe not. But tell me this. Do you have different names? As a strictly tactical matter, I can't call you both Anya. That could get confusing with a lot of violent Martians around."

A laugh broke through. "My name is Happy. We're going to save Lovely. And..." Her voice caught. "Joyous."

"Unusual names."

She rolled her eyes heavenward. "Yeah. I know. We had unusual parents."

Happy had been tailing Lovely. Lovely knew all about it. The sisters had been tailing each other for a short while. They had suspected someone was paying them too much attention. They had hoped to turn the tables.

"Bit risky, both of you in the same room."

"It was a big restaurant. I was mostly at the bar. Besides, she had the pearls; I didn't. I had the ponytail; she didn't. Very different make-up and very different clothes. We're girls. We put on disguises all the time."

Becker chuckled. "True enough. So you shot Stigs?"

She closed her eyes. "I shot... at him. He was brutalizing you. And no one was stepping in."

Bitterly he said, "Angry Martians make sheep of some people. Why didn't you shoot the one taking Lovely?"

"I might have hit her!"

"You might have hit *me*."

"You're not my sister."

"Ah."

"Besides, you were being killed." She sighed. "I intended to get the other Martian. Threaten him at least. But by the time I got to the alley he was packing Lovely into a car. He got in and the driver backed up to hit me. I jumped out of the way. No one noticed my tiny gun."

The Martians had taken Lovely to a house just within the Martian district. Drawn by Lovely's locator, Happy caught up to them. She hesitated a few doors down. The sisters had a dataspheric link, and Lovely, panicked and blindfolded, warned that she sensed a lot of Martians in the house. Happy was frightened. Much as she loathed leaving Lovely alone, she retreated to get Gorelov's help. Wary of being overheard and intercepted – and unsure how to explain the triplet thing over the phone – she had not called ahead, and arrived at Gorelov's without warning.

Becker asked, "Why not call the cops?"

"Habit. Anya keeps a low profile. Besides, Rodion has some resources."

"Criminal?"

She made a face. "Borderline. Rodion has... tastes and ambitions. Not everyone he deals with is respectable."

"Are you borderline, too?"

She smirked. "Not really. Secret life, yeah. Not criminal, though."

"You let Gorelov handle the dirt."

She raised her eyebrows. She blushed, too.

Becker watched her blush. "So why would Martians kidnap you?"

Slowly she answered, "I imagine it has something to do with Rodion."

"He seemed unaware. Why haven't they contacted him?"

She started to speak; then did not.

Becker scowled. "Just a simple girl from Geneva Cove."

"Don't be snarky. Lovely is blameless. *I* am blameless."

"And Anya?"

Her face hardened. "And Anya."

"Uh-hm. Lovely still think she's alone in that room?"

"Mm..." She avoided his look. With her implant she sent *<literal> :: <query> :: alone*. Lovely replied *<literal> :: <answer> :: yes*.

"...Yes."

Lovely then added, as she had repeatedly that evening, *<emote> :: <imperative> :: rocket* and *<emote> :: <statement> :: spiders*. The packets were barely kilobytes but, being tiny and barely energetic, made less noise in the datasphere than cosmic rays. Low profile, indeed; enough to escape the attention of authorities and foes, Terran and Martian. Resourcefully, though, the sisters had – over the years – imbued each dictionary crumb with flavorful connotations. *Rocket* when emoted meant *I don't care what you're doing you have to come now*; and *spiders* meant *I am overwhelmed and viscerally terrified*.

"She still think there's lots of Martians?"

"Mm... Yes."

Becker nodded. "Then it's a good thing I have lots of ammo."

Martians, at the time of the Terran arrival, had not been *primitive*. Their civilization had rather been indifferent to mechanisms and the relentless manipulation of Nature. Even now they kept their distance from Terran technology; at least within their own remaining territories. The high caste, however, had encouraged the low to live among the Terrans and, to one extent or another, succumb to the animate metals of Earth.

Terrans had differing opinions about the wisdom of Martian districts. As successful conquerors, though, most Terrans had become indulgent of the beaten indigenes. Meanwhile there were no Terran districts in Martian territories; the high caste was allowed to disallow them. Which might seem a double standard. But then, Mars was occupied by Earth. Strictly speaking, there were Terran districts *everywhere*.

Since the intent of the Martian districts was a stand-offish assimilation (and no doubt a guileless infiltration), the homes looked more or less Terran; not only in structure but in upkeep and decoration. A Martian district had the flavor of any genteel, urban slum on Earth. Clean, well-minded, but poor. On top of that, not a few Terran outcasts, down-on-their-luckers, and Areophilic posers lived in a Martian district. So, as Becker walked casually toward the house that held Lovely, he did not feel or seem so very out of place. Only the Gneiss would have given an onlooker pause; and most onlookers were now inside and asleep.

He walked past the house and, in the streetlight, assessed what he could. There were no guards or the like. This was just an innocent home, after all; no thugs or cabals or kidnapped girls – no sir. He turned the corner. He said a prayer to St. George and, staying in the shadow, hopped a couple of fences and eased into the house's backyard.

Although more domesticated than his ancestors, Becker retained a few items and kept them close. There was the Gneiss, of course. And just as he had been prepared to do at Anya's house he now broke into Lovely's prison, quietly squatting at the back door and using his grandfather's pick. The pea-sized EMP disabled the lock. A few artful wiggles undid the physical catch. The door was ready to give way.

He took a moment to collect himself.

Becker had no *plan* to kill anyone. He intended, if possible, to spirit Lovely away. But he expected resistance. And even if, for now, the Gneiss in his grip was manifested as a dart-taser, he had it configured for instant reversion to its lethal default.

With a breath he slipped into the house.

Becker huddled silently in the mudroom, out of reach of the kitchen lights. He peered out and saw no one. Something pungent simmered on the stove. Packages of snacks – some Terran, some Martian (manufactured by Terrans, of course) – lay opened and spilled on the table.

To the front of the house there seemed to be two groups of Martians. One was closer – in the dining room, he guessed – and, given the repetitive and rhythmic utterances and spots of laughter, was probably playing a game. The other group was in a further room, going on about something, as the TV blared some Terran comedy. The quantity of voices confirmed for Becker that there were indeed a lot of Martians. They seemed *distracted*, however. Were a girl not captive nearby, Becker would think he had invaded a mere soiree.

Lovely had been taken to the back of the house. Becker was at a corner; to his right was a hallway. He sprinted through the light like a roach.

The hallway turned to his left. He presumed that, when he followed it, he might finally encounter something suggestive of a kidnapping. Gneiss high, he went wide, and sure enough there was a guard at a door. A bored guard, leaning against the wall, reading a tablet. It looked up and its eyes swirled green with bewilderment. It made no move. Guarding was clearly not its vocation. Then all four eyes snapped wide into whiteness as Becker's dart suffused the Martian with electric debilitation.

Becker bounded and caught the Martian before it could noisily crumple to the floor.

He quickly dragged the Martian through the door. The room was unlit. There was blackness once he shut the door. He whispered, "Lights, low," and the room became dimly lit.

The room was small, apparently used for storage of household items, including discarded and broken appliances. Lovely had been placed on the floor. Her ankles were bound, her legs to her side. Her wrists were bound behind her back. The same sort of rags used to bind her had been used to gag and blind her. Having heard Becker's voice she left her slouch, the anticipation of rescue perking her up.

Incited by Lovely's condition, a part of Becker desired to stomp the unmoving Martian. The rest of Becker reined in unfocused retribution and instead hastened to free Lovely's eyes and mouth. He crouched before her and removed the rags. She licked her lips, blinked into the light, and whispered hoarsely, "Hamlin, thank you."

For a moment he forgot his task. There was a way that her lips tucked into her cheeks – tiny dimples in a soft, rosy breadth – that entirely tripped him. Her lashes were rich and her nose straight and fine. Lovely allured him. It was an odd thing. Happy had the very same face, but only Lovely distracted him like this. Maybe it was the curls.

He reached for her ankles and unbound them. A moment of his admiration for the foot that was shoeless prodded a sensible thought. As she started to rise he raised his hand; and she paused, questioningly. He withdrew her lost shoe from his belt and, putting it to her little foot, found it slipped on very easily, fitting her as if it were made of wax.

She laughed sweetly. "Thanks."

They rose together. She turned and he freed her hands. She turned back, reached up with both hands, and gently held his face. On tiptoes she met his lips. Her kiss was generous. Only prudence made him end it.

Suddenly and robustly optimistic, he prepared to take her away.

Happy had had no illusions about joining Becker. She had stayed with the car as their getaway gal. She was parked up the street but could still see the house. So she was able to send a warning.

Lovely grabbed Becker's forearm. "Wait." He watched her listen to the datastream. Her face darkened. "A car is here. More Martians. Happy thinks two are high caste."

That couldn't be good.

And it wasn't. The soiree had ended. They heard Martians approaching the room. A name was yelled – presumably that of the downed Martian guard. Becker hissed to Lovely, "I'll go out first. You go right, right again, then left out the back." Fearfully she nodded. Without a farewell Becker opened the door and hurled himself out. Behind him Lovely ran.

He neatly tased two of the Martians. They became useful obstacles in the narrow hallway. He retreated quickly towards the kitchen. None of the Martians in the vanguard were armed. One enthusiastic Martian leapt at Becker and tackled him. Lovely was alone when she appeared in the kitchen. Two Martians were already there, refreshing their pungent stew. Although surprised, they blocked her way and nabbed her. She struggled in frustration. More Martians poured into the kitchen and hallway.

There really were a lot of them.

The furniture was rearranged. Everything was pushed to the far wall, except the couch and two dining-room chairs. The couch was placed so that Martians (a couple with shotguns) could stand behind it. In front of the couch the chairs were placed, together and close, like thrones. On the couch sat Lovely and Becker. In the chairs sat the high-caste Martians.

In public, high-caste Martians always came in twos, a male and a female, whether or not the two were betrothed, married, or even especially known to each other. Neither of the Terrans had ever met a high-caste Martian, but of course they knew what the high caste were like. The two Martians in this case were typical. Each was clothed in loose swaths of fabric. The swaths, piecemeal like vestments, were dyed with drawings of beasts and blossoms and were visually striking; but, of course, they were only a flourish to the glass they left exposed.

Glass sprouted upon the temples and crowns of the Martians; grew from their forearms and over their wrists; covered the chest of the male, and the shoulder blades of the female; and traced a bit of the outer hip and thigh. The glass of the male was tiled and etched; of the female, filigreed. And although the glass was indelicate, hard to the strike, and grounded in the skeleton, it was wholly *fluid*. It was bone enspirited with water. Literally so. Upon coming of age, a high-caste child – who had no glass but only bony growths – was immersed in the rapids of a Canal; all but drowned, in fact; and childhood ended when bone became glass.

Glass changed with the years; it changed with the weather; it changed with the mood. It was a distinctive plumage, a distinguishing elaboration of the self. Any Terran could be awed by its beauty and complexity. Few Terrans, however, could read the *social* signals of shifting glass. Becker didn't even try.

The male had taken Becker's papers. And the Gneiss. He was turning the Gneiss in his hands as if it were a delicate work of art. His eyes a pondering blue, he remarked, "This is an unusual weapon, Mr. Becker. I've never seen it in use before. You must tell me where I can get ammunition for it." Like all Martians he seemed to be singing, his syllables pursuing a chant; yet his accent was muted and his English methodical. He looked directly at Becker. "I do wonder what an SUSF operative could want with these women. Why is the SUSF meddling in this business?"

Becker retorted, "I'm not SUSF."

The male ignored him, saying, "I admit *sohunni* Stigs gave you cause to meddle. He and *sohunni* Nurg and Grak acted ineptly. Prematurely. Quite against our plans." His eyes pulsed orange. "All this fuss! I should thank you for *chastising* Stigs. The SUSF doesn't often do me such favors."

Irritably Becker said, "Look, pal. I'm as much SUSF as you are *sohunni*. And I don't get the feeling I'd *ever* want to do you a favor. I really don't care about your plans. I'm sure you can perfectly rationalize kidnapping an innocent girl. Why don't rationalize letting her go? She's done nothing to you."

The male was instantly incensed. "Nothing? Innocent!" Flustered he grasped the Gneiss as if it were a rock and, in a spasm, nearly threw it at Becker; then, having passed (mostly) through the unthinking part of his anger, he gripped the Gneiss properly and aimed it. The female touched his forearm, cautiously tightening her fingers. She trilled something in Martian. The male calmed. He set the Gneiss in his lap. Then, composing himself, upright in the chair, he leaned over to the female and whispered what Becker knew were the words of transition. The female now spoke. Her voice was like her partner's, pitched higher but nonetheless a methodical, near enough chant. She addressed Lovely.

"Your mate – I apologize. Your *boyfriend* Gorelov has recently come to distrust you. He hired a PI – a private investigator, yes? – to confirm your fidelity. This worried us. A PI might complicate our *own* investigations of Gorelov. We were wary of stopping him. We watched him, however. We soon realized he had learned something that excited him. We wanted control of this news. We paid the PI very well – you Terrans are *so* corruptible – to tell Gorelov the trivial truth that you were casually dating other men. Meanwhile we kept the greater truth. Frankly we're embarrassed. We had dismissed you as a secondary concern."

Becker glanced to Lovely. She was striving to seem bewildered.

The female lifted her hand, opened it like a bloom, and, with the other hand, lifted a necklace from her palm. It was the necklace Becker had seen on Joyous. Or, rather, one like it. It must have come from Lovely.

"Two of you," the female continued, "would retreat from life, while the third would live it. For a while. And when the third was done, she would give the other two her necklace. And the two would drink from the crystal." She shuddered. "The PI thought it was a 'weird religious thing.' We, on the other hand, knew Gorelov regularly gave you vials of the *Norikuam*." She used the Martian word for the *Waters* of a Canal; which were truly not the mere waters of a rainfall or a lake. "We were investigating him because we knew he was a collector. You Terrans! You can't stop despoiling anything..." The shadows in her eyes were suddenly *furied*. Then, calming, she pondered the necklace. "And now we see that what we feared is true. The *Norikuam* have heard your Being. Haven't they? And the *Norikuam* have spoken your Being. You Terrans are exchanging lives lived. It's... foul." She glared at her. "What sort of Terrans *are* you?"

There was a knocking behind Becker and Lovely. It was at the front door, which led directly into the room. The female huffed and tilted her head impatiently. A thug moved to the door, exchanged a few words through it, and then let in a neuter. The new thug scurried in and obsequiously stood before the male and the female. It gave the female something, and then the male. It also gave some brief report. The male, who seemed a little perturbed, gave it some orders; and then it scurried out of the way.

The female leaned towards the male and whispered transition. The male tapped briefly on the Terran phone that the thug had given him. He turned it to show the screen image. It was Joyous as Becker had found her. Lovely already knew, through Happy, that Joyous was dead; but to see Joyous so...

Lovely started to sob. The male narrowed his eyes at Becker and said, "One sister eludes us. When we found the other, we... ah, a terrible thing. She is now dead. Not quite our intention, but you can appreciate, now, the seriousness of this business."

Becker tried hard not to smirk. The Martian was trying to intimidate them by claiming the killing of Joyous. He was late to that party; but Becker let him play his bluff.

The male continued, "My *ayoatu* holds the *Norikuam* of the dead woman." The female was showing what the thug had given her: the necklace from Joyous. "These *Norikuam* are tainted. They need mercy above all. But I wonder if they might serve a purpose." His eyes darkened. "The Being within them is not told. Give me any more trouble, Mr. Becker, and this woman who lives will drink the *Norikuam* of a death."

Becker caught the lavender smugness that washed through each eye of the male. The male paused so that Becker might *consider the import*. Threats had a protocol, after all; and Becker was given his *sanctioned moment* to understand the consequence of his resistance. He knew he had a moment to consider the damage threatened; he knew he had a moment to consider the welfare of the threatened woman. So while the male smugly awaited Becker's resignation, Becker lunged at him.

The male didn't have a moment to remember he was sitting. When he realized Becker was coming at him he hastily tried to back away. He only launched himself into his chair. His chair began to topple. He did have the wit to raise an arm, to ready a strike against Becker. As it was, Becker had never meant to *impact* the male. With his right hand he snatched the Gneiss from the male's lap and twisted, right shoulder first, between the male and the female. With his left hand he clamped onto the female's right shoulder and, continuing his twist, spun and dragged her down. The male, tangling with the air, was knocked aside, hard.

Of course, there on the floor like a sack of sand, the female frantic atop him, Becker was hardly formidable, nor even well positioned to do much of anything. *But*, he was assaulting a couple of high-caste Martians – one a female, no less! – and was making himself the center of attention. *And*, he had the Gneiss. The thugs couldn't help but converge on him. Lovely had an opportunity to run away. God bless her, she took it. She didn't hesitate in fear or foolishly join in. She scrambled over the back of the couch, getting behind the Martians who had moved to save their betters; and when Becker saw her bolt, he took a few potshots with the Gneiss, causing the thugs around them to flinch, dodge, trip, and spasm. Lovely disappeared through the front door. Becker resisted as long as he could, kicking and generally making it difficult for the thugs to end his lock on the female.

Becker didn't have a plan for his own escape. Bracing himself, he prayed the Martians were not vindictive.

They weren't, precisely.

It had clearly been a mistake not to bind Lovely and Becker. Yet it was simply the case that when dealing with anyone, high-caste Martians – who bathed in hubris – preferred intimidation to restraint. It was easy to restrain someone. In any event, after Becker was pummeled and subdued he was returned to the couch and, this time, tightly bound.

He slumped, growing bruises. The male cursed the ineptitude of his *sohunni* thugs. The thugs grumbled. The female scalded Becker with the angriest eyes he had ever seen on any woman of any species.

Lovely had escaped. Presumably, as she fled, she had alerted Happy, and Happy had been ready to scoop her up. Becker liked to think that the getaway car had waited a *little* while for him. At least the girls got away.

And, once they were out of the picture, they had also helpfully called the police.

Flashing lights appeared in the window.

The male spat a few words. The thugs scattered out the back. The female sighed. The male then dithered over Becker with an exasperation that was almost pitiable. Becker could tell he didn't want to explain a captured Terran, nor did he want to release a witness and the evening's only prize.

Stolidly Becker said, "Give me my Gneiss and let me go."

The male blinked. "Whyever would I do that? So you can *shoot* me?"

Becker snorted. "With the cops outside? No."

The male stared.

"Look," said Becker, "you're not running. I'm sure the cops are a big nuisance but they aren't precisely *worrying* you. I don't know what you have up your sleeve. I don't care. But let me sweeten it. *I won't say a word.*" He sat back confidently. "As long as you give me my Gneiss and let me go."

The male squinted in bemusement. Running out of time – and moved by Becker's brazen guile – he silently unbound Becker and gave him the Gneiss. He returned Becker's phone and papers, too. Becker stood up,

haltingly, and left it to the high-caste Martians to answer the knock at the door.

Outside, Becker moved quickly through the yard and over the fence, but once he was away and in the darkness, he slowed, tired of tamping down all the scattered pains. His phone chirped.

I'm wide awake and thinking of you. We should meet again. Are you wide awake, too? How about that coffee shop on 14th? – Susan

Becker didn't know a Susan. He did know a 14th Street. There was indeed a coffee shop there. He couldn't recall its name, but he could picture the neon mug and its animated steam. He made his way to a corner and called for a ride.

He nearly nodded off in the cab.

At the shop, his car was in the lot. The girls were not in the car, nor in the shop. He ordered a coffee just to be polite to the waitress. He waited for a while, wearily tapping his straw in his cooling drink. Was he meant to wait? Had the girls simply run off? More than anything else, he bristled at their simple *ingratitude.* Eventually he returned to his car. It was unlocked, the keys in the cubby. He went home.

At home, he sat on his bed and removed his shoes. He lay back and, despite his whirling thoughts, instantly fell asleep.

Two days later, the police had still not called on Becker. He assumed the Martians had wiggled their way out. He also assumed the girls had been unspecific in their 911. Surely no mention of a Terran held captive by Martians! Just, oh, a disturbance of some sort, some arguments and crashing, or something; just enough to prod the police and monkey-wrench the whole affair.

He had not even heard anything further of Stigs. He *might* suppose the police had simply not identified the Terran couple involved. He suspected, however, that the fix was in. The Martians had hardly been wrong about the corruptibility of Terrans. Whether the fix had come from criminal or diplomatic forces, Becker really didn't care.

He heard nothing about the murder of an Anya Day, either. Her house was locked; her phone disconnected. Someone had cleaned all that up, too. The Martians again? Or Gorelov, who had the resources? Or perhaps Happy and Lovely had recovered their poor sister and...

moved on. They apparently had the experience hiding and sneaking and disappearing.

Everything was unduly calm.

That afternoon, as Becker worked through his pains, he received a message from "L."

I'm sorry. H thought we had other priorities the other night. She wasn't wrong. Please know we weren't casting you aside. At least I wasn't.

Another important thing.

I did love R.

I/We. You know.

At first he was just a friend. A source of what I needed to drink. He always wanted more of me than I intended. But I want you to know that my dating wasn't just a way to sidestep R, let alone hurt him. He and I had never made vows.

Yes, I handled it poorly.

One more thing.

Since my necklace is gone, I can't properly give my recent life to H. She is miffed. You know

what? I'm not.

Thank you. Thank you.

Words aren't enough.

Meet me.

Becker gazed at the message for a long time. He remembered their kiss; he felt it anew. He sighed. Lovely had provided a time and a place. He wryly supposed that this might count as their second date. At least it wouldn't be blind this time.

Not as much, anyhow.

"*Some Things Missing from Her Profile*" is copyright © David Skinner.

David Skinner has been writing steadily (though not prolifically) since he was twelve years old. His most recent book is the novel "The Giant's Walk." He has also had three books of fantastical juvenile fiction published by Simon & Schuster (most notably "The Wrecker"). He loves science fiction. He lives in Michigan and blogs at www.davidskinner.biz.

In 947 A.D.   ROLF OF THE GOLDEN HORN, A VIKING, REPELLED AN ALIEN INVASION. # PULPHISTORY

*What strange power could cause wealthy men to suddenly give away their
fortunes and commit suicide?*

Dream Master

BY GENE MOYERS

On Tuesday morning at just after eleven o'clock, Stanley Kincaid walked out of the midtown branch of the State Bank of New York. He was a distinguished-looking older man wearing an expensive suit and carrying a small paper-wrapped package. Tucking the package under one arm he strolled casually three blocks to a branch post office. While he waited in line he addressed the package with a gold-plated pen. After he had mailed it he exited the bank and stepped to the curb. He waited patiently for a few moments then calmly stepped off the curb in front of a city bus.

The impact threw Kincaid nearly twenty feet. Immediately a crowd gathered. Some were in shock by the sudden violence, while others excitedly told each other what had happened. In less than a minute a beat cop had shouldered his way through the crowd to the injured man. He was too late. Kincaid had died the moment he struck the pavement.

On Wednesday morning Thaddeus Van Dorn emerged from the 34th Street exit of First City Bank of Manhattan. He too was expensively dressed and had a small package under one arm. He stepped to the curb and hailed a passing cab. The cab dropped him at the main post office downtown. Quickly addressing his package he mailed it, and walked briskly through the main entrance onto the street. At the curb he glanced around. He looked to his left and waited patiently as the noisy traffic passed by him. Soon he sighted a city garbage truck approaching. Belching diesel smoke, the rumbling truck sped up to beat a yellow light at the corner and roared through the intersection.

Van Dorn stepped off the corner into the path of the accelerating truck. At the last second the garbage truck's driver saw him step off the curb. He stood on the brakes but was too late. Calmly Van Dorn awaited the impact but instead a strong arm reached out and jerked him toward the curb. He almost made it. The truck's right corner bumper struck him in the arm and shoulder. Spun around he ended up in a tangled heap with the quick-thinking man who had saved him.

Another crowd quickly gathered. Someone ran to telephone for an ambulance while the quick thinking savior examined the unconscious Van Dorn. He wasn't dead... yet.

Thursday morning Thomas Manning was in his office. He did not look up from his patient's notes as the intercom buzzed. He pressed a button down on the intercom with his left hand as he continued to write, "Yes, Alexis."

A pleasant voice spoke formally from the small speaker, "Telephone call for you, Doctor."

"Take a message Alexis, I have a lot to do this morning."

A laugh came through the speaker, "Not today, Tommy. I don't think this guy's going to take 'no' for an answer."

Manning stopped writing. His pen poised above the paper, he looked at the intercom and said, "Ohhhh?"

"Yes, this gentleman says he's with the FBI and it's important."

Manning put down his pen, "Thank you Alexis, I'll take it."

As he reached for the phone he thought he heard a chuckle and sotto voce comment that sounded like, "Thought you might."

Not for the first time Manning smiled thinking about his complicated relationship with his secretary, as he picked up the telephone, "Thomas Manning." A calm voice spoke on the other end, "Tom? This is Frank Drew. How are you?"

Manning nodded, "I'm fine Frank, How are you? Still running the Bureau?"

"I'm fine. I'm working out of the New York field office now."

"Sounds like a promotion. What can I do for the Bureau today?"

"We need you to take a look at a uh... very disturbed man."

"In New York? Frank, I have a very busy schedule."

A pause, "Do you have rich, amnesiac businessmen throwing themselves in front of buses?"

Manning replied thoughtfully, "No. No, I don't. I'll come as soon as I can."

"Thanks Tom. I knew I could count on you." After a few more moments to work out details Manning said goodbye. He stood up and walked to the window in his private office. The view of downtown Baltimore was quite spectacular from here. Absently he pulled his watch from its snug pocket by its gold chain. He flipped open its lid and glanced at the time. After eleven o'clock. Closing the watch, he replaced it in his vest.

Manning turned and walked across the room. His office was large and comfortable. Three walls were covered in bookshelves. One side of the room was furnished with comfortable armchairs, small tables and shaded lighting. He walked to one of the bookshelves and reached out for a wooden box. It was over a foot long, about ten inches wide and perhaps four inches deep. Made of mahogany, it was highly polished and hinged at the rear. Set into the lid was a brass plaque with the words "Thomas Manning" engraved into it. Manning hesitated for a moment before he shoved the box back in place. Turning, he crossed to the outer office door, fingering his watch chain as he went.

The tall, attractive brunette at the typewriter looked up from her machine as the inner door opened. Alexis's attention was immediately drawn to where Manning was fingering the small key on his watch chain. She immediately picked up a pencil and slid a note pad toward her. Manning stopped in front of her desk. "Alexis, I have some work for you."

She nodded pencil poised, "Of course, Doctor."

"First, I need a ticket on the first available train to New York, this afternoon if you can get it." Alexis scribbled furiously. "I'll also need a hotel room in New York. Next, reschedule my appointments for the rest of the week. Cancel everything. I should be back by Monday, if not I'll call." He turned toward his office again as Alexis reached for the phone.

A half hour later Alexis handed Manning

a piece of paper. "Here's your reservation for the *Northeastern Limited* and compartment number on the train. I'm canceling all your appointments now. I've also booked you into the *Biltmore*. Is there anything else, Doctor?" Shrugging into his overcoat Manning took the paper and shook his head, "No. As usual I don't know what I'd do without you." He smiled, "When you're finished there, take the rest of the week off. Take your mother to the opera or something." He put on his homburg and turned toward the door. Alexis spoke quietly as he opened the outer office door, "Be careful, Tommy."

"I will." He nodded and was gone.

As the door closed behind him Alexis looked thoughtfully at it. With his average looks and quiet, polite manner Thomas Manning looked anything but formidable. Alexis knew differently. Despite being just short of thirty years old, he was perhaps the most intelligent and capable man she had ever met. Still, she worried about him. He had a tendency to get started in one direction and keep going no matter what got in his way. One of these days he would come up against something that didn't move. She sighed and turned back to the phone.

"What do you mean he's not dead?" Both men quailed in front of the gold-robed figure. The smaller was almost dwarfishly short, standing not even five feet tall. He had black hair and a swarthy complexion. His normally shifty look was now replaced by one of fear. The taller of the two was more athletically built. He had a rough face and a nose that had been broken in the past. Despite his tough looks his forehead was covered in sweat. He spoke respectfully, "The cops are hiding it but Van Dorn is alive and under guard at a hospital."

The robed figure stood up from a mahogany chair that was more like a throne than a normal chair. The chair was in the shadows near a tapestry-covered wall. Soft music played over hidden speakers. As he stood, he whipped the glass he was holding over his head and smashed it to the stone floor in front of his two henchmen. The crystal shattered into a thousand pieces making the two jump. "How did this happen? He should have obeyed my commands like the others! He must suffer as the others have! I have waited too long for my vengeance! They..." The man in the shadows stopped, took a deep breath and got control of himself, "Where is he being kept?"

The two exchanged looks before the taller answered, "Manhattan General, but he's under guard and he has no memory of..."

"Memories are not the most important thing. Van Dorn cannot be allowed to live."

"But the specialist..."

The robed man's eyes pinned the taller man, "What specialist?"

"Well, the word is there's a specialist in amnesia on the way."

"It does not matter." He pointed at the larger of his two henchmen. "Hendricks, go back to the hospital. Learn everything you can." He turned to the small man, "Trusseau, we will use the powder of Ampuri."

As the two men scurried to do their master's bidding, the gold robed figure, his features obscured by an opaque veil, walked away from his chair. He moved toward a curtained alcove. From behind the curtain came the sound of a soft female voice.

As Manning crossed the huge lobby of Grand Central station he was accosted by an athletic-looking man in a dark suit holding out a hand as he approached, "Tom, thanks for coming. Good trip?"

Manning shook the strong hand of Agent Frank Drew, FBI. Drew certainly looked like one of J. Edgar Hoover's fair-haired boys; he was tall, clean cut, athletic and all-American. As Drew led them outside to a waiting car, he looked at Manning. "What's so funny?"

Manning smiled. "Nothing, just thinking. What do you have for me, Frank?"

With the sedan under way, Drew consulted a small notebook. "Let's see, Thaddeus Van Dorn: age 57, married, two children. He's a successful investment banker who did well even during the"crash." Two days ago, Wednesday, Mr. Van Dorn went to one of his banks and drew out one hundred thousand dollars in cash. He expressly asked that the money be wrapped in plain brown paper. He then left the bank and went to a post office where he mailed a package, to an unknown address. He then left the post office, walked out to the street, and stepped in front of a garbage truck." He shut the notebook and looked brightly at Manning.

Manning said carefully, "A terrible tragedy."

"It would have been if an off-duty policeman hadn't been standing there. He jerked Van Dorn out of the way but he still got clipped pretty hard. He's lucky to be alive but he's got a broken arm and collar bone."

"And he has no memory of anything?"

"Nothing that happened that morning, anyway. It's funny because all the docs at the hospital say he has absolutely no head injury."

"That *is* interesting." Manning replied.

"No, what's interesting is that this is the third time this has happened here in Manhattan." Manning gave him a questioning look. "Yep, the first one happened Monday morning. Same thing, some rich businessman withdrew a boatload of cash, went to a post office where he presumably mailed it somewhere and then stepped in front of a speeding taxi and was killed. It happened again on Tuesday, same withdrawal same kind of death." Manning said nothing but Drew could see the wheels turning in the psychologist's mind as he leaned back in his seat.

At the hospital Drew's federal badge cut through much red tape. They were quickly shown to the psych floor where Manning spoke at length to both Van Dorn's medical doctor and a psychiatrist. They both agreed that there was no physical reason for Van Dorn's suicide attempt or any memory loss. Other than the events of that morning Van Dorn's memory was intact and his health had been good with no signs of depression or mental illness. Finally the psychiatrist offered, "We're putting the memory loss down to hysteric reaction to near death trauma. He may be resisting any memory of his near accident."

Manning nodded and politely thanked both physicians. Before meeting Van Dorn, Manning questioned the floor nurse and asked for some favors. While they waited he spoke to Drew. "Frank, I'd appreciate it if you wait here while I speak to Van Dorn. I need some private time to evaluate whether he is lying about the amnesia and assess his mental state. I also may want to hypnotize him." Drew looked surprised at this last statement, "Hypnotize? Is that kosher?"

Manning smiled. "Hypnotism is not really recognized much in the medical fraternity but I have found it very useful in retrieving repressed memories. Something is keeping this man from remembering. I'd be willing to bet if they were alive the other men would have the same memory loss." He smiled. "I'm sure this is exactly why you called me here, isn't it?"

Drew was still thinking of a reply when the nurse returned. As they walked toward Van Dorn's room she said, "I've arranged Mr. Van Dorn's room as you asked, doctor."

He smiled at her, "Thank you for your trouble, Nurse." He shook her hand and, nodding to the police guard, entered the room.

The overhead light had been turned off. Instead a shaded lamp had been placed on a nightstand next to the bed. A comfortable-looking but worn armchair had been scrounged up from somewhere, probably the Doctor's lounge, and placed near the bed. The dim light showed the injured man reclining in bed. His arm was in a cast and elevated. An elaborate bandage covered his neck and shoulder.

Manning introduced himself. "Mr. Van Dorn, I'm Doctor Manning. Do you feel up to talking with me?" The pale man turned to Manning and nodded his assent. Manning sat in the armchair bringing him down to the patient's level so they could see each other's faces in the warm light.

"Firstly, let me say I'm very sorry that all this has happened to you. I'm not a medical doctor but I believe I may be able to help you sort things out."

The pale man seemed confused. "Not a doctor? But you just said…"

"I'm a psychologist, and I know a good bit about amnesia."

"Then they told you I can't remember anything about what happened."

"Yes. Can you tell me the last thing you do remember?"

Van Dorn frowned. "The last thing I remember is going to bed on Tuesday night."

"Alright. Are you seeing a therapist or other counselor?"

"No. I'm not crazy, you know."

"Of course not. I didn't mean to offend; I'm just trying to establish your state of mind lately. Have you ever been hypnotized?"

"Hypnotized. Of course not, I don't believe in that kind of hokum."

Manning smiled slightly while inside his mind worked swiftly. He was a trained observer. He had been involved in thousands of counseling sessions and interviews. Over the years he had learned to evaluate things like breath, eye movement, body language, pupil dilation and other subtle signs. With practice he had become adept at telling whether people were lying or telling the truth. It wasn't foolproof but it was very difficult to lie to him successfully. Everything he was now seeing was telling him that Van Dorn was being honest. He had not been hypnotized; at least he thought he hadn't. Thoughtfully Manning continued, "Do you sleep soundly, Mr. Van Dorn?"

"Uh, well, I guess so."

Manning nodded. "Do you ever dream?"

Van Dorn hesitated for a moment before answering brusquely, "No, never. Or at least almost never, I can't remember the last time I dreamt anything." For the first time, Manning detected uncertainty in Van Dorn's response. Thoughtfully he pulled his watch chain from his vest. He held it loosely in his right hand so the gold watch dangled below his hand swinging slightly.

Standing up so his head was out of the direct light but his torso and hands were still brightly illuminated, he continued questioning Van Dorn. Now though, his voice dropped to a lower, softer tone. His questions changed as well. He now asked friendly, easy questions about Van Dorn's family and life. All the time he continued to play with the watch chain in his hand, causing the watch to sway slightly back and forth. In Munich years before, Manning had studied hypnotism from an old doctor who had sworn by his techniques. He had also taught Manning tricks about using his voice in subtle ways to influence his listeners. Manning had polished these techniques when he returned to the US from sources as varied as carnival barkers and stage magicians. Very quickly, Van Dorn would be in a light trance without even realizing it.

In minutes the injured man's responses became slower and finally stopped. Manning pocketed his watch and sat down. Continuing the interrogation, Manning questioned Van Dorn closely. He was looking for any sign of hypnotism; hypnotic blocks, post hypnotic suggestions and the like. To his surprise he found nothing. Van Dorn had been truthful; he had never been hypnotized as far as Manning could tell.

The psychologist then questioned him about the money and his suicide attempt. The answers came quickly and were very interesting. Under hypnosis Van Dorn remembered everything. He had been told to withdraw the money and mail it to a City address. He had then been instructed to walk into the path of a speeding vehicle. Most interestingly, he recognized the names of the other two victims. He had been involved in business transactions with both of them many times.

Unfortunately the investor could not name or describe the man who had ordered him to his death. This surprised Manning. He probed deeper into Van Dorn's unconscious mind but the only answer he could get was "the dream." When he questioned Van Dorn about this dream, he received a shock. It was very clear that all of Van Dorn's self-destructive actions stemmed from a dream. A dream where a mysterious, shadowy figure had appeared and given him specific instructions; instructions so strongly worded that Van Dorn had no choice but to obey them, even if they involved robbing himself and committing suicide. Since it had happened in a dream the only clues were deep in his subconscious.

Manning sat back, nonplussed. In all his experience he had never even considered the idea of invading someone else's dreams. This would rewrite psychological text books, possibly law books as well. Were there even laws covering this? Suddenly, Manning decided, the world had gotten a whole lot more complicated.

He gently extricated himself from Van Dorn's subconscious, brought him out of the trance and into a gentle sleep. He left quietly. Agent Drew was waiting for him at the nurse's station. Manning needed to tell him what he had found, or at least part of it. Then he had an errand; because he had learned one more thing while probing about in Van Dorn's subconscious memories. He had learned the address the money had been mailed to.

Manning paid off the driver of his cab and looked around the narrow street. He was southwest of Central Park in a neighborhood of rooming houses and older apartments. He was just wondering how to get past the locked vestibule door of the apartment building in front of him when an elderly woman carrying two grocery bags started up the front steps. Stepping briskly up the steps he reached her just as she attempted to get her key in the lock while juggling her bags. Manning smiled as he took one of her bags. "Let me help you there, ma'am."

She smiled back. "Why thank you, young man."

Once inside the door, he handed her back the bag and tipped his hat. She nodded and moved toward the elevator. Taking the stairs, he quickly climbed to the fourth floor. The dimly lit hallway was empty and quiet. Squatting, he examined the lock of the flimsy door. He sighed, reached into a vest pocket, and pulled out a small pen knife and opened its thin blade. Grumbling once again, about buying a set of skeleton keys, he set about manipulating the cheap lock.

A minute later the lock turned and Manning let himself into the apartment. Looking around after he had relocked the door, he could see few personal signs of occupancy. The closet was empty save for a worn leather jacket. Entering the kitchen he opened the refrigerator. It was empty except for several bottles of beer and a half-eaten sandwich wrapped in a white takeout sack. The sink held more empty beer bottles. Under the sink Manning found a trash can with a wad of crumpled brown paper in it. Still wearing his gloves he pulled the paper out. Examining it, he could see the address of this apartment handwritten on it just below a post mark. He nodded; this place was full of evidence for Drew's lab boys. He replaced the paper in the waste can and put it back under the sink.

Manning then moved to the single bedroom. The bed was unmade but had been slept in recently. There was practically nothing in the dresser; some workmen's clothing and a change of underwear was all he found. The closet contained a worn set of work boots but more interestingly there was a large metal toolbox. Dragging it out, Manning opened it and found a full set of electrician's tools: pliers, wire strippers, electrical tape, and several spools of wire. Most interesting was a folded sheet of thin yellow paper. Opening it, Manning recognized the flimsy carbon copy of a work order from a Manhattan based electrical contractor. He frowned. He did not recognize the address or name on the order, but memorized it anyway. Then, replacing the work order in the toolbox, he shoved it back

into the closet.

Manning was heading for the front door of the apartment when he heard a floorboard creak in the hall. With no other choice but the closet, he lunged for it as a key rattled in the lock. He silently closed the door as the hallway door opened. Manning heard keys rattle and footsteps crossing the room. There came the noise of what sounded like the refrigerator door closing. He crouched down and put his eye to the keyhole.

His vision was narrow but he saw a man standing in the living room. He had removed his jacket and was in shirt sleeves. He was tall and well-built for a man who Manning guessed to be about forty. His face was rough and he had a broken nose. He was loosening his tie with one hand. The other held a beer bottle. As he turned and entered the bedroom Manning could see the butt of a revolver tucked into his waistband. Manning had no idea that this man, Hendricks, was working with the mastermind behind the murders. Whoever he was, he was certainly a danger. Waiting with his eye to the keyhole, he heard noises from the bedroom. Minutes later the broken-nosed man emerged from the bedroom, now wearing workman's clothes and boots. He carried the toolbox. As the man walked toward the front door, Manning stood up carefully. His shoulder brushed against some metal coat hangers that jangled metallically. Manning tensed as he heard footsteps drawing near. As the door knob rattled he leaned back against the rear wall and lashed out with his foot against the door.

The toolbox in his hand, Hendricks was just reaching for the hall door when he heard a noise across the room. Setting it down, he drew a revolver from under his work shirt and stepped quietly toward the closet. Just as he touched the door knob the door slammed open just missing his face but smacking hard into his outstretched gun arm, pushing it wide. Hendricks squeezed the trigger involuntarily. Manning lunged forward as the slug dug into a wall. He pounded his left fist down on the outstretched wrist at the same time he landed a punch to hendricks's jaw. Dropping the gun, Hendricks staggered back but immediately came back swinging.

Manning stepped forward with his hands up. He blocked the first swing and responded with a jab to hendricks's jaw that pushed him back. In college Manning had boxed for two seasons before deciding that fighting was too serious to be considered a sport. He still remembered his training and his reflexes were excellent. He blocked a punch to his face but missed another to his stomach. He grunted and bent forward protecting his midsection. As Hendricks stepped in to finish him, Manning kicked him as hard as he could in the shin with his hard-soled wingtip. Howling in pain Hendricks hopped back, his weight on one foot. Manning stepped in and drove a punch at his face. Hendricks avoided it but lost his balance and fell over.

The dropped revolver was five feet away from Hendricks at that point. He lunged for it but Manning took two steps forward and kicked the revolver away from his fingers and under the sofa. He turned and aimed a kick at Hendricks who had got to his knees but Hendricks grabbed his foot and threw him backwards. There was a momentary pause as both men regained their feet. Hendricks was heavily favoring his right leg and Manning circled him throwing out jabs to keep him off balance. Then in a furious exchange of blows, Hendricks slipped a right hook past Manning's guard and caught him on the chin. Manning staggered back two steps and tripped over the toolbox. He went sprawling and rolled into a small table that held a lamp. As Hendricks limped around the box and came for him Manning grabbed the lamp and threw it. Holding his hands up to protect his face, Hendricks was shocked when the ceramic lamp crashed into his already injured shin. He howled and hopped back.

Holding his jaw Manning attempted to get to his feet. As he did, he was surprised to see his opponent grab up the toolbox and head for the apartment door. He shook his head to clear it and staggered to the doorway. Once there he could hear Hendricks cursing as he clattered down the stairway. Manning considered pursuit but decided it wasn't really necessary. Instead he reentered the apartment. Getting down on his hands and knees he groped around under the sofa until he felt something heavy. Grunting he pulled out the lost gun and stood up.

It was a heavy, short-barreled revolver. Examination showed it was a standard Smith & Wesson police model that had been professionally modified. The barrel had been shortened to a manageable three inches and the front sight had been enlarged. As he hefted it, Manning decided with a bit more wood on the grip to accommodate his long fingers it would handle very nicely. He shoved it into a coat pocket. He would hang on to it... just in case.

Straightening his tie and brushing dust from his suit Manning left the apartment. Once on the street he went looking for a telephone. He soon found a drug store with a phone booth in the back. It took a few minutes to be connected but finally he was able to bring agent Drew up to date on his findings. Drew promised to send a team to the apartment at once. Manning then hailed a taxi and gave the cabbie the uptown address he had memorized.

While Manning was cabbing uptown, things at the hospital were quiet. The guard outside Van Dorn's room was absorbed in the sports section of his newspaper. Two nurses spoke quietly at the nurse's station near the elevators while a short janitor mopped the floor at the other end of the corridor. The elevator opened and a man exited. The policeman looked up but resumed reading when the stranger approached and spoke to the nurses. The janitor continued mopping.

Suddenly there was a scream. The man at the nurse's station had collapsed. One nurse bent over him while the other began speaking urgently into a phone. Throwing down his newspaper the guard strode toward the commotion. Both nurses were now crouched over the man, loosening his tie and checking his pulse. A nurse looked up and told him, "He was just talking to us and collapsed."

While this was happening, the short janitor left his mop bucket and glided swiftly to the door of Van Dorn's room. Pushing inside, he drew something from his overall pocket as he looked around. Van Dorn was asleep. The room was empty. The janitor took a deep breath and held it. He then stepped to the bedside and, holding the small atomizer near the sleeping man's face, squeezed the rubber bulb once, twice and three times. A fine reddish mist sprayed forward over Van Dorn's face and head. The janitor backed away quickly as he replaced the atomizer in his pocket. He opened the door into the corridor and stepped out, closing the door silently behind him. He reached his mop bucket in a few steps and pushed it quietly down the corridor. He had been inside Van Dorn's room less than ten seconds.

Leaving the nurses and unconscious man, the policeman returned to his post. As he reached for his newspaper he heard a crash from inside the hospital room. Opening the door he leaned in. A pitcher of water had been knocked off the nightstand onto the floor. Van Dorn was awake and thrashing around in his bed. The officer stepped toward him but was shocked into immobility by Van Dorn's appearance. His face was purple and getting darker by the second. It was swollen and his blackened tongue protruded from his wide open mouth. His hands clawed at his throat. He gasped for breath but was only able to make pathetic hacking noises. Sickened, the officer drew back to the doorway, a move that probably saved his life. He turned to run for the nurse's station. Once there, he grabbed the telephone and started yelling into it as the nurses ran for Van Dorn's room. He didn't notice until much later that the man who had collapsed was nowhere in sight.

After paying off his cab, Manning looked up at the tall building in front of him. The *Hudson Arms* was a new high rise full of luxury apartments. The doorman greeted him at the door. Manning handed him one of his business cards and spoke confidently. "The renovations you have underway, I'm trying to get hold of the electrical contractor doing the work. Is there anyone here I might speak to?"

Glancing from the business card to Manning's expensive suit and back to the card the doorman hesitated. Then, no doubt convinced by the *Dr. Thomas Manning, PhD* written on the card he spoke. "I'm not sure that the electrical people are working today, sir, though there was someone there yesterday."

Manning pulled his pocket watch out to check the time and then frowned. "I really do need to get word to the contractor. It concerns some expensive renovations that were done to my office building. Would it be possible for you to show me to the construction site? Perhaps I could leave a message with someone."

The doorman hesitated for only a moment before nodding. "Certainly, sir. The apartment under construction is 706. If there is no one there, I would be glad to accept a message for the electricians." Manning smiled, nodded his thanks and headed for the elevator.

Once on the seventh floor, he walked down the hall to 706. He never got there because as he passed the door marked 704 he stopped cold. On a small plaque next to the door was the name *Stirling*. Manning looked at the door thoughtfully for a few moments before moving on to 706. It was locked, as expected, with a lock far too complicated for his pen knife. Looking closely he could see signs of construction, though. There was dust on the carpet near the doorway and a scrape on the jamb.

He crossed the hallway and knocked on an apartment door. Moments later the door was opened by a well-dressed elderly woman. Hat in hand, he spoke respectfully. "I'm sorry to disturb you, ma'am but I'm trying to locate the contractors working in 706. Have you seen anyone working there today?"

The grey-haired woman smiled and opened the door a little wider. "Why no, young man. I don't think anyone has been there today. I haven't heard anyone coming or going."

Manning nodded. "Thank you ma'am, perhaps I shall try to reach them tomorrow." He started to turn away and then stopped. "Oh, one more thing ma'am. How long have they been working on the apartment?"

The woman frowned in thought for a moment. "A week or more... I think, but they aren't there every day. They certainly aren't in any hurry to get things completed, if you ask me. Why, I don't see any workmen for two or three days at a time. Then they just seem to bang around over there all day. I hope they have things finished before Mr. Johnson returns."

Smiling, Manning asked casually, "And how long has Mr. Johnson been gone?"

"Well, he left suddenly just before the workmen showed up. He said he had been called away for a family emergency and might be gone quite a while."

Manning nodded once more. "Thank you again, ma'am. You've been very helpful."

He tipped his hat and headed for the elevator. Thoughts ran through his mind quickly as the operator took the car swiftly to the lobby. He tipped the operator a dime and crossed briskly to a phone booth in the lobby. He dropped in a nickel and had the operator connect him to the local FBI office. He gave his name and waited for Drew to answer. "Tom? Where have you been? Big things have been happening."

Manning came back quickly with, "And I've got big things for you. How quickly can you get over to the Hudson Arms?"

"The Hudson Arms? I've got to get down to the coroner's office. Van Dorn's dead."

"Dead? How?"

"We're not sure how, but the circumstances were definitely suspicious. We think he was poisoned. That's why I need to talk to the coroner."

Manning thought quickly. "It's terrible about Van Dorn but if you want to stop the next death, you'd better get over here right away. I've discovered who the next victim is going to be and I think it's happening tonight."

He was answered by silence for several moments. "Alright, Tom. I'll meet you there as soon as I can. What's the address?"

Manning told him, then hung up and left the booth. He thanked the doorman for his kindness before he left the building.

Locating a coffee shop nearby he settled in to wait.

The light was low and the classical background music matched it. The robed figure sat on his throne-like chair; in front of him stood his two lieutenants. "Are you sure Van Dorn is dead, Trusseau?"

The short figure nodded eagerly. "Yes, master. I used the powder just as you said, and I saw them take the body downstairs later."

From behind his veil, the man barked out a laugh. "Ha! Now he has gotten what he deserved. With his death there is only one man left to kill here in New York." He turned to the taller man. "Hendricks, all is ready for tonight?"

Hendricks nodded. "Yes, sir. The apartment is ready, including the cot. I've scouted the building and exits as well."

"Very good. We leave at ten o'clock. Now tell me about this man you encountered? Are you sure he did not follow you from the apartment?"

"No, sir. I checked carefully. No one followed me. I crossed all over town to make sure before I came here."

"Who do you think he was? A policeman?"

Hendricks reached down and rubbed his swollen shin. "No. He was too well dressed to be a city cop, and he fought too well."

A pause. "FBI then?"

Hendricks nodded. "Maybe, but he was all alone. Where was his partner? Those guys are never alone."

The veiled mastermind thought for a moment. "How did he find out about the apartment?"

Hendricks shrugged. "Van Dorn must have told him."

The veiled man slammed his fist down on the arm of his chair. "Impossible! When I left his dreams he remembered nothing. He could have told them nothing." He paused. "Unless... What about this specialist you spoke of? What did you learn about him?"

Hendricks frowned. "Not much, I'm afraid. At the hospital they said he was some kind of psychologist from out of town. Supposedly the FBI called him in."

"A psychologist, hmmm. He shouldn't have been able to probe Van Dorn's dreams. Still, we must learn more of this 'expert.' By tomorrow my revenge will be complete, and we shall have all the funds we need to move on to bigger things. We will also have time to find out all we need to know about this stranger. No doubt he is the one who confronted you at the apartment. You must never return there. The FBI will be searching it as we speak. No matter; they'll be too late."

He paused as a tall blonde woman passed behind his underlings. She was dressed in a floor-length, black, nearly sheer gown. She wore nothing else underneath. Carrying a bottle, she disappeared beyond a curtain. If the two men noticed anything they certainly knew better than to let on. They kept their eyes glued to their master.

He stood up. "Leave me now, but be ready. Tonight we end it."

The two nodded and silently left the room. The robed figure picked up a glass from the table next to him. Carefully lifting his veil he sipped from it. He then stood up, crossed the room, then passed through the curtain. A moment later came the sounds of gentle laughter.

When Drew arrived in front of the *Hudson Arms* Manning was waiting for him. He came right to the point. "Alright, what's going on and where have you been all afternoon?"

Manning had mentioned his theory about dreams before he left the hospital earlier that day. He picked up from there, telling of his trip to the package's address and his fight with the unknown man. Drew interrupted to remind him sarcastically about search warrants; Manning smiled but quickly continued. When he mentioned the second address he had found in the toolbox Drew looked interested. He looked up the front of the tall building. "And I suppose this is the address?"

Manning nodded. "Yes, I found out there is some work being done on an apartment whose owner left town suddenly. The interesting part is the apartment where this work is being done is next door to an apartment owned by a Samuel Stirling. That was one of the names that Van Dorn mentioned under hypnosis. Van Dorn and the other two victims were all involved in some shady deals years ago. A fourth man was also involved; his name was Samuel Stirling. I'm sure he's the next intended victim."

Drew was thoughtful for a moment. He nodded. "Let's go in and check out these apartments... or have you already done some more breaking and entering?

Manning smiled and shook his head. "Just asked a few questions, Frank." He held the door open for the agent to precede him into the lobby. The doorman stepped up to them with a smile, but before he could speak Drew flashed his badge and asked for a telephone. They were immediately shown to the building manager's office. Drew got on the phone and was quickly connected to his office. Manning listened as men were sent to research Stirling and the others. When he hung up, he requested that the manager accompany them to Stirling's apartment with a passkey. On the way up in the elevator, Manning questioned him about Johnson. "When did he leave town?"

The manager frowned as he fingered his keys. "Ten days ago, about. He said he had been called out of town on business and would be gone a couple of weeks."

"And the work in his apartment?"

"He said he had decided to do some renovations while he and his wife were away."

"His wife?"

"Yes, she's been away visiting family for several weeks."

Manning continued thoughtfully, "What about the workmen? Have you seen any of them?"

The manager nodded. "I have seen one man, an electrician, I think."

"What did he look like?"

"He was tall and well built, rough looking with a broken nose." A look crossed between the investigators. As the elevator doors opened on the seventh floor and they stepped out, the manager said, "Oh yes, there was that short fellow." This earned him another look. He saw the interest and continued, "He was really short, not even five feet tall, I'd say. Dark looks and coloring. Twice I saw him carrying things into the building with the tall fellow."

Manning thanked him for the information as they reached apartment 706. The manager opened the door for them and was motioned back by Drew. Drew entered first with his hand on his holstered revolver. The apartment had an empty feel to it but they proceeded carefully. They found drop cloths down and tools and materials scattered about. The only room that seemed to have any work done was a bedroom that had been converted into an office. All the furniture had been piled to one side. Against the wall a narrow cot had been set up. Near it was a table. On the table were a doctor's stethoscope and a pad of paper and pencil. There was also a large hole knocked in the plaster and wooden laths exposing the inner wall of the apartment next door.

Drew looked at Manning. "What do you think?"

Manning looked around. "Obviously the renovations were just a cover to get in here for an extended period of time." He pointed to the cot. "Here's why." He picked up the notepad and tipped it to the light. Using the pencil he rubbed the side of the lead gently across the top sheet. Gradually legible indentations showed up. He handed the pad to Drew.

The agent examined it and frowned. "Times. Lots of times." He brightened as understanding flooded him, "Someone used the stethoscope to listen in on Stirling through the wall. He was noting down times, probably of comings and goings. But why did they need the cot?"

Manning replied, "I told you, it's the

dreams. Somehow, whoever is behind this has learned how to enter and manipulate a person's dreams. He needed this apartment to get next to Stirling and learn his movements. I think he intends to use this cot tonight to enter Stirling's dreams and manipulate him into robbing himself and committing suicide as he did the others. I'd guess that he somehow got near the other men when they were sleeping to enter their dreams as well."

Drew looked grim. "Maybe so, but we're going to put a stop to it. I can have a team of agents here in half an hour. Now that we know where he's going to be, we'll get him."

Manning held up a hand. "We'll get him all right, Frank. But hear me out. We need to find out how he does what he does. This is unique. It's important we find out more about this dream stuff."

Drew looked thoughtful but suspicious. "What do you have in mind?"

Manning smiled. "First let's have a talk with Stirling. I have a plan for a trap."

"Are you sure about this?" Drew stood in the door of the luxuriously decorated bedroom looking at the psychologist. Manning smiled at the agent. "I know what I'm doing, Frank, and it's important to the plan. Do your men have their orders?"

Drew nodded, "Two of my best men are downstairs in the manager's office staying out of sight. Two more are staked out in the building behind this one watching the alley. Two more in a car ready to pursue or reinforce as needed."

Manning nodded as he sat on the edge of the bed. He bounced a little bit to test it. He considered removing his shoes, decided against it, and swung his feet onto the bed. Leaning back on the propped up pillows he asked, "You remember what I told you?"

Drew nodded. "Watch carefully but don't wake you unless you start thrashing about or crying out in your sleep. Listen carefully to what you say and take notes if possible." He held up a notepad. "I still say this is crazy. If this guy can do what you say he can, what's to stop him from getting to you like he did the others? I don't want you walking in front of a bus tomorrow."

Manning plumped his pillow and smiled at Drew. "I'm sure I can hold him off. I know

how he's going to attack; the others didn't. Plus I have a trained and disciplined mind. Besides, if he's asleep and sneaking into my dreams he'll be vulnerable. He'll have people with him. As soon as you think he's in my dreams you call in the cavalry. Maybe we can catch them unaware."

Drew frowned but nodded. He picked up the telephone on the nightstand and pulled it toward an easy chair the cord trailing behind. He sat down with the phone on his lap. "The lab boys found plenty of stuff at that apartment, but it's gonna take a few days to get the fingerprint results back. And I talked to the policeman at the hospital; he reported seeing a short, dark-haired janitor near Van Dorn's room about the time he was killed. Nobody with that description works for the hospital."

Manning raised an eyebrow. "Do they know how Van Dorn was killed?"

Drew shook his head. "It's got the docs stumped. The coroner said his lungs and throat were totally blocked by some kind of gunk. He said it looked like it was made of tiny spores. Weird, huh?"

Manning shook his head. "Whoever he is, this... this... Dream Master is certainly deadly." He leaned back and closed his eyes. "Let's get started." Drew reached over to turn out the light. He then leaned back to wait.

Just yards away in the Johnson apartment, Hendricks wiped his .45 automatic with a cloth and holstered it. He mentally grumbled at losing his revolver but the .45 had carried him through his marine days and would do alright if he needed it. His companion didn't notice; he was dozing on the sofa. Hendricks glanced at his watch and then toward the darkened bedroom where the Master had just settled down. It was nearly eleven.

Manning woke up with a start and looked around. The room was dark; he could barely make out the bed and nearby walls. There was no sign of Drew. He frowned and listened for a moment before walking toward the dimly outlined doorway. As he reached the next room, someone began pounding on a door in the opposite wall.

Surprised, he started toward the door when he was suddenly overwhelmed by a sense of danger. Somehow, he knew that the Dream Master was behind that door trying to force his way in. Startled, he realized this must be his dream. He spun about, ran back to the bedroom, slammed the door behind him and turned. The bedroom was gone. Instead he was faced by a wall of thick, gray mist that swirled and eddied as if it was alive.

Dream or not, Manning knew he was in great danger. Behind him he heard a door crash open. He plunged into the mist, holding his hands out in front of him cautiously. The mist felt greasy and was filled with vague, unrecognizable sounds.

He heard footsteps and changed directions, moving off at an angle. The footsteps faded but he soon heard the sound of multiple voices. Manning felt a chill on his neck as he realized the voices were in German. One voice was barking out orders. Soon he could hear multiple steps moving through the mist toward him. He turned and ran in another direction. As he did, a rifle shot rang out behind him, followed by a flurry of rifle shots. He heard more shouted orders. He was shocked; Nazis? No it couldn't be. That was all years ago. Still... it was his dream, driven by his memories... anything could happen.

The pursuit faded and he was alone once more. He changed direction again. A figure materialized in the mist. He moved toward it carefully and soon realized it was a dark-haired, middle-aged man with a strong Roman nose. He was rather shabbily dressed in an inexpensive suit. He stood there with a hand in his pocket and a thin smile on his face. Manning's face hardened as he recognized Charles Herfford. Herfford had been a traveling salesman who worked the mid-Atlantic states. He had been fond of murdering strangers, mostly women. He was also dead. Manning had helped the FBI find him and had been there when Agent Drew himself had put three bullets in the man's chest.

He wanted to tell this dream figure that he was not real but before he could speak the smiling figure of Herfford pulled a knife out of his pocket and stepped toward him. Manning turned and fled back into the mist.

He slowed when he felt the danger fade. As he continued moving forward he soon could make out dim shapes in the mist ahead. He moved toward them, and gradually they took the form of a man and woman standing together. Manning stopped. He recognized the middle-aged couple ahead, the mist curling about their feet. He had seen the woman's warm smile many times. She was his mother. His father stood with one arm around his wife looking down protectively at her. Manning's heart seemed to catch in his throat. He reached out toward them but hesitated; it couldn't be real. The two people who had adopted him at birth and raised him as their loved and cherished son had been dead for nearly ten years. He couldn't help himself; he took a step toward the figures, then another.

Then he stopped. His parents were dead. This was some kind of trap to weaken and slow him. He took a breath and forced himself to turn away. As he did his father called out to him. He glanced over his shoulder and saw his father looking at him proudly. The dream figure nodded and waved him away. Dashing a tear from his eye, Manning turned away into the mist.

Deciding that he somehow had to take control of this dream Manning stopped, took a deep breath and closed his eyes. As he did he held his hands up in front of his face, fingers spread. He opened his eyes. The hands were there before him but they seemed blurred at first. Then his hands snapped into sharp focus.

He looked around. Everything seemed more vivid. Sounds were more distinct. Even now he could hear footsteps approaching. It had to be the Dream Master stalking him. "Enough," Manning decided. It was time to confront the villain on his own terms.

He looked around. The mist still surrounded him but was now less opaque. Knowing where he had to go Manning stepped off confidently. Soon he came to a dark curtain that stretched away in the mist. He pushed through its heavy folds and found himself standing on a vaudeville theatre stage. The house lights were down and the stage was only illuminated by the footlights.

Manning turned at a noise behind him and saw a dark-robed figure push through the curtain. His features were covered by a veil all except for his bright, light blue eyes. He held a knife in his hand and moved slowly toward the psychologist.

Manning didn't know much about knives but he was familiar with blades. He held out his hand and concentrated. Recalling his fencing days in college, he watched as a long dueling sword materialized in his hand. He smiled as he whipped the sword around getting a feel for it. If the Dream Master could manipulate the dream world, then so could he. All it took was concentration.

Manning moved forward confidently now. The Dream Master stopped and began to back away. Manning lunged forward and the Dream Master dodged to his left. The psychologist laughed as he turned to follow his enemy. Now he had the upper hand. He smiled as he attacked again. As his sword plunged toward his enemy, someone grabbed him from behind...

"Tom! Tom! Wake up!" Manning awoke to a stinging slap to his cheek. He stared hard into the concerned face of Agent Drew. He sat up as Drew spoke on the telephone. He was back in the Stirling bedroom. Things seemed unreal for a moment as he stood. How long had he been asleep? He turned as Drew slammed down the receiver. "My men are moving in. What happened in there?"

Manning shook his head. "Tell you later. They're getting away." He headed for the doorway. Drawing his revolver, Drew pushed past him, gritting out, "Let me go first."

Manning crowded out into the hallway close behind him. Thirty feet away the husky figure of Hendricks was shepherding a cloaked and hooded figure down the hallway. A third figure was just closing the door of 706. Drew threw up his gun and commanded, "FBI! Halt right there!"

Hendricks pivoted around, putting himself between the cloaked figure and the agent. He and the third man both fired. Drew ducked and crashed into Manning, who was struggling to get his "borrowed" revolver out of his pocket. The bullets screamed overhead. Drew got off an unaimed shot that hit nothing. The third man fired again and ducked back into 706. Manning got his gun clear. Drew took aim and fired just as a fire alarm began ringing through the hallway. Startled, his shot went wide. hendricks's return fire chipped plaster over their heads.

Hendricks fired again. Manning ducked and darted forward. As he did so the lights went out. Doors opened and people flooded into the hallway, yelling. Drew shouted for

Manning awoke to a stinging slap to his cheek. He stared hard into the concerned face of Agent Drew.

them to keep back. There were more screams and curses in the darkness. Manning moved along the wall and came to the open door to 706.

The hallway was now illuminated by dim emergency lights, but the apartment not at all. Manning could make out only dim shapes by moonlight coming through the windows. He slipped inside and called out, "Throw down your gun! It's all over!"

He was answered by a stab of flame from across the room. Manning fired once at the flash and threw himself to the carpet. Two answering shots slammed overhead. There were more screams and shouts from the hallway behind him. As he crawled forward, Manning saw movement in the shadows. He fired once and was answered by another shot. Then he heard the gunman's revolver click on an empty chamber. In a flash Manning was up and across the room. A shadowy figure loomed in front of him and he dove at it. Head down, he caught his unknown assailant just below the sternum and momentum carried the two backward, crashing through a pair of French doors onto a balcony in a shower of glass.

Scrambling to his feet, Manning faced his opponent and brought his hands up. He led with his left and followed up with a right hook that his opponent took on the shoulder. The man replied with a flurry of punches, one of which got past Manning's guard and caught him on the point of his chin. Manning staggered back two steps and landed on his backside, his head snapping back to hit the metal railing with a jar. He pushed himself upright as the gunman rushed him, hands reaching for his throat. At the last second Manning sank down against the railing and grasped his attacker's thighs. He rose up quickly and the man's momentum carried him up and over Manning's shoulders.

The gunman screamed as he went over the rail and grasped wildly for any hold. Manning twisted and grabbed one of his legs as it went past. His grab slowed the gunman enough so one of his flailing arms could wrap around the top rail. Manning let go. The gunman ended up hanging by his hands to the top rail of the balcony. His feet dangled in mid-air.

Slowing his breath Manning leaned over the rail and looked into the gunman's terrified face. He pleaded, "Help me!"

Manning looked past him at the distant sidewalk. "It's a long drop. I'd like to help but I need something."

The man gasped out, "Please! I can't hang on much longer."

Manning nodded. "Good, then tell me where the Dream Master is hiding, and I'll help you up."

The gunman shook his head. "I can't... he'll kill me."

Manning leaned closer. "Who? The Dream Master?"

The man licked his lips and begged, "Please!"

Manning hardened his gaze. "Tell me where I can find him."

His face pale in the moonlight the man shook his head again. Manning leaned over him. "We can protect you. Tell me where he is!"

The man's sweating face was pale as he gasped out, "You don't know what he can do. I've seen things, horrible things... I can't."

Suddenly remembering the dream Manning took a wild shot. "It's a theatre, isn't it?"

Manning could see surprise in the terrified man's eyes but he again shook his head. Suddenly deciding, he let loose of the rail but Manning grabbed the man's left hand in both of his, "What are you doing?"

The man screamed, "Let me go! I'm dead anyway!"

The man's dead weight was tremendous. Manning knew he couldn't hold on for long. He gritted his teeth and heaved backward. As he did he heard Drew's voice from somewhere behind him. "Manning! Where are you?"

"Out here! Help!"

The terrified man dangling below pushed at the railing with his free hand. "Let me go!"

"What theatre is it?!"

Drew appeared behind them.

"Help! I can't hold on much longer!"

Drew lunged to the rail reaching for the man's free arm. The gunman pulled hard against the psychologist's grip. Manning yelled, "Where is he?!" As Drew's hand closed on the man's free wrist the gunman jerked his hand free and fell away. Both Drew and Manning

were leaning over the railing and could clearly see the terrified man's face as he fell away screaming out, "Excaliiiiiiiii....!"

The two stood up and Drew looked at Manning. "What was that all about?" The psychologist just shook his head.

Minutes later the FBI team was comparing notes in the lobby. Drew told Manning, "Our boy had someone in the basement who pulled the circuit breakers and cross-wired the fire alarm to cover his escape." He shook his head. "I can't believe we had the place sewed up tight and they still got away clean." He looked closely at the psychologist. "You alright?"

Manning had been staring off into space. He brought his eyes down to meet Drew's, "Do you know of any theatre called the Excalibur?"

Drew looked at him in surprise. "Theatre?"

"Yes. I believe we're looking for a theatre."

The FBI man's eyebrows drew together for a moment then he raised his voice. "I need a phone book over here! Now!"

Manning stood up as Drew came through the office door along with half a dozen other agents. He handed his Tommy Gun to a fellow agent and came over to the psychologist. Manning didn't have to ask. "He was gone."

Drew nodded tiredly. "Yeah, they'd been there, though. They must have cleared out in a hurry. We found some of the money, but a lot of it is still missing. They left plenty of evidence scattered around, though. Maybe we can get a line on this Dream Master guy from fingerprints." He wiped a hand tiredly across his face. "That's the frustrating part, we don't even know who this guy is." He frowned. "You should have seen the place; it's decorated like something out of Arabian Nights. Your dream buddy has a real flair for the dramatic."

"He's overcompensating; probably an ego problem. I have no doubt he's a megalomaniac with repressed hostility and a whole lot of other issues. And I wouldn't worry about his identity. We'll get another shot at him."

Drew looked surprised. "You think so? I bet this guy is long gone. He'd be a fool to come back now that we're on to him."

Manning shook his head. "We may have disrupted his plans for now but sooner or later he'll turn up again. I'm certain of it."

"His name is Thomas Manning. I got it from a stoolie at the federal building."

The shadowy figure of the Dream Master brooded on this for a moment. "So we have a name for our new adversary."

"Do you want me to track him down?"

"No, Hendricks, not yet. While this was a setback it is not the end of our plans. It is time to move on. But there will be plenty of time later to find out everything there is to know about this Mr. Manning. Then he will be sorry he tried to interfere in my affairs."

"Dream Master" is copyright © Gene Moyers.

Gene Moyers has had many careers; from a stretch in the U.S. Army to Licensed Massage Therapist. For many years, from his sanctum deep in the forests of the Great Northwest he has been writing mystery, adventure and horror stories for various publishers. For Airship 27 he has written stories starring Domino Lady, Purple Scar, Black Bat, Phantom Detective and one published in the award winning Legends of New Pulp Fiction. He has also had stories published by Moonstone Books and Pre Se Press. He is latest project is a full length alternate history novel set in Africa in the 1930s to be published soon by Airship 27.

WHEN IN DOUBT, HAVE A MAN COME THROUGH
A DOOR WITH A GUN IN HIS HAND.
CHANDLER'S LAW

A young man with a possessed gun that can't miss collides with an aging gunslinger that can't be hit. Trouble and death can't be far behind.

Under the Gun

BY DAVID J. WEST

"**P**ick me up," called the Six-Gun from a dead man's hand.

The boy, almost a man, heard the voice despite the buzzing drone of gunfire and whoops of the warriors who triumphed over the hated blue-coats.

The hillside was littered with the bodies of the blue-coats and their fallen horses—shot if only to give cover for the white men from the rain of fire coming from the valiant Sioux, Cheyenne, and Arapaho. The dead all looked the same to the boy except for the one still clutching the Six-Gun. This dead white man wore buckskins like the Sioux, and his yellow hair was shorn close to the scalp, save for a curly lock now hanging in his dead eyes. The dead man retained a large handlebar mustache drooping beneath an open mouth.

"*Use me,*" said the Gun. "*I never miss.*"

It was beyond even complying as the boy realized he wanted to pick the Gun up more than he had ever wanted anything before in his whole life. He pried the Six-Gun from the dead man's hand.

"*I am power.*"

The boy held the Six-Gun for what seemed an eternity, forgetting his once precious coup-stick. He stroked the long barrel as he had dreamt of stroking a woman.

"*Taste what I can do.*"

The boy took a careless limp-wristed aim. He had never held a pistol before.

"*Feel what I can give you.*"

The boy pulled the trigger. With wicked thunder, a red mist appeared behind the final blue-coat on the hill. Reeling like a drunk, the blue-coat went down.

They were more than a hundred paces away. An impossibly fine shot for a pistol.

"*Told you, Boy. I never miss.*"

An older brave trotted up, hunting for valuables among the dead. He had a fresh bloody scalp at his belt. He wanted more and was uninterested in the boy until he noticed the Six-Gun. "Moon-Wolf, where did you get the pistol? Give it to me; you are not worthy of such a prize."

"No," answered the boy, pointing the Six-Gun at him.

"*Shoot him,*" said the Gun.

"You are not worth it. Go away or I shall hit you," he said, but the brave was the one who backed away to continue his rummaging of scalps and loot amongst the dead blue-coats.

The boy spoke to the brave. "Did you hear that, Wolf-No-Kill-Him?"

"Hear what?" answered the brave.

"My gun."

"*Shoot him!*"

"I heard you pointing it at me."

"Did you hear it speak?"

Thoroughly offended, the brave answered, "Are you going to shoot at me? Keep it, let my teasing go. Or I will beat you again."

"*Shoot him!*"

"It speaks," said the boy.

"Is your mind broken? What do you want?" asked the brave, as he sheared a scalp from a still moaning blue-coat.

The boy then knew the voice was only in his head and for his ears alone. "Spirit of the Gun, are you there still?" he asked, unsure that he would yet hear a reply.

"*I am.*"

"Do you whisper to me alone?"

"*As you do to me.*"

"Are you the trickster?"

"*No. Call me George.*"

"That's a strange name for a gun."

"*I wasn't always a Gun. Besides, Moon-Wolf is a strange name for a killer.*"

"I was not always a killer."

"*You are now. Shoot the man beside you.*"

"No!" shouted the boy, as he side-eyed the warrior. "He is part of my tribe," he whispered.

The brave cast an evil glare at the boy, then

returned to his work looking for loot among the fallen.

"*You don't like him. He stole your father's horse once. He beat you three moons ago.*"

"How do you know that?"

"*I know what you know. Kill him. Who will know the difference? Shoot Wolf-Not-Kill-Him. Then his name will be a lie.*"

"I don't want to," pleaded the boy, but his finger itched, and a burning filled his bosom to fire the gun and destroy. To gain power and feel himself conquering his enemies.

"*Do it!*"

Moon-Wolf turned and shot the older brave as he rummaged through the pockets of the dead blue-coats. The wounded brave clutched his heart, fell, quivered a few seconds then was still. His eyes were wide with horror. They stared at the boy, accusing him, silent and final.

The boy shook his head and stared at the Six-Gun and then the dead man. The chaos around him still swelled like roiling thunderheads even with all the blue-coats slain. Braves covered the hillside, taking scalps and loot from the fallen blue-coats. Many whooped in joy of the victory, some few chanted their death-songs. But Moon-Wolf just ran.

"*You forgot to get more ammunition. We need the ammunition.*"

Keeping a tight hold on the Six-Gun, the boy ran down into the coulée to be away from the battle, fearing the temptation to shoot more of his kinsmen. He thought he heard the Six-Gun laugh, but his heart was pounding even louder.

Entering the mass of teepees, the Six-Gun burned in the boy's hand. "*So many targets. Use 'em up.*"

"No," said the boy.

"*Use me. I never miss.*"

"No," said the boy, looking at an old squaw and then the gun. The barrel shook in his hand, up toward the white-haired woman.

She stared at him. Eyes unafraid and dark. "Little man went to battle and stole a gun? You think you are a brave now?"

"*Shoot her.*"

The Gun's barrel leveled and the hammer cocked.

The old woman spat.

"Moon-Wolf! What are you doing? Where did you get that gun?" shouted an older brave riding up on a painted pony. The old squaw

turned and went back to her teepee.

"*Now!*" The Six-Gun erupted in his hand and took the brave square in the chest. He fell from the startled pony.

"Iron-Shirt. I did not mean to shoot," cried the boy, leaning over him.

The Six-Gun grinned, still exhaling smoke, and still hungry.

"It was a good day," said Iron-Shirt. "But get rid of the Gun. I see the spirit of the Long-Hair upon it. Throw it in the river... away with it," he gasped.

The barrel rang out again, silencing Iron-Shirt. "*There's more of them to shoot, you know. Lots more.*"

"No, George, no more of my people," he said, trembling. His heart beat like the sun-dance drums; his ancestors screamed for him to throw the Gun away. But he made his own choice.

The boy thrust the smoking gun into his belt and emptied the pockets and satchel of Iron-Shirt of his cartridges, tobacco and buffalo jerky. He took the pony and satchel and rode away, circling wide toward the Rosebud.

The smell of copper and ash blanketed the hills and he could not drive the scent from him. The stink of death and murder. The accusing eyes of Wolf-Not-Kill-Him and Iron-Shirt. The guilt rested on his heart like a buzzard, ripping and tearing, devouring the goodness there. And the desirable, all-powerful Six-Gun laughed.

P orter found himself in the Montana territory badlands, far afield of his usual routes. He couldn't explain why he had let himself go this far north of Cheyenne. Hell, he was almost to the Little Bighorn River. Still, there was something whispering on the wind to him. Something calling mournful like, as if it was afraid he might not come. It was most urgent even if he couldn't put a word to it.

Porter was old now, well past his prime, but even a legendary old gunslinger and horseman has to keep moving or else the joints start to ache more than regular. Keep 'em working, he told himself, or they won't want to work no more at all.

He kicked spurs to his paint horse and had her galloping through the sage. He wasn't sure where he was going just yet, but knew he had to get there sooner than later.

"Moon-Wolf is no more. He is Man-Killer-Wolf now, and he has gone crazy from the victory over the blue-coats. He has killed two of our tribe and stolen from us. Calf-Woman cries for her dead son. Who will feed her now when the snows come? It gives me a heavy heart but we cannot let him do these evil things. I am Buffalo-Stands', his grandfather, and I have spoken," said the old man.

The men sitting about the fire were silent a moment in honor of Buffalo-Stands words, and each waited longer to allow another to speak.

An older man with a buffalo-horn headdress spoke. "Man-Killer-Wolf has brought shame to the tribe on this great day over the blue-coats. Today we slew Crook and may yet keep our enemies out of the sacred lands."

"It was not Crook!" argued another warrior. "It was the general Bear-Coat."

"It was not Miles either," said yet another.

Buffalo-Stands turned to a middle-aged, broad-shouldered brave and gestured for him to speak by giving him his pipe.

"I have known Man-Killer-Wolf since he was born. He is my dead brother's son. I will go and return him," said the brave, "that he will care for Calf-Woman at least one more winter, or I will kill him."

"It is good that you will do this, Bear-Paw," said Buffalo-Stands. "A man should take care of his brother's family always."

Bear-Paw nodded and stood. The rest of the men, save one still seated, nodded their approval. "I will bring him back. I will speak to him, and he will choose to do the right things."

With that, Bear-Paw exited the teepee. The only man who had not sustained him still sat cross-legged with a scowl across his face.

Buffalo-Stands said, "Many-Elk is angered, but this council has spoken."

"I did not speak for Bear-Paw to do this. Man-Killer-Wolf shot my son, and I should have my chance to avenge him."

"That is not the way."

"Killing our own people is not the way," said Many-Elk, scowling as he exited the teepee. "I will have justice."

Buffalo-Stands shook his head, but let him go.

Man-Killer-Wolf's sleep was held together by horrific dreams, bound in rawhide soaked in his own sweat and then burned out dry by fever. Blue-coats came and massacred his village and slew his people, mowing them under with gunfire as burning teepees belched acrid smoke. He watched from above in the clouds, a helpless spectator with eyes that could not be shut. The thunder of guns slapped him in the face. A deep laughter was beside him, malevolent and cruel.

"*See how they run? I almost did that at Trevilian Station. But you got to stand to survive and be remembered. Kept the colors in my coat so no one could say I gave up.*"

Man-Killer-Wolf said nothing, but stared in tearful horror at the murder before him. The Six-Gun continued speaking, but the boy would not listen anymore. The cries of the dying filled his ringing ears. Children torn from their mothers' grasp, braves trampled under horses' hooves, ponies shot with feral delight.

"*Reynolds did right to get between you and the ponies.*"

"Why do you make me watch what happened at the Powder River?"

"*To make you hard. When you have witnessed all the horrors of men, you can do anything. I see you as you truly are and I wish to help guide you, give you power.*"

"Yours does not seem the Medicine of light, but of shadow."

"*Is there a difference? There is not one without the other. Is there? Besides, strong is strong. Vengeance is coming.*"

The boy twisted the Six-Gun in his hand and pointed it at a blue-coat far below and pulled the trigger.

"*Awake and dream no more, but live and kill.*"

The snorting of horses brought Man-Killer-Wolf roaring awake. He looked about in a daze. Not twenty paces from where he lay, a dozen riders meandered past, not noticing him or his pony in the gulch. It was several hours beyond the dawn, and he was surprised at himself for sleeping so late. His pony whinnied, and a few of the blue-coats turned and saw him for the first time.

"*Have at 'em. Use 'em up. We need their cartridges.*"

Man-Killer-Wolf raised the Six-Gun, his eyes blank and cold.

They in turn saw a wild-eyed youth leveling a pistol, and they returned in kind.

The Six-Gun didn't lie this time. Six shots took six men and Man-Killer-Wolf had to drop down in the muddy gulch and reload.

"*Better hurry and reload or they'll take me away.*"

He only had three bullets loaded, and he had to look up and use them on three men. Three shots rang out, and three fell dead. He whooped in sudden excitement and bloodlust, fumbling with the last four cartridges he had.

"*Hurry! Before they get away.*"

Jumping on the embankment, the boy saw the other three riders swiftly departing, alarmed at their nine companions' sudden death.

"*I never miss, shoot, shoot!*"

He took careless aim, yet again letting the spirit of the Six-Gun do his work, and two shots rang out. Two men fell, and the third spurred his mount to even greater speed.

At an incredible distance for the pistol, the terrified soldier believed himself safe and chanced to look back at his foe. A bullet took him between the eyes, and he fell from the saddle, twitching and shaking, and then went still.

"Scalp them and gather all their cartridges."

Man-Killer-Wolf went about scalping all twelve soldiers, taking their cartridges and tobacco. All of them had curious green paper rolled into their pockets.

"What is this?"

"*The white men use it to trade with. It is valuable. Keep it to trade with.*"

"I will not trade with white men," said Man-Killer-Wolf, as he threw the papers to the ground and let the breeze blow them away across the sage and blood-covered field.

"*I suppose not. We will take whatever is required until–*"

"Until what?"

"*Until a greater warrior for me is to be found.*"

"You would betray me?"

"*Never. But if you were to fall dead, I would be picked up by the next person to hear my call, and they would be my weapon.*"

"You mean, you would be their weapon."

"*Did I mean that?*"

"You are mine."

"*And you are mine.*"

"Together we will take back these sacred lands. I will have many ponies and become a chief of my own clan."

"*Anything is possible.*"

"You are a trickster, George."

"*That I am.*"

Porter spent a rough night amongst pillars of sandstone. The wind had carved interesting shapes in the stony hillsides, mimicking an anthill to Porter's sight. It reminded him of the Utah badlands, though that was a red land and this was yellow.

He got up and stretched, then took a long draw on his canteen before chasing that with his Valley-Tan whiskey. It was late. He was getting a whole lot slower with age; he never would have slept so long years ago. But it was time to get moving rather than fret over the time left. He meant to catch a Missouri flatboat to carry him to St. Louis. He guessed this would be the last time he would head that far east. Maybe that was why he was allowing this ride to last so long. He was putting off the inevitable. He wasn't going to be riding the range anymore come next year. He was too damn sore for that.

Bear-Paw found the dozen dead blue-coats. They had been stripped of their cartridges, food and water. Green paper was tossed about them, being carried away in the wind. This bloodshed was impressive. There was only one wound per man, and he found no other sign of battle. It appeared that this was where Man-Killer-Wolf had camped, but to take on a dozen blue-coats by himself and prevail was incredible. He wondered how he might be able to defeat a foe blessed by such power. This was not done by the Great Spirit, but something else, something dark.

He mounted his pony and followed the sure sign of Man-Killer-Wolf's passage. He was heading away from the tribes and toward the sacred mountain of Heammawihio, 'the wise one who sits above'. Once he reached the sacred mountain, he would ask for a vision of what should be done. He feared that only bloodshed could bring Man-Killer-Wolf back from the path he was on now.

Man-Killer-Wolf waylaid a pack of Crow scouts that had fled from the blue-coat battalion when it was seen that they would surely fall under the knife of the tribal confederation. One sang his death song as George silenced him with a crack of thunder. There was no mercy here, no forgiveness, and the wind echoed the death song for far longer than it should have.

"George, have I done wrong?"

"*There is no wrong. There is only power. With me, you have that power, and that makes everything right.*"

The boy studied the Gun, and for a brief moment, it almost seemed like he would toss it away. But the dark power within the spirit of the Gun was stronger, and the fingers holding the ivory handle gripped all the tighter.

"*We will not be separated until I find someone stronger than you.*"

"Then what will happen to me?"

"*You'll go the way of all things.*"

"That's not fair."

"*There is no fair, boy. Just power.*"

Man-Killer-Wolf moved the end of the barrel to his own temple and pulled the trigger. An empty click seemed loud as a gunshot.

"Hahaha," the Gun laughed. "*Not until the time is right. Don't worry, there is still time for the road you're on.*"

"Why do you mock me?"

"*You need to learn. You need to gain the strength to wield me. Let's move on. I sense more opportunity for us following the creek.*"

Man-Killer-Wolf mounted his pony and rode upstream alongside the winding serpentine creek. He didn't know what he would find, but was lost in a haze of confusion as the will of the Gun dominated him with a spectral malignancy, overpowering his own sense of self just as dusk overtook the bloody land.

Bear-Paw rode up to the sacred mountain just as dawn was rearing its head. He walked amongst the sacred glyphs that his people had carved on the stone in eons past and placed his hands in the grooves therein. He stood there all day from when the sun first touched him, until the last ray left his body to disappear in the west. Then he let go in a sweat-filled aura of peace. His vision had been answered by the Great Spirit—and while he was pleased he had answers, he was saddened as well, for he knew what had to be done, and that filled him with regret.

Man-Killer-Wolf knew he was close to his tribe's sacred mountain. He wondered why he had ended up here. It was usually deserted except for ceremonies and vision quests and wouldn't be a place to demonstrate his bravery to the Gun.

"Why are we here?"

"*I sense a great killer is coming.*"

"You wish that I should defeat him?"

"*If you can. If not, I go to another.*"

The boy's anger flushed his face. "With you I can defeat anyone! You told me yourself!"

The Gun laughed without humor. "*Keep me. If you can.*"

Man-Killer-Wolf stalked from the copse of trees that hugged the creek. The flat-topped mountain loomed above him. It was reddish with sprouts of green here and there, as well as splashes of the light brown sandstone all about its base. Glyphs of his people were carved there, denoting their devotion to the Great Spirit and to heroic deeds of yore. He knew many from his tribe had come here shortly before the battle with the blue-coats to pray and make their pilgrimage, that they might be invincible. It had worked for many; their victory had been beyond reckoning.

He prowled toward the mountain, ever watchful. "George, will I find my enemy here?"

"*Oh, he is here, all right. He is watching us even now.*"

Man-Killer-Wolf looked about, but saw nothing. He went down a ravine and back up as arrows suddenly shot through the air, gouging a hunk of flesh from his shoulder, another just missing his ear.

"Why didn't you warn me?" he cried as he hit the dirt.

"*I did,*" answered the Gun with a mocking laugh.

Man-Killer-Wolf howled at the pain in his shoulder and fired wildly, emptying the Six-Gun. He quickly reloaded and peeked up from behind his shallow cover within the ravine. He couldn't see anyone. But whoever had shot at him was very skilled, and he knew that it was but one man. The arrows were a matching set. He scanned the fletchings and paint circling the ends. He knew them. It was his uncle's mark. Bear-Paw!

"I don't want to kill you. But I will!" shouted Man-Killer-Wolf.

"I was going to tell you the same,"

returned his uncle. "I know what you bear, and it must be destroyed. If it has stolen your spirit, I must destroy you both so that you can walk the winds in peace."

"*Stand and shoot him!*" ordered the Gun.

"He'll be ready to hit me with an arrow."

"*I never miss. Let this be a contest.*"

The boy didn't like those odds, but he was compelled beyond reason and the Gun had never failed him yet. He sprang up and fired. An arrow flew straight at him, but only grazed his ribs. The archer standing above him fell to the dust with a pained cry.

Man-Killer-Wolf rushed toward his fallen uncle. Bear-Paw lay on his back. Blood leaked from his mouth, but gushed from the great hole in his chest.

"I have failed you, my brother's son. I beg you. Destroy the Gun before it destroys you."

"*End his miserable existence and prepare, for the true killer comes.*"

The boy was puzzled at that, for he had thought Bear-Paw was his only opponent. He hesitated.

"*Shoot him and let us deal with the great killer. He is coming.*"

Bear-Paw gave a weak nod, urging, "Throw the Gun away. It will destroy you."

"I can't." Man-Killer-Wolf pointed the Gun at his uncle's forehead and pulled the hammer back with a violent shake.

"*Hurry, the killer is coming. He is here. Shoot him!*"

He pulled the trigger as a shadow loomed over him. Man-Killer-Wolf heard the echo of the Gun's report, then saw a rifle butt as it took him in the face.

P orter made camp along the Rosebud in a copse of gnarled trees with branches like witches' fingers. He tied the horses up beside the creek and set about making a fire. He then took Man-Killer-Wolf down off the back of his own horse and laid him beside the fire. He tried to give the boy some water but he wasn't quite awake yet, so he let him sleep while he made himself supper.

It was dark when the youth began to stir. Porter watched him with a wary eye while he cleaned the Gun.

Man-Killer-Wolf felt his own body and wondered at being alive. He knew he should have been dead, but here he was, without the Gun.

He could still hear its voice calling to him.

"*He won't listen to me. He is a great killer but he won't listen to me! You have to take me back and use me! Kill him and take me back!*"

Porter quietly continued cleaning the Gun while the boy watched him. The fire was starting to get low, so Porter leaned over and fed a few more thick branches to it. The flames began feasting on the dry wood in a ravenous repast.

"I'm sure you can't understand me kid, but I try and do the right thing whenever I can. I had to take this here piece from you. It's got an evil way about it. We're going to have to work together and find a way to get rid of it."

Despite knowing what the Gun spoke, Man-Killer-Wolf could not understand the long-haired white man. So he told him what he thought of him. "You're a foolish old white man, and if I had my Gun back you would die!"

Porter just stared at the kid. "I think I might have got your meaning," he drawled. "But you and me are gonna have to get along in this world. I've got a notion on how to end this evil, but you've got to do your part and be you. No more trying to kill anyone, or it'll hurt."

"*Take me back. Kill him!*" pleaded George.

Man-Killer-Wolf watched Porter a long time. The old man was meticulous in cleaning the weapon, and if not for the other Navy Colt on his belt, Man-Killer-Wolf would have launched himself at the old man a long time ago. Instead, he sat and watched and waited, all the while hearing the incessant cry of George to take him back and kill the old man.

Porter was starting to get tired. He was ready to nod off right there on the stump beside the fire. He looked at the kid once again. "You feeling any more neighborly? Can I trust you to just be a person and not listen to what this demon Gun tells you?"

Man-Killer-Wolf's dark eyes stared, unflinching. They could have been lumps of coal for their steadiness.

Porter was still passing the time cleaning the pistol. Oh, how it sparkled now, gleaming silver and ivory upon its handle. A more beautiful gun never was made, and it cried for Man-Killer-Wolf to take it in hand.

"*He ignores me! Take me back! Make me do what I was made for! Kill him!*"

Porter leaned hard to the right on the

stump and caught himself just before he fell off. His method of easing his weariness was to take a quick pull on his bottle of Valley-Tan whiskey. He looked at the anxious kid. "You're just raring to go, aren't ya? Think this old man ain't ready for the likes of you? Huh?"

Man-Killer-Wolf said nothing; he could hardly hear anything but the continual screaming of the Gun. The blood cry, the death song—many names for the same relentless maddening desire.

Porter was still polishing the Gun.

"Take me back! Kill him!"

Porter's eyes drooped, and he leaned forward, catching himself just as Man-Killer-Wolf was ready to spring. Their eyes locked, and there was a confrontation of silent wills. "I'm telling you, boy. You better settle down. We are gonna have to settle this, and I'm afraid it won't end well for you. I ain't tying you up because it's gonna have to be your decision to end this. I just hope you got the sand to choose the right path. But if you don't..." He shrugged.

"He's old! He's weak! He can hardly sit up straight, he is so old and drunk! Take me back! Kill him!"

Porter was still polishing the Gun with his silken hanky, even as his eyes blinked from exhaustion, flickered awake like a dying flame, then fell closed again.

Man-Killer-Wolf lunged and yanked the pistol away from Porter. He put a cartridge in and drew back the hammer.

"No, not yet! Not now! Wait! No!" cried George, in a sudden twisting of his previous instructions.

The Six-Gun exploded. Shrapnel flew back and ripped Man-Killer-Wolf's hands apart. Shards of steel flew into his face and neck. Blood spurted from the grievous wounds. He fell to the ground choking, drowning on his own lifeblood.

Porter was miraculously unhurt from the exploding six-gun. He looked over the damage to the gun and youth.

The cylinder was bent and flexed on one side. But worse was the barrel, twisted open and peeled back. The gun was ruined, and George's brief incarnation as a weapon was done. Porter picked it up and tossed the piece of steel into the Rosebud, where it vanished with a gulping splash.

George's voice was silent. Man-Killer-Wolf was done, but his former self, Moon-Wolf, could go walk upon the winds in peace.

Porter looked the dying kid over. "I tried to tell you to let it go. But you had to do it yourself, didn't cha? You weren't the only one who could hear that gun. I could too. That's why I had to find it and get it, so I could destroy it. I couldn't let anyone else live under the gun."

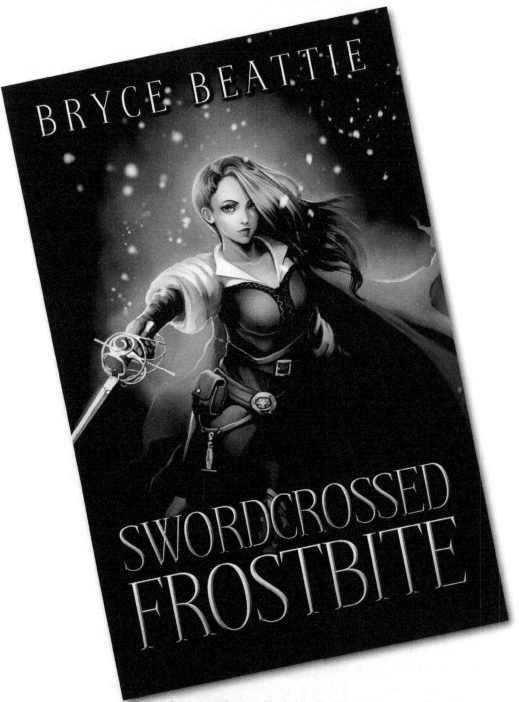

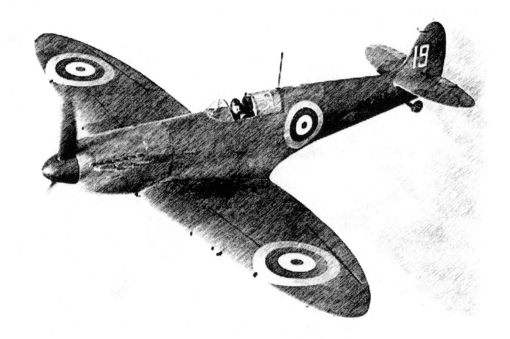

A WWII pilot is shot down over enemy-controlled territory. Will he survive and sneak across enemy lines to make it home? Or will he spend the rest of his days as a prisoner of war?

Circus to Boulogne

BY MIKE ADAMSON

From the Memoirs of Squadron Leader Jonathan "Johnnie" Carstairs, DSO DFC, RAF (Ret'd)

Nineteen forty-one came in bleak; it felt like both sides were taking a breather after the exhaustion of the summer and autumn of '40. The chance of the Germans renewing their large-scale air offensive against Britain was still very real and the RAF was hampered by awful weather and poor range. Our best fighters had been designed as defensive weapons, in which role they had served admirably during the Battle of Britain, but now we were taking our first steps on the front-foot we found all the natural advantages of fighting at home switched to the enemy.

On December 21st, 1940, Air Vice Marshal Trafford Leigh-Mallory had issued orders that committed us to offensive operations across the channel; indeed the first such raid had been the previous day when a couple of Spits from 66 Squadron at Biggin Hill flew the very first tip-and-run harassment raid into France, relying on high speed and going in at wave-top height for the element of surprise. This was the first of what were to be code-named 'rhubarb' raids, and all of us on the south coast flew our share of those. The other main ploy was the 'circus' raid, in which a small formation of bombers, too many for the Germans to simply tolerate, were sent against tasty targets, towing as many as a couple of hundred fighters to pay out the Germans when they came up against the bombers. That was the theory, at least, but they didn't prove very successful at first.

Now, I'd missed the Battle of Britain, I was still ploughing through my qualifications at No. 1 Flying Training School as 1940 trudged to its weary close, but by the time the cross-channel offensive was starting to gather steam I was a freshly-minted Flying Officer. I was posted to No. 610 (County of Chester) Squadron at Tangmere, part of the new wing-structure incorporating 145 and 616 Squadrons, plus the squadrons from Middle Wallop, under the able hand of Wing Commander D. R. S. Bader (now Sir Douglas). We were the 10 Group wing, and wings from 11 and 12 Groups completed the available force. We were rostered into close, medium and high-altitude cover formations to trail the bombers, and as March unfolded the raids began to develop a rhythm. Targets were varied but our critical range penalty meant we could reach no more than seventy miles beyond the French coast, so naturally we initially struck at German maritime assets and the infrastructure of their occupation. We all knew French civilians were copping it in the process and we felt very bad about that, but besides being scrupulously careful in the doing of our jobs what more could we do?

According to my log books, it was March 14th when flights from the various squadrons took off at 10:22 to form up into echelons above and behind a flock of Blenheim bombers from 105 Squadron at Honington; they were tasked with going after German merchant shipping in the port of Boulogne, some 25 miles south and west of Calais. This was my third circus operation. Now, in March '41 the Spitfire V had yet to reach units in any numbers and 610 was flying the still fairly new Mk II, an improved Mk 1 with the Merlin XII series engine. My trusty steed was a Mk IIa with the original eight-gun armament; indeed our redoubtable Wing Commander did not trust the 20mm cannon armament of the B-wing variants due to prolonged jamming problems encountered during the summer

battle, and was among the last to stand by the rifle-calibre Browning setup. Be that as it may, I launched into the channel haze in patchy sunshine, my engine thrumming sweetly as the fighters climbed out from Tangmere, just back from the West Sussex coast and we set course almost due east to the Dover narrows, picking up the bombers *en route*.

March had begun very wet and cold. The first ten days had been a misery, with severe snow in the north, while down on the south coast it was wet, day after day. Things fined up in the middle few days, though, and our circus was taking advantage of the first fair conditions. The sea-haze cleared as we went, our echelon settling at 18,000 feet, looking down on scattered cloud over the sea and wispy cirrus overhead.

We kept radio silence once we were away. The Germans were installing their own radar along the French coast at this point but there was no call to give them any extra assistance. We listened for our Sector Control stations to give us updates as necessary with regard to weather conditions, enemy activity and so forth, and of course our "steers" to rendezvous with the bombers. When it came time to speak up, my callsign was Redfox 3, third aircraft of a "finger-five" formation. Our leader was a brilliant chap, Flight Lieutenant Herbert Wallace, solid as a rock, looked after his boys, was a great third-wicket bat and could run a rugby ball half the length of the field. Crack shot, too. He lead us over the channel in company with elements from several other squadrons and we had fair visibility–if I looked over my left shoulder I could see back into the South Downs, while off my starboard nose France stretched away into a cloudy distance.

At this point I thought back on my last holiday across to France–the family had taken a daytrip to Boulogne by steamer from the south coast in the interwar years as so many did, and I had thought France in summer a most wonderful place. Little had I imagined I would be back one day, in deadly earnest.

I recall those minutes of cruise being the peace before the storm. Every pilot was tense as a mainspring, watching his instruments for any problem with electricals, radio, armament or engine that would force a turn-back–every mission saw aborts for technical reasons. The radios at that time, for instance, were particularly unreliable. I clearly recall feeling the thrum of the engine through the fuselage, reflecting on how strong and solid it felt, the confidence it gave a pilot to know he had such a mount under him. It all served to keep our minds off how cold and uncomfortable we were in the narrow cockpits, rugged up in our sheepskin-lined jackets and boots, thick gloves, leather helmets with oxygen mask, goggles and throat mike–none of which was any protection if that engine in front of us should burn.

Of course, the Spitfire developed a mythology, and rapidly became a national symbol–there are those who say it was partly an image created for public morale, but as a pilot who took the Spit to war I can say with absolute conviction it was the finest aeroplane I have ever flown. On that day in March 1941, I more trusted that this was the case than believed it with the sort of conviction I would in the years to follow. We downy-cheeked young knights had to believe we had a fair chance of coming back, and the sleek Spitfire imbued one with confidence. She was the sort of aeroplane that looked fast standing still, and if the Jerries had half the respect for her we did then she was doing her job.

Thoughts like those helped pass the minutes as we cruised high and fast for occupied Europe. We knew the French coast like the backs of our hands, had intelligence briefings of enemy activities, weather data, departure heading from the general target zone, radio codes–lots to think about and stay focused on. All too soon the French coast was ahead, a long pale strip between the dark spring sea and the newly-greening fields beyond, and the city of Boulogne-sur-Mer was laid out like a map at our feet, the huge docks in its midst.

That's when the Germans took an interest. They had moved plenty of ack-ack to surround the port and their eighty-eights began to lay a carpet of flak ahead of the bombers, but the real threat–the real reason we were here at all–was the Luftwaffe. Drawing them up for a scrap was the object, and as the Blenheims went in to lay their load on the merchantmen unloading in the heart of the great port, we found them coming at us. This was it –the *tally-ho* moment that made every fighter pilot's heart race!

Like specks of silver far off in the blue, the Bf 109s appeared from the haze, solidified into savage shapes with glittering props, their yellow engine cowlings visible from far out. These were the Bf 109 E-4s of JG 51, under the redoubtable Werner Mölders, hard-bitten veterans that they were. Now we were "bounced" there was no point keeping silent and the air lit up with reports and the kind of exuberant chatter we were not supposed to engage in but sometimes couldn't help. We broke formation in a wild melee as the brawl developed. It looked like there was plenty for all. I remember someone calling out, "Dig in, chaps! Fill your boots!" I went with Lieutenant Wallace as his wingman as he tore after a Hun. I covered his sunward arcs, keeping my eyes peeled, but it looked like we had the altitude on them today. Most of our echelons went diving after the Germans setting about the bombers. In moments we had lost thousands of feet, trading it for speed, and I clung to my leader with clenched teeth.

Lieutenant Wallace got his man after a tight, hard chase. I confirmed the kill, having distinctly seen flashes and sparks along the fuselage before the 109 went into a dive. In the adrenalin of the moment, my leader and I wasted precious seconds watching the enemy fighter streaming glycol vapour from its exhausts in its death-plunge, and–as most who engage in aerial combat do, or did at that time–silently hoping the other chap would get out. In that instance I was relieved to see a parachute against the rooftops of Boulogne, but an instant later my heart slammed into overdrive as I realised I had a Hun knocking at my door. I jabbed my throttle to full and pulled out of the lazy turn I had instinctively entered after the kill–time was compressed, the event was likely no more than seconds earlier but already felt like old news as I struggled for my life.

The E-series Messerschmitt was ubiquitous at this time but we had heard reports of a new mark on the way–the "Emil" was giving way to the "Ferdinand," the first had been brought down just a month before, and I was now unlucky enough to find myself on the receiving end of the new model. It was fast, had a redesigned, much more streamlined nose, with rounded wingtips and heavier armament. The Spitfire II was, to be frank, ever so slightly out-classed, and longing for the Mark V did not help in that instant. I reacted like a startled hare, banking and jinking, pulling every trick I knew to break contact, but it felt like I had one of the *experten* on my tail. I remember calling for help, but the battle was a chaos of intersecting contrails, flashes of flame, puffballs of flak following the bombers as they pulled out and around for the sea and home, and it began to feel like I was on my own.

I broke contact momentarily with a diving turn that pushed me close to blackout, I banked hard and held full pressure, and almost miraculously found myself turning onto the Hun's tail. Perhaps his concentration broke at some point, I have no idea what gave me that fractional advantage, but I exploited it, pulled in a sighting–with admittedly much more angle-off than desirable–and squeezed the trigger at top left of the ring-grip. The eight Brownings juddered in the wings and a storm of shells chased away, surrounding the target as if with a swarm of hornets, and though I was sure I had sent no few through his tail the 109 came out of it meaner than ever, performed a sharp split-S and dived away. That was typically the disengagement maneuver of German tactics, and, like a raw beginner, I let him go rather than stay on him–hard as it would be. It was the only time I ever made that mistake, because he recovered, came out of the dive and was after me before I could fix my attention elsewhere.

As they say, some things are just a blur, and those moments of sweating, straining effort to hold off my attacker, feeling in my guts I might just be about to drop off the proverbial perch, are such. It stood to reason, every pilot knew, the Hun would sooner or later chalk up one for the Führer and you'd be the unlucky one today. I can't really say what was going through my mind, a confused tumble of ideas and half-formed thoughts; I remember wondering if those heavy shells of the new model would punch right through the armour plate behind my seat, and preferring that to burning. *If my number is up then let's get it over with...*

A string of holes were blown through the aircraft around me but mercifully none in myself. My engine gauges went into the red as oil pressure dropped like a stone and cylinder temperature soared–the coolant lines had purged and the Merlin was effectively dead. I was unsure quite where I was, but I saw the sea to one side, the land to the other, and threw a prayer of thanks on high as I realised the pilot behind me was not vindictive. My nose was going down as white vapour billowed and the Merlin seized a few seconds later, the prop freezing with a jarring shock.

Now my only thought was to get out while I had the chance. I called "Redfox Three, hit and going down, I'm bailing out!" I struggled to bring the nose up, letting speed bleed off as I released my harness, unplugged the radio lead and oxygen mask, then unlocked the canopy and entry door and sent the blown Perspex "Malcolm-hood" back in the roaring windstream. With a gentle forward pressure on the stick the aircraft nosed over into her final dive and negative G force helped me on the way out, a not-so-graceful dive over the starboard trailing edge with a fervent prayer to not collide with the tail in the process.

All the noise abated at once and I was in cool, rushing weightlessness, a tipping, rolling world of cloudy blue and the land and sea below, of streaking aircraft and trails of white and dark smoke. I did not see what became of my Spitfire as I tried to judge my altitude and knew the ground was coming up frighteningly quickly. I had the ripcord in hand and waited, waited – getting down smartly reduced the odds of a cowardly shot while helpless under the parachute, and gave those on the ground less time to react. Picking the exact moment was more instinct than learning, though, and when the parachute banged open over my head, slowing me in a wicked deceleration, I found green country below and the sea some way off. I looked around, got my bearings and realized I was well north of Boulogne; I saw a dully shining strip of road winding along the coast and a couple of fishing villages threaded to it like pearls on a string, and fought to recall the details of the target area. These would be the villages of Ambleteuse and Audressselles, and I was falling into scrubby privet country just back from the sea more or less between them.

The surviving bombers were out and heading home by now, hopefully they all made it, while the fighters would keep up the scrap over the city until they hit their safe fuel limits, then disengage any way they could. A few fingers of oily smoke reached into the spring noon, marking the last resting places of aircraft from each side, and a moment after registering this I brought my feet together and prayed hard I would not snap an ankle as I touched down in the soft, sandy terrain–if I did I would probably spend the rest of the war as a POW.

Landing was rough, a massive impact that jarred me from head to foot, but at least nothing broke. I lay for a few desperate moments, my head spinning as I grasped the fact I was down and alive, but on the wrong side of the channel. Training rapidly took over and I fought to my feet to haul in the lines and gather the wind-rippled white silk, rolling it down into a ball, then releasing the harness. I pushed it all away under the dense, wild privet, crouched low as I struggled out of my helmet, goggles and life jacket. The bright yellow, kapok-filled vest I pushed under the bushes with the silk, then stripped off my gloves and opened my jacket as the relative warmth of the day hit me. I could not leave them—March on the Channel coast could be pretty cold after dark, and, besides, some of my survival supplies were stored in the pockets.

I bundled my jacket under my arm and thrust the gloves into my uniform pockets as I crept through the scrubby bushes and coarse grass, eyes peeled for trouble—I soon found it. Coming down the coast road was a small German patrol, an open command car, followed by two troop trucks, all in the weathered blue-grey paint they used at the time. They were probably well-versed in prisoner round-up after raids, as well as locating and recovering their own people—our parachutes were white, the German equivalent was beige, so in this situation these chaps always knew who they were after. One thing I remembered from briefings on the target area, just a mile or so north of the villages was a construction site, the Germans were building something pretty hefty, probably some sort of coastal defence installation—big guns in a hardened protective housing—which of course later proved to be the Todt Battery. The site was busy with labourers under military guard, so heading that way was asking for trouble.

I was maybe a hundred yards inland of the road. I stayed low as the patrol went by, and they pulled over a couple of hundred yards further on. They must have seen my descent from up at the construction site and come at once with a rough idea of my touch-down point. As the soldiers in their field-grey uniforms and coal-scuttle helmets poured out of the trucks I began to creep away from them on hands and knees, being particularly careful not to disturb the bushes. They would doubtless find the parachute and I must be far from it when they did. I heard a barked order and sun glittered as bayonets were fixed to their bolt-action Mauser rifles, and the soldiers spread out, beginning to prod through the scrub with naked steel.

About this point I started to ask myself what I thought I was doing. Might it not make more sense to simply put my hands up and be delivered to a prison camp? But—the huge *but* that factored against that—England was due north, Cape Gris Nez to the point of Dungeness in Kent was about 22 miles. People had swum that far! The problem was, I was no Olympic swimmer. I could not see England, it was below my horizon from here, but I knew it was there, so close I could almost reach out and touch it.

What I needed was a boat...

I heard German voices, their quick-fire guttural exchanges sounding permanently angry. To hear the language spoken it was hard to believe English was descended from it, yet I knew they had great similarities as well as differences. We had been told the local French people were chafing at their occupation, just nine months ago France had still been fighting gamely, but now it was they who suffered from every near-miss as *we* went after the German war machine. Not only had Frenchmen been compelled to swallow their pride, but they were suffering daily from both antagonists in this conflict; how, I wondered, would that affect how they viewed us? Could I expect help if I approached the locals, or would they consider me as much an enemy as the Jerries? I honestly did not know, and our escape and survival briefings had no definitive guidance for us. It came down to gut instinct in any situation, and my gut was telling me to lie low, stay alone, and make my way to the nearer village, because where there were fishermen, there were boats; we knew the Germans were allowing traditional fishing to continue on this coast, so, just maybe, there might be a boat going spare for an enterprising young Englishman far from home.

I clung to this idea with fierce conviction as I tried to put some distance between me and the troopers, but they were making a thorough job of searching and sooner or later they would flush me out and the game would be up. I just could not see any way to avoid them... until I stumbled when a small, ephemeral watercourse opened under my boots. It was a seasonal creek or tributary of one, carved through the gentle dune by winter rains but now quite dry. It was sandy and overhung completely by the privet... Here was my chance. My heart thumped painfully as I considered it, kneeling to look into the black shade, all the while hearing the German voices growing closer.

It was the only opportunity fate was about to bring me, so, with a sense of fatalism, I decided to accept. I made sure I had not dropped anything in my falter, found all present, and passed my bundled jacket ahead of me into the cool shade, then crawled in, finding the washaway barely wide enough for my shoulders. I did not even think about what might live in here, some sort of sand spiders or biting ants? Were there snakes in France? None of this mattered, I simply must lie still and quiet and, with the help of providence, they might pass me by.

I heard a yell go up from not far away and knew the soldiers had found my abandoned gear. They were like bloodhounds on the scent now, and redoubled their efforts, stabbing with their bayonets through the leafy tangles. I hardly dared breathe, checking over and over that my boots were far enough into the deep shadow to escape notice – I *hoped* they were. If I crawled any further my head would near a patch of light between bushes; come what may, I was in the deepest cover I could find and they either missed me... or they didn't.

What's it to be, I remember thinking, *a prison camp in a few days, and put your feet up for the duration, or stay free and do your best?* The uncertainty was an agony and I steeled myself for the bushes to be dragged apart and a ring of stern, Teutonic faces to stare down at me, rifles presented. If that was my fate, there was no more I could do.

I heard hob-nail boots approaching, the chatter of tense voices, a calmer officer's voice sending the search line one way or another, and the insidious ripping of the blades as they stabbed into the undergrowth. They might skewer me before I could move... I think I prayed rather intensely as the rustle of the bushes came closer and then held my breath as a shadow crossed the dappled light above me. I saw German boots in the bright light level with the washaway and for a moment the tip of a bayonet appeared through the stems of the privet, flashing within an inch of my chest... Then again near my hip. If I had been lying on the ground surface they would have probably done me to death in that moment, but the depth of the washaway saved me and, little by little, I heard the search party moving on.

Now I breathed a shuddery sigh of relief and closed my eyes, thanked providence sincerely, and let myself rest. I guessed the time and knew my squadron mates would be landing back at Tangmere by now, hopefully all safe and sound, with debriefing to go through, then put a meal under their belts. I had my "escape box" and some extras, a water bottle and a couple of chocolate bars, but my mouth was already dry from fear.

But I was safe in my hole, and decided to stay right there. The voices faded out and a while later I heard a whistle shrill, calling the men back to the trucks. They started up and moved off, probably to try their luck further on, and I knew I was momentarily in the clear. The aftermath of tension had its chance to set in and I shook like a leaf for a while, turned over in the now chilly-seeming hole, and huddled rather miserably. I hunted out my pocket watch and turned the face to the dim light, surprised to find the hands at 1.30 already. Sunset here was not due until about seven o'clock at this time of year, so I had a long, anxious wait ahead of me before I could emerge and creep toward the waterfront of Audresselles. I turned my jacket and fished a

> *What's it to be, I remember thinking, a prison camp in a few days, and put your feet up for the duration, or stay free and do your best? The uncertainty was an agony and I steeled myself for the bushes to be dragged apart and a ring of stern, Teutonic faces to stare down at me, rifles presented.*

chocolate bar from a deep pocket along with the small, soft plastic water bottle I carried, a twin of the one in the escape box but already filled. The snack helped calm me and after a while I felt carefully for the special pocket in my blue battledress trousers, reassured myself my kit was undamaged, then composed myself to rest... Mercifully, as I relaxed, I found sleep to pass the hours.

Sunset was glorious over the channel, stretching away west into the Atlantic Ocean. The weather was being kind, very different from the appalling rain and cold a week ago. Had I been faced with that, I'm not sure what I would have done. Still, daytime highs were not much above 60° F, it was a far cry from summer.

As I cautiously came out of my foxhole I sniffed the sea breeze and enjoyed the deep colours of day's end. I crouched down, kept an eye out for a while–anyone on the road would be an unwelcome observer. As night thickened I left my hiding place and, staying low, made my way toward the beach. I pulled on my jacket, fastened and belted it, checked my gloves were secure, and set out for the village. I crossed the road in a flat run, went down among vegetation on the other side, and crept on toward the shore. When I found the sea I turned north and followed the edge of the dune country toward the few lights showing in the village, probably six or seven hundred yards at most, no reason to pull out the maps in my jacket. It seemed they had no call for full blackout conditions here–a fishing village in the Pas de Calais was hardly a strategic target.

Ancient sea walls fronted rocks and tide pools below the long white houses with their red roofs, which I made out in the last light. A fine, grey stone medieval church was visible over the rooftops, away on the landward side, and I heard the faint sound of music from houses, perhaps a public house. Unless I was going to appeal to the locals for help, I had to stay unseen in the darkness, and that suited me fine.

There is a stretch of sandy beach south of the town, and a few fishing boats were drawn up on the shore, awaiting tomorrow's tide. Among them was a fairly large craft, an equivalent of an English "smack," I suppose, and I made a fast run into its shade, listened hard, and when I was satisfied I was alone I heaved over the side and sheltered from the wind below the freeboard. Everything was done with the greatest caution, and I explored the vessel carefully before opening the door of the narrow cabin abaft the catch wells. This was a wheel house and retreat from the weather, and I fetched a box of matches from my pocket, turned my back on the windows and struck one for light. There were books and charts in wall holders, a medical kit–nothing to eat or drink, unfortunately. I found a handwritten note on a clipboard hanging on the wall and my high-school French was just good enough to translate something useful–a German patrol boat was due down the coast about 8.30 and every thirty minutes thereafter, as it patrolled back and forth between Calais and Boulogne. The fishermen were curfewed, it seemed, all civilians off the water by sundown. I checked the time and nodded.

The most useful things I found were an old-fashioned cork-float life jacket and a Verey pistol and cartridges, and I "liberated" them, scrawling a note in my poor French to the effect the owner would be recompensed after the war. *Appologies - attendre une récompense après les hostilités*. With something of a sinking feeling, I knew what I had to do. I could never shift a boat this size, nor was I skilled in its handling, but I could certainly manage a rowboat–I had done plenty of rowing with my high-school team just a couple of years ago, enough to know I could purloin the dinghy that lay on the sands nearby, get it launched and put some space between me and occupied Europe during the night. With the alternating eastward or westward set of currents in the channel at different points in the tide a small boat would be rather at the mercy of the elements, and I doubted I could make it all the way to England anyway; but our rescue launches patrolled the channel every day when the RAF was up, and in the good weather I would expect the Command staff to squeeze in two "shows" a day. That meant the British side of the narrows would be well patrolled, and, if I could get near enough, a flare might reasonably bring help.

It was a gamble, of course. My life was in my hands, and I stayed in the wheelhouse of the boat to enjoy what protection it offered. I opened the small clear plastic package of the escape box, brought out the nutritious but not terribly appetizing "liver toffee" and boiled sweets, saving my other chocolate bar for the hard hours I knew were to come, and made myself save the water. By the light of a match I transferred the Benzedrine tablets from my escape box to a pocket, it would save some fumbling for them when the exhaustion started to bite, and added several cubes of the toffee—besides energy, it would fight thirst by stimulating saliva. At 8.15, seen by the luminous hands of my watch, I made myself step out, drop to the quiet beach and listen intently out over the rush and roll of the dark waters. Germans were typically very punctual; more or less on-time, I heard the growl of powerful engines as a fearsome *Schnellboot* eased past maybe half a mile out, no lights showing. That was it, I now had half an hour until it was back after turning around off Boulogne, and I cast a last glance at the few cheery lights of Audresselles before proceeding with my theft. I was not happy to abandon dry land, I was an airman, not a sailor, but practicality was at a premium. All I prayed for now was that the sea was not too rough out there. If I swamped, I was likely a gonner—the cork vest over my jacket would keep me afloat but the cold would strike deep.

I examined the dinghy, chancing a struck match with my back turned to the town and my hand cupped around it. I found it empty of all but a rather rank-smelling net, which I turfed out. Then I put the Verey pistol and flares aboard, unsnagged the bow line from the sand, bent my back to shove it down to the incoming water; finally I paused to toss my boots and socks aboard, roll up my trousers, then shove her in. I was wet to the knees by the time I was aboard. I dropped the oars into the locks and got her under control, and with my feet freezing, I bent my back to row directly away from the town lights.

When the shore was far enough away for me to be in a regularly undulating swell, I came about for the north. I had taken the compass on its thong from around my neck under my uniform and it now lay open on the bench before me, luminous green markings glimmering softly, and settled to make time. I wanted to be well beyond the patrol boat's track before she came back, and when I heard the engines growling up from the south I hunched low, hoping the crew's attention would be mostly on the shoreline...

Once again I was supremely lucky. I saw the seaward stab of a small searchlight from the long, low craft, then it extinguished. Someone on the open bridge was playing it randomly back and forth in brief snatches, and it would be down to pure bad luck if I got in the way of one. Perhaps my bold plans would come to nothing and I would be guest of the Kriegsmarine for the evening before being packed off by rail to a Navy *Stalag...* I stayed low, though what use that was I did not consciously imagine, and gritted my teeth, but the next time the light stabbed out over the black waves it had moved on a little to the north, and the widest sweep saw the patch of glare arrest a dozen boat-lengths from me. I breathed easier and as the engine sound of the S-boat receded I bent my back and headed on into the dark.

To be careful what you wish for is wise counsel. I had felt smugly clever as I launched my tiny craft and set out boldly, but as an hour became two and the faint sparks of what lights showed along the French coast faded into the darkness, the world felt awfully big, and I felt awfully alone. If I was swamped by a tall wave I would probably die... After an hour I could not feel my feet—whether dry or damp no longer mattered. I struggled into my thick wool socks and boots, and soon regained some circulation. I was very thirsty and sipped a little water before indulging in my other chocolate bar, and rowed on with single-minded purpose. It was going to get very cold and my jacket collar was up around my ears, which ached with a dull pain in the sea wind. I had tied my silk neck scarf around my head to help. My gloves were on now, protecting my hands from both the cold and chafing. The oars would have blistered me raw otherwise.

Before midnight I had called myself all kinds of idiot I could lay tongue to. This may be one of the most-travelled waterways in the world but the chance of meeting friendly shipping was about nil, while being run down by some craft daring a fast passage was far from remote. If I had given myself up, I had reasonable chances of surviving, and the idea of making it back to England had begun to look like a fool's errand as clouds hid the stars and the long groundswell of the channel lifted and lowered me with a mesmeric rhythm. I doubtless fell asleep occasionally, but mercifully the oars were still in my hands when

I woke each time, and I rowed again.

I remember being desperately afraid the current was sweeping me eastward, in which case I was simply travelling in an arc which would bring me back toward Cape Gris Nez and Calais beyond–I might still be looking at a German patrol at daybreak. If I was, I could say I gave it my very best try and there was no shame in that.

I heard boat engines out in the dark once more in the early hours, and aero-engines far overhead as night-bombers headed off to do damage in one direction or the other. I felt insignificant, like a flea on a dog's back, and made my way with the utmost care in the hopes the dog would not scratch. I suppose when you're about twenty years old you think you're at least slightly immortal; one of greater years would think twice or three times before attempting something so patently foolish. But, there I was, rowing slowly now, tired out and cramped, mind almost blanking with the effort of staying awake and pulling one stroke after another. Benzedrine helped, washed down with a sip of precious water, and followed by sweets to keep the juices flowing.

But fatigue was fatigue, and an hour became two more, and 3 am became 4 and then 5, and I rowed in a mesmeric state of mechanical repetition, trying to ignore my blisters. I dreamed all sorts of nonsense, found myself up in the blue sky, flinging my fighter around clouds for the joy of being alive, such a quantum difference from the chill, the dark, the endless motion, fatigue and thirst that clawed at me, the sting of dollops of water that came aboard from wave tops... I thought I had nothing with which to bale, and to do so I would sacrifice the warmth and protection of my gloves, but in desperation I struck a match for the company of light and found to my delight an enamelled can on a short lanyard attached to the middle bench just behind my feet, and thanked a thoughtful French fisherman for the small mercy. I soon had the water in the bottom over the side and took a short rest before I adjusted the oars in their locks and rowed again. My whole existence had taken on the aspect of rowing, baling, shivering, listening, hoping to catch a glimpse of stars, and wondering where I would be when there was light to see by.

"Here lies Johnny Carstairs, Flying Officer and fool," I murmured to myself, composing the inscription for my gravestone in some corner of an English country churchyard. "Went to a watery grave because he thought he was indestructible." I laughed, a miserable sound over a salt-sore throat, and hardly the derisive cackle it was meant to be. *Oh, Johnny*, I thought, *you've really done it this time.*

I think I faded out again for a short while, because when I snapped back I had light to see by. Sunrise was due about ten to seven at this time of year and when I found a grey haze through early mist I had my bearing on east. I put it off my left side and rowed again with a will, knowing only that England was out there somewhere behind me and I wanted to be far from France when this haze lifted.

The chill haze persisted as 7 am came and went. I rowed until I thought I could row no more, then found strength from somewhere and rowed again. I had started to lose hope, and despaired of ever seeing dry land again. I think I wept for a while, head down on the oars and feeling very sorry for myself, almost too stiff with the cold to bend my back, legs cramped and numb.

Engines droned above me, far away through the fog, and I looked up. I recognized the sweet timbre of V-12s and knew our boys and theirs were mixing it up there, wherever this was. Maybe the Germans were intercepting a circus raid before it could get near its target, hoping to disperse our chaps–a potentially costly tactic for them, their odds were best if they fought over France itself. Nevertheless, I heard the battle, miles above, and the splash as spent cannon and machine gun shell cases rained into the sea around me. How I wished I was up there with them, and the distant sounds reminded me of my role in all this–I was a fighter pilot, not a ferryman! Now I rowed again, though only defiance powered me, and when, some time later, I heard a marine engine through the lifting mist I knew I was approaching the limits of my endurance. I had stimulants left but I was growing dehydrated, I needed warmth, and in desperation I would accept relief from anybody. Maybe I gave up too soon, but I knew if the current swept me east or west away from the narrows, I may be effectively lost at sea, and a rowboat was a very small thing to spot out here.

I had quarter-mile visibility by this point, the sun would burn off the mist completely in another hour, and the low, dark silhouette that detached from the goldy-grey haze was both welcome and ominous. The craft was moving slowly, heads turned on the open bridge, and a whistle was blown repeatedly, as if inviting a reply. A whistle had been attached to my life jacket but that was far away now, and I loaded the Verey pistol with numb hands that would hardly flex any more. I looked at the boat through the mist, the outline firming up as the moments went by, and reached the most difficult decision of my life.

I could not tell if it was ours or theirs, but I did not expect one more stroke of luck to come my way, and I wanted to live. I raised the pistol and thumped off the flare, and a moment later the lurid pink-red fireball lit up the mist in surreal glare. I heard shouts across the water and a nudge-up of throttle, the craft came about and in one minute my heart was broken at last, as a German pennant fluttered from the bow. I put my head down and indulged in my despair, but when the Germans came alongside and a line was thrown across to me I found a brave face for the Hun – never let it be said an Englishman was less than composed.

The dark-uniformed German sailors– actually airmen, as the civilian *Seenotdienst* had been absorbed into the Luftwaffe–hauled me aboard and I collapsed in the rear well, my legs unable to carry me. I found myself face to face with a German pilot, soaked to the skin, his life jacket at his side, and a blanket around his shoulders as he clutched a tin mug that steamed in the morning air. He was glassy-eyed from his own ordeal–bailing out over the channel after one of our chaps did the deed, coming down to a water landing, getting out of his chute harness and swimming clear, then waiting– hoping–as the cold ate into him. I smiled and nodded, all the understanding I could communicate, and a moment later I found a blanket coming my way, and a mug placed in my hands. The coffee was black, sweetened with honey, and I gulped it down, my bared hands soaking up the heat as if I had never felt it before. In that moment I was grateful for any mercies, and thankful to have my life back, especially in view of the British belligerence toward the enemy Sea Rescue Service since the middle of 1940. It would be a prison, then, I thought, and was happy with the trade–my life for sitting out the conflict.

The launch cruised on, and I heard much radio chatter, the signalman was monitoring the talkback from the battle, and soon they pulled another of their own from the sea. This was the daily round of the action, and I did not envy the crews who performed this duty in the sort of appalling weather just gone by. We squeezed through operations whenever the weather permitted, and that meant the rescue teams had to be out in it as well, on both sides.

The sounds of battle faded. The mist was clearing and we had a horizon. I saw the dark line of France off to the south and, achingly, England to the north. I stared at it and felt very melancholy. I came so close... The crew were still intent on their sweep, however, and cruised a search pattern under the area of action for another half hour. As the morning wore on, however, there was increased radio activity, including some two-way chatter, and from the cockpit I could have sworn I heard a few words of English. Perhaps they were simply reporting they had picked up an *Englander*, and I thought no more of it, simply huddled miserably in my jacket.

A little while later, I was tapped on the shoulder by a big German non-com and he gestured. "*Bitte, komm mit mir*," he said quietly, and I did not need a translation. I rose unsteadily and hung onto the safety rail at the gunwale to watch another craft emerge from the background of streaky cloud and tossing swells–and a moment later I could have wept as I recognised an RAF rescue launch. Each craft was showing a white flag, some silently- arranged unofficial signal, it seemed, and the soft radio contact was clearly just between the boats. The crewmen on both sides were armed but kept their hands clear of their pistols as the craft came alongside, and there were tight smiles and silent waves. Two pilots had been rescued by the British boat, one of them German, and I suddenly realised what was happening–a little give and take. A prisoner exchange was performed without a word, I got to go home, and so did a young German whom I might have faced in the air at some point.

There had been a hotline between antagonists during the Battle of Britain to provide humanitarian information, guiding rescue services to the location of each other's downed pilots, and it seemed the crews out here at sea had not forgotten that simple courtesy. A code of conduct existed between men, even if it was evaporating between governments, and when I stepped across and was welcomed by my countrymen I found at least some faith in humanity restored. The boat skippers had clearly done this before, they spoke a few quiet words and shook hands before the craft parted company, and I found myself headed for Folkestone once the patrol was over.

I was initially debriefed by an intelligence chap at the rescue station but failed to mention being retrieved by the Germans, it simply looked better for our own crew and avoided difficult questions. It took me a day or two to make my way back to Tangmere by railway and Red Cross car, dishevelled and care-worn, looking like a drowned rat when I arrived back minus my Spitfire, but I was more glad to see the base than I could possibly put into words. I received a check-up, was fed again, debriefed again by our wing's Intelligence Officer, and was given all sorts of free advice by my squadron mates. They considered henceforth calling me "Dinghy," but the best news was, I was allowed a 48-hour leave to recover. I packed my gas mask and kitbag and was off to Cambridge by train from nearby Chichester within the hour, home to the joys of blackouts and rationing.

Bizarre as it may seem from the perspective of thirty or forty years on, one never felt more alive than when tomorrow was not guaranteed and any bomb might have your name on it, and people pulled together for the common good.

Ah, the war years... Misery that they were, they had their good points, and I know I'm not alone in missing them.

"Circus to Boulogne" is copyright © Mike Adamson.

Mike Adamson holds a PhD in archaeology from Flinders University of South Australia, where he has both studied and taught for some twenty-four years. Born in England, his family immigrated to Australia in 1971; after early aspirations in art and writing, Mike returned to study and secured degrees in both marine biology and archaeology. Mike currently lectures in anthropology, is a passionate photographer and a master-level hobbyist, and has rediscovered a passion for writing speculative fiction, with 29 placements to date. Interests embrace science fiction, fantasy, horror, historical and military fields, while pass-times include model building and airbrush art.

"Don't fret, chum! This issue might be over, but StoryHack will be back with more great fiction before you know it."

Thanks for Reading!

storyhack.com/thankyou – for a list of those wonderful folks who helped kickstart this great magazine.

storyhack.com/subscriptions – soon you'll be able to subscribe.

storyhack.com/newsletter – stay up to date with the magazine

And if you can find the time and the love in your heart to give the magazine a review *anywhere*, I'd be even more grateful. Seriously, Amazon, GoodReads, your own blog, the blog of a friend, a public announcement board at the grocery store, *anywhere*.

Credits

Edited / formatted / assembled by Bryce Beattie.
Published by Baby Katie Media, LLC.
Additional editing by: Julie Frost, Mark Thompson, Jon Mollison, & Dean McSmith.
This issue was funded by a bunch of great people via Kickstarter.
This Magazine is copyright © 2017, Baby Katie Media.
Authors retain copyright to their stories.
Cover art was sponsored by Gene Moyers of genemoyers.com

Made in the USA
Las Vegas, NV
25 July 2021